APPLY IT *NOT*
ERE I GIVE THE WORD!

As if answering a challenge, a deep grunt rumbled down the trail. While Jillo secured the horses, Eudoric laid out his new equipment and methodically loaded his weapon.

"Here it comes," said Eudoric as he detected the vibrations of a heavy tread through his boot soles. "Stand by with that torch. Apply it not ere I give the word!"

The dragon came into view, plodding along the trail and swinging its head from side to side. Having newly shed its skin, the creature gleamed like fresh paint, its hide bearing a reticular pattern of green and black. Its great, golden, slit-pupiled eyes focused keenly on the hunters.

The horses screamed; the dragon speeded its approach.

"Ready?" said Eudoric, settling the weapon in its rest.

"Aye, sir. Here goeth!" Without awaiting further command, Jillo applied the torch to the touchhole.

With a great boom and a cloud of smoke, the device discharged, rocking Eudoric back a pace. Through the dissipating smoke, the dragon appeared still rushing towards them.

"Idiot!" screamed Eudoric. "You were not to give fire until I commanded! You've made me miss it clean!"

"I'm s-sorry, sir. I was palsied with fear. What shall we do now?"

"Run, fool!"

THE INCORPORATED KNIGHT

L. Sprague and Catherine Crook de Camp

BAEN BOOKS

THE INCORPORATED KNIGHT

A Baen Book

Baen Publishing Enterprises
260 Fifth Avenue
New York, N.Y. 10001

First Baen printing, September 1988

Chapters I and II first appeared as the story "Two Yards of Dragon" in the anthology *Flashing Swords! #3*, copyright © 1976 by Lin Carter.
Chapter III first appeared as "The Coronet" in *The Magazine of Fantasy and Science Fiction*, v. 51, n. 5, Nov. 1976, copyright © by Mercury Press, Inc.
Chapter IV first appeared as "Spider Love" in *The Magazine of Fantasy and Science Fiction*, v. 53, n. 5, Nov. 1977, copyright © 1977 by Mercury Press, Inc.
Chapter V first appeared as "Eudoric's Unicorn" in the anthology *The Year's Best Fantasy Stories: 3*, copyright © 1977 by Daw Books, Inc.
All these stories have been revised for the present volume.

ISBN: 0-671-65435-7

Cover art by Dan Horne

Printed in the United States of America

Distributed by
SIMON & SCHUSTER
1230 Avenue of the Americas
New York, N.Y. 10020

To Jeanne and Paul Maguire,
whose lively imagination
gave us our title

CONTENTS

I

Two Yards of Dragon

Eudoric Dambertson, esquire, rode home from his courting of Lusina, daughter of the enchanter Baldonius, with a face as long as an olifant's nose. Eudoric's sire, Sir Dambert, said:

"Well, how fared thy suit, boy? Ill, eh?"

"I—" began Eudoric as his stocky, muscular body slumped into a chair in his father's castle hall.

"I told thee 'twas an asinine notion, eh? Was I not right? When Baron Emmerhard hath more daughters than he can count, any one of whom would fetch a pretty parcel of land with her. Well, why answerest not?"

"I—" said Eudoric, his serious face gatherng into a frown beneath his dark hair.

"Come on, lad, speak up!"

"How can he, when ye talk all the time?" said Eudoric's mother, the Lady Aniset.

"Oh," said Sir Dambert. "Thy pardon, son. Moreover and furthermore, as I've told thee, an thou were Emmerhard's son-in-law, he'd use his influence

1

to get thee thy spurs. Here thou art, a strapping youth of three-and-twenty, not yet knighted. 'Tis a disgrace to our lineage."

"There are no wars toward, to afford opportunity for deeds of knightly dought," said Eudoric.

"Aye, 'tis true. Certes, we must all hail the blessings of peace, which the wise governance of our sovran Emperor hath given us for lo these thirteen years. Howsomever, to perform a knightly deed, our youthful gallants must needs waylay banditti, disperse rioters, and do such-like fribbling feats."

As Sir Dambert paused, Eudoric interjected: "Sir, that problem now appears on its way to solution."

"How meanest thou?"

"If you'll but hear me, Father! Doctor Baldonius has set me a task, ere he'll bestow Lusina upon me, which should fit me for knighthood in any jurisdiction." Eudoric's old tutor Baldonius, a wizardly scholar who eked out his pension by occasional theurgies, lived in semi-retirement in a house in the forest.

"And that is?" said Sir Dambert.

"He's fain to possess two square yards of dragon hide. Says he needs 'em for his magical mummeries."

"But there have been no dragons in these parts for more than a century!"

"True; but, quoth Baldonius, the monstrous reptiles still abound afar to eastward, in the lands of Pathenia and Pantorozia. Forsooth, he's given me a letter of introduction to his colleague, a Doctor Raspiudus, in Pathenia."

"What?" cried the Lady Aniset. "Thou, to set forth on some year-long journey to parts unknown, where, 'tis said, men hop on a single leg or have their faces in their bellies? I'll not have it! Besides, Baldonius may be privy wizard to Baron Emmerhard, but it is not to be denied that he be of no gentle blood."

"Well," said Eudoric, "so who was gentle when the Divine Pair created the world?"

"Our forbears were, I'm sure, whatever the case with those of the learned Doctor Baldonius. Young people are always full of idealistic notions, like those that stirred the serfs of Franconia to wicked rebellion against their natural lords. Belike thou'lt fall into heretical delusions, for I hear the Easterlings have not the true religion. They falsely believe that God be one, instead of two as we truly understand—"

"Let's not wander into the mazes of theology," said Sir Dambert, his chin on his fist. "To be sure, the heretical Franconians believe that God be three, an even more pernicious notion than that of the Easterlings—"

"If I meet God on my travels, I'll ask him the truth of't," said Eudoric.

"Be not sacrilegious, thou insolent whelp! Still and all and notwithstanding, Doctor Baldonius were a man of influence to have in the family, be his origin never so humble. Methinks I could prevail upon him to utter spells to cause my crops, my kine, and my villeins to thrive, whilst casting poxes and murrains upon mine enemies. Like that caitiff Rainmar, eh? What of the arid seasons we've had, the God and Goddess know we need what supernatural help we can get. Else we may some fine day awaken to find that we've lost the holding to some greasy tradesman with a purchased title, with pen for lance and tally-sheet for shield."

"Then I have your leave, sire?" cried Eudoric, a broad grin splitting his square, bronzed, serious young face.

The Lady Aniset still objected; and the argument raged for another hour. Eudoric pointed out that he was not an only child, having two younger brothers and a sister. In the end, Sir Dambert and his lady agreed to Eudoric's quest, provided that he returned in time to help with the harvest and took along a manservant of their choice.

"Whom have you in mind?" asked Eudoric.

"I fancy Jillo the trainer," said Sir Dambert.

Eudoric groaned. "That old mossback, ever canting and lecturing me on the duties and dignities of my station?"

"He's but a decade older than thou," said Sir Dambert. "Moreover and furthermore, thou shalt need an older man, with a sense of order and fitness, to keep thee on the path of a gentleman. Class loyalty above all, my boy! Young men are wont to swallow every new idea that flitters past, like a hoptoad snapping at flies. Betimes they find they've engulfed a wasp, to their scathe and dolor."

"He's an awkward wight, Father, and not over-brained."

"Aye, but he's honest and true, no small virtues in our degenerate days. In my sire's time there was none of this newfangled saying the courteous 'ye' and 'you' to mere churls and scullions, as I hear thee doing. 'Twas always 'thou' and 'thee'. . . ."

"How ye do go on, Dambert dear," said Aniset.

"Aye, I ramble. 'Tis the penalty of age. At minimum, Eudoric, the faithful Jillo knows his horses and will keep your beasts in foremost fettle." Sir Dambert smiled. "Moreover and furthermore, if I know Jillo Godmarson, he'll be glad to get away from's nagging wife for a spell."

So Eudoric and Jillo set forth to eastward, from the banneret knight's holding of Arduen, in the barony of Zurgau, in the county of Treveria, in the kingdom of Locania, in the New Napolitanian Empire. Eudoric rode his palfrey and led his mighty destrier, Morgrim. The lank, lean Jillo bestrode another palfrey and led a sumpter mule. Morgrim was piled with Eudoric's panoply of plate, nested into a compact bundle and lashed down under a canvas cover. The mule bore the rest of their supplies.

For a fortnight, they wended uneventfully through the duchies and counties of the Empire. When they reached lands where they could no longer understand the local dialects, they made shift with Helladic, the tongue of the Old Napolitanian Empire, which lettered men spoke everywhere.

They stopped at inns where inns were to be had. For the first fortnight, Eudoric was too preoccupied with dreams of his beloved Lusina to notice the tavern wenches. After that, his urges began to fever him, and he bedded one in Zerbstat. Thereafter he forbore, as a matter not of morals but of thrift.

When benighted on the road, they slept under the stars—or, as befell them in the marches of Avaria, under a rain-dripping canopy of clouds. As they bedded down in the wet, Eudoric asked his companion:

"Jillo, why didst not remind me to bring a tent?"

Jillo sneezed. "Why, sir, come rain, come snow, I never thought that so sturdy a springald as ye be would ever need one. The heroes in the romances, like Sigvard Dragonslayer, never traveled with tents."

"To the nethermost hell with heroes of romances! They go clattering about on their destriers for a thousand cantos. Weather is ever fine. Food, shelter, and a change of clothing appear, as by magic, whenever desired. Their armor never rusts. They suffer no tisics and fluxes. They pick up no fleas or lice at the inns. They never get bees in their helms. They're never swindled by merchants, for none does aught so vulgar as buying and selling."

"If ye'll pardon me, sir," said Jillo, "that were no knightly way to speak. It becomes not your station."

"Well, to the nethermost hells with my station, too! Wherever these paladins go, they find damsels in distress to rescue or have other agreeable, thrilling, and sanitary adventures. What adventures have we had? The time we fled from robbers in the Turonian Forest. The time I fished you out of the

Albis half drowned. The time we ran out of food in the Asciburgi Mountains and had to plod fodderless over those hair-raising peaks for three days on empty stomachs."

"The Divine Pair do but seek to try the mettle of a valorous aspirant knight, sir. Ye should welcome these petty adversities as a chance to prove your manhood."

Eudoric made a rude noise with his mouth. "That for my manhood! Right now, I'd fainer have a stout roof overhead, a warm fire before me, and a hot repast in my belly. If ever I go on such a silly jaunt again, I'll find one of those verse-mongers—like that troubadour, Landwin of Kromnitch, who visited us yesteryear—and drag him along, to show him how little real adventures resemble those of romances. And if he fall into the Albis, he may drown for all of me. Were it not for my darling Lusina. . . ."

Eudoric lapsed into gloomy silence, punctuated by sneezes.

They plodded on until they came to the village of Liptai, on the border of Pathenia. After the border guards had questioned and passed them, they walked their animals down the bottomless mud of the principal street. Most of the slatternly houses were made of logs or of crudely hewn planks, innocent of paint.

"Heaven above!" said Jillo. "Look at that, sir!"

"That" was a gigantic snail shell, converted into a small house.

"Knew you not of the giant snails of Pathenia?" asked Eudoric. "I've read of them in Doctor Baldonius' encyclopedia. When fullgrown, they—or rather their shells—are ofttimes used for dwellings in this land."

Jillo shook his head. " 'Twere better, had ye spent more of your time on your knightly exercises and less on reading. Your sire hath never learnt his letters, yet he doth his duties well enow."

"Times change, Jillo. I may not have the learning

of Doctor Baldonius, or clang rhymes so featly as that ass Landwin of Kromnitch; but in these days a stroke of the pen were oft more fell than the slash of a sword. Here's a hostelry that look not too slummocky. Do you dismount and inquire concerning their tallage."

"Why me, sir?"

"Because I am fain to know, ere we put our necks in the noose! Go ahead. If I go in, they'll double the scot at the sight of me."

When Jillo came out and quoted prices, Eudoric said: "Too dear. We'll try the other."

"But, Master! Mean ye to put us in some flea-bitten hovel, like that which we suffered in Bitavia?"

"Aye. Did you not prate to me on the virtues of petty adversity, to strengthen one's knightly mettle?"

" 'Tis not that, sir."

"What, then?" asked Eudoric.

"Why, when better quarters are to be had, to make do with the worse were an insult to your rank and station. No gentleman—"

"Here we are!" said Eudoric. "Suitably squalid, too! You see, good Jillo, I did but yestereven count our money, and lo! more than half is gone, and our journey not yet half completed."

"But, noble Master! No man of knightly mettle would so debase himself as to tally his silver, like some base-born commercial—"

"Then I must needs lack true knightly mettle."

For a dozen leagues beyond Liptai rose the great, tenebrous Motolian Forest. Beyond the forest lay the provincial capital of Velitchovo. Beyond Velitchovo, the forest thinned out *gradatim* to the great grassy plains of Pathenia. Beyond Pathenia, Eudoric had been told, stretched the boundless deserts of Pantorozia, over which a man might ride for months without seeing a city.

Yes, the innkeeper told him, there were plenty of

dragons in the Motolian Forest. "But fear them not," said Kasmar in broken Helladic. "From being hunted, they have become wary and even timid. An ye stick to the road and move yarely, they'll pester you not unless ye surprise or corner one."

"Have any dragons been devouring maidens fair of late?" asked Eudoric.

Kasmar laughed. "Nay, good Master. What did maidens fair, traipsing round the woods to stir up the beasties? Leave them be, I say, and they do the same by you."

A cautious instinct warned Eudoric not to speak of his quest. Two days later, after he and Jillo had rested and renewed their equipment, they set out into the forest. For a league they followed the Velitchovo road. Then Eudoric, accoutered in full plate and riding Morgrim, led his companion off the road and into the woods to southward. They threaded their way among the trees, ducking branches, in a wide detour. Guided by the sun, Eudoric brought them back to the road near Liptai.

The next day they did the same, except that their circuit curved off to the north of the highway.

After three more days of this exploration, Jillo became restless. "Good Master, what do we, circling round and about so bootlessly? The dragons do dwell farther east, away from the haunts of men, they say."

"Having once been lost in the woods," said Eudoric, "I would not repeat the experience. Therefore do we scout our field of action, like a general scouting a future battlefield."

" 'Tis an arid business," said Jillo with a shrug. "But then, ye were always one to see further into a millstone than most."

At last, having committed the nearer byways of the forest to memory, Eudoric led Jillo farther east. After casting about, they came at last upon the unmistakable tracks of a dragon. The animal had beaten a path through the brush, along which they could ride about as well as on the road. When they had followed the track for above an hour, Eudoric became aware of a pungent, musky stench.

"My lance, Jillo!" said Eudoric, trying to keep his voice from rising with nervousness.

The next bend in the path brought them into full view of the dragon, a thirty-footer facing them on the trail.

"Ha!" said Eudoric. "Meseems 'tis a mere cockadrill, albeit longer of neck and of limb than those that dwell in the rivers of Agisymba—if the pictures in Doctor Baldonius' books deceive me not. Have at thee, vile worm!"

Eudoric couched his lance and put spurs to Morgrim. The destrier bounded ponderously forward.

The dragon raised its head and peered this way and that, as if it could not see very well. As the hoofbeats drew nearer, the dragon opened its jaws and uttered a loud, hoarse, groaning bellow.

At that, Morgrim checked his rush with stiffened forelegs, spun cumbrously on his haunches, and veered off the trail into the woods. Jillo's palfrey bolted likewise, but in another direction. The dragon set out after Eudoric at a shambling trot.

Eudoric had not gone fifty yards when Morgrim passed close by a massive old oak, a thick-girthed limb of which jutted into their path. The horse ducked beneath the bough. The branch caught Eudoric across the breastplate, flipped him backwards over the cantle of his saddle, and swept him to earth with a clatter.

Half stunned, he saw the dragon trot closer and closer—and then lumber past him, almost within touching distance, to disappear on the trail of the fleeing horse. The next that Eudoric knew, Jillo was bending over him, crying:

"Wellaway, my poor heroic master! Be any bones broken, sir?"

"All of them, methinks," groaned Eudoric. "What's befallen Morgrim?"

"That I know not. And look at this dreadful dent in your beauteous cuirass!"

"Help me out of the thing. The dent pokes most sorely into my ribs. The misadventures I suffer for my dear Lusina!"

"We must get your breastplate to a smith, to have it hammered out and filed smooth."

"Fiends take the smiths! They'd charge half the cost of a new one. I'll fix it myself, if I can find a flat rock to set it on and a big stone wherewith to pound it."

"Well, sir," said Jillo, "ye were always a good man ơ your hands. But the mar will show, and that were not suitable for one of your quality."

"Thou mayst take my quality and stuff it!" cried Eudoric. "Canst speak of nought else? Help me up, pray." He got slowly to his feet, wincing, and limped a few steps.

"At least," he said, "nought seems fractured. But I misdoubt I can walk back to Liptai."

"Oh, sir, that were not to be thought of! Me, allow you to wend afoot whilst I ride? Fiends take the thought!" Jillo unhitched the palfrey from the tree to which he had tethered it and led it to Eudoric, who said:

"I accept your courtesy, good Jillo, only because I must. To plod the distance afoot were but a condign punishment for bungling my charge. Give me a boost, will you?" Eudoric grunted as Jillo helped him into the saddle.

"Tell me, sir," said Jillo, "why did the beast ramp on past you without stopping to devour you as ye lay helpless? Was't that Morgrim promised a more boun-

teous repast? Or that the monster feared your plate
would give him a disorder of the bowels?"

"Meseems 'twas neither. Marked you how gray
and milky appeared its eyes? According to Doctor
Baldonius' book, dragons shed their skins betimes,
like serpents. This one neared the time of its change
of skin, wherefore the skin that covers its eyeballs
had become opaque and thickened, like glass of inferior quality. Therefore it could not plainly discern
things lying still and pursued only those that moved."

They got back to Liptai after dark. Both were
barely able to stagger, Eudoric from his sprains and
bruises and Jillo footsore from the unaccustomed
three-league hike.

Two days later, when they had recovered, they set
out on the two palfreys to hunt for Morgrim. "For,"
Eudoric said, "that nag is worth more in solid money
than all the rest of my possessions together."

Eudoric rode unarmored, save for a shirt of light
mesh mail, since the palfrey could not easily carry
the weight of the plate all day. He bore his lance and
sword, however, in case they should again encounter
a dragon.

They found the site of the previous encounter but
no sign of dragon or destrier. Jillo and Eudoric tracked
the horse by its prints in the soft mold for a few
bowshots, but then the slot faded out on harder
ground, and despite diligent search they failed to
pick it up again.

"Still, I misdoubt Morgrim fell victim to the beast,"
said Eudoric. "He could show clean heels to many a
steed of lighter build, and from its looks the dragon
was no courser."

After hours of fruitless searching, whistling, and
calling, they returned to Liptai. For a small fee,
Eudoric was allowed to post a notice in Helladic on

the town notice board, offering a reward for the return of his horse.

No word, however, came of the sighting of Morgrim. For all that Eudoric could tell, the destrier might have run clear to Velitchovo.

"He'll probably pass his remaining days," said Eudoric, "in pulling some peasant's plow. Now then, good Jillo, you're free with advice. Well, rede me this riddle. We've established that our steeds will bolt from the sight and smell of dragon, for which I blame them little. Had we all the time in the world, we could doubtless train them to face the monsters, beginning with a stuffed dragon; and then, perchance, one in a cage in some monarch's menagerie. But our lucre dwindles like snow in the spring. What's to do?"

"Well," said Jillo, "if the nags won't stand, needs we must face the worms on foot."

"That seems to me to throw away our lives to no good purpose. For these vasty lizards can outrun and out-turn us and are strongly harnessed to boot. Barring the luckiest of lucky thrusts with the spear—as, say, into the eye or down the gullet—that fellow we erst encountered could make one mouthful of my lance and another of me."

"Your knightly courage were sufficient defense, sir. The Divine Pair would surely grant victory to the right."

"From what I've read of battles and feuds," said Eudoric, "methinks the Holy Couple's attention often strays elsewhither, when they should be deciding the outcome of some mundane affray."

"That is the trouble with reading, sir; it undermines one's faith in the True Religion. But ye could be at least as well-armored as the dragon, in your panoply of plate."

"Aye, but then poor Daisy could not bear so much weight to the site—or, at least, bear it thither and have breath left for a charge. We must be as chary of our beasts' welfare as of our own. Without them, 'tis a long walk back to Arduen. Nor do I deem that we should like to pass our lives in Liptai."

"Then, sir, we could pack the armor on the mule, for you to do on in dragon country."

"I like it not," said Eudoric. "Afoot, weighted down by that lobster's habit, I could move no more spryly than a tortoise. 'Twere small comfort to know that, if the dragon ate me, he'd suffer indigestion thereafter."

Jillo sighed. "Not the knightly attitude, sir, if ye'll pardon my saying so."

"Say what you please, but I'll follow the course of what meseems were common sense. What we need is a brace of those heavy steel crossbows for sieges. At close range, they'll punch a hole in a breastplate as if it were a sheet of parchment."

"Such arbalests take too long to crank up," said Jillo. "By the time ye've readied your second shot, the battle's over."

"Oh, it would behoove us to shoot straight the first time; but better one shot that pierces the monster's scales than a score that bounce away. Howsomever, we lack these little hand catapults fell, and they make them not in this barbarous land."

A few days later, while Eudoric still fretted over the lack of means to his goal, he heard a sudden sound, like a single thunderclap, from close at hand. Hastening out from Kasmar's Inn, Eudoric and Jillo found a crowd of Pathenians around the border guard's barracks.

In the drill yard, the guard was drawn up to watch a man demonstrate a weapon. Eudoric, whose few phrases of Pathenian were not up to conversation, asked among the crowd for someone who could speak Helladic. When he found one, he learned that the demonstrator was a Pantorozian. The man was a stocky, dish-faced, snub-nosed fellow in a bulbous fur hat, a jacket of coarse undyed wool, and baggy trousers tucked into soft boots.

"He says the device was invented by the Sericans," said the villager. "They live half a world away, beyond the Pantorozian deserts. He puts some powder into that thing, touches a flame to it, and *boom!* It spits a ball of lead through the target as neatly as ye please."

The Pantorozian demonstrated again, pouring black powder from the small end of a horn down his brass barrel. He placed a wad of rag over the mouth of the tube, then a leaden ball, and pushed both ball and wad down the tube with a rod. He poured a pinch of powder into a hole in the upper side of the tube near its rear or closed end.

Then the Pantorozian set a forked rest in the ground before him, rested the barrel in the fork, and took a small torch that a guardsman handed him. He pressed the wooden stock of the device against his shoulder, sighted along the tube, and with his free hand touched the torch to the touch hole. Ffft, *bang!* A cloud of smoke, and another hole appeared in the target.

The Pantorozian spoke with the captain of the guard, but they were too far for Eudoric to hear, even if he could have understood. After a while, the Pantorozian picked up his tube and rest, slung his bag of powder over his shoulder, and walked with downcast air to a cart that was hitched to a shade tree.

Eudoric approached the man as he was climbing into his cart. "God den, fair sir!" began Eudoric, but the Pantorozian spread his hands with a smile of incomprehension.

"Kasmar!" cried Eudoric, sighting the innkeeper in the crowd. "Wilt have the goodness to interpret for me and this fellow?"

"He says," said Kasmar, "that he started out with a

wainload of these devices and hath sold all but one. He hoped to dispose of his last one in Liptai, but our gallant Captain Boriswaf will have nought to do therewith."

"Why?" said Eudoric. "Meseems 'twere a fell weapon in practiced hands."

"That is the trouble, quoth Vlek. Boriswaf says that, should so fiendish a weapon come into use, 'twill utterly extinguish the noble art of war, for all men will cast away their weapons and refuse to fight, in lieu of facing this devilish device. Then what should he, a lifelong soldier, do for his bread? Beg?"

"Ask Goodman Vlek where he thinks to pass the night."

"I have already persuaded him to lodge with us, Squire Eudoric."

"Good, for I would fain have further converse with him."

Over dinner, Eudoric sounded out the Pantorozian on the price he asked for his weapon. Acting as translator, Kasmar said: "If ye strike a bargain on this, I should get ten per centum as a broker's commission, for ye were helpless without me."

Eudoric got the gun, with thirty pounds of powder and a bag of leaden balls and wadding, for less than half of what Vlek had asked of Captain Boriswaf. As Vlek explained, he had not done badly on this peddling trip and was eager to get home to his wives and children.

"Only remember," he said through Kasmar, "overcharge it not, lest it blow apart and take your head off. Press the stock firmly against your shoulder, lest it knock you on your arse like the kick of a mule. And let not fire come near the spare powder, lest it explode all at once and blast you into gobbets."

Later, Eudoric told Jill: "That deal all but wiped out our funds."

"Even after the tradesmanlike way ye chaffered that barbarian down?"

"Aye. The scheme had better work, or we shall find ourselves choosing betwixt starving and seeking employment as collectors of offal or diggers of ditches. Assuming, that is, that in this reeky place they even bother to collect offal."

"Master Eudoric!" said Jillo. "Ye would not really lower yourself to undertake menial labor?"

"Sooner than starve, aye. As Helvolius the philosopher saith, no rider wears sharper spurs than necessity."

"But if 'twere known at home, they'd hack off your gilded spurs, break your sword over your head, and degrade you to base varlet!"

"Well, till now I've had no knightly spurs to hack off, but only the plain silvered ones of an esquire. For the rest, I count on you to see that they don't find out. Now go to sleep and cease your grumbling!"

The next day found Eudoric and Jillo deep in the Motolian Forest. At the noonday halt, Jillo kindled a fire. Eudoric made a small torch of a stick whose end was wound with a rag soaked in bacon fat. Then he loaded the device as he had been shown and fired three balls at a mark on a tree. The third time, he hit the mark squarely, although the noise caused the palfreys frantically to tug, rear, and roll their eyes.

Leading their mounts, the hunters proceeded to the place where they had met the dragon before. Jillo rekindled the torch, and they cast up and down the beast's trail. For two hours they saw no wild life save a fleeing sow with a farrow of piglets and several huge snails with boulder-sized shells.

Then the horses began to plunge and whinny. "Methinks they scent our quarry," said Eudoric, trying to quiet them.

When Eudoric himself could detect the musky

odor of dragon, he said: "Tie the nags securely. 'Twould never do to slay our beast and then find our horses had fled, leaving us to drag this terrestrial cockadrill home afoot."

As if answering a challenge, a deep grunt rumbled down the trail. While Jillo secured the horses, Eudoric laid out his new equipment and methodically loaded his weapon.

"Here it comes," said Eudoric as he detected the vibrations of a heavy tread through his boot soles. "Stand by with that torch. Apply it not ere I give the word!"

The dragon came into view, plodding along the trail and swinging its head from side to side. Having newly shed its skin, the creature gleamed like fresh paint, its hide bearing a reticular pattern of green and black. Its great, golden, slit-pupiled eyes focused keenly on the hunters.

The horses screamed; the dragon speeded its approach.

"Ready?" said Eudoric, settling the weapon in its rest.

"Aye, sir. Here goeth!" Without awaiting further command, Jillo applied the torch to the touchhole.

With a great boom and a cloud of smoke, the device discharged, rocking Eudoric back a pace. Through the dissipating smoke, the dragon appeared still rushing towards them.

"Idiot!" screamed Eudoric. "You were not to give fire until I commanded! You've made me miss it clean!"

"I'm s-sorry, sir. I was palsied with fear. What shall we do now?"

"Run, fool!" Dropping the bronzen device, Eudoric turned and fled, with Jillo close behind him.

Then Eudoric tripped over a root and fell sprawling. Stopping to guard his fallen master, Jillo turned to face the dragon. As Eudoric scrambled up, Jillo hurled the torch at the onrushing monster's open maw.

The throw fell short of its target. It happened, however, that the charging dragon was at that instant lumbering over the bag of black powder. The whirling torch, passing beneath the creature's gaping jaws, struck this sack.

BOOM!

When the dragon hunters returned, they found the monster writhing in its death throes with its underbelly blown open and blood and guts spilling out.

"Well!" said Eudoric, drawing a long breath. "That's enough knightly adventure to last me for many a year. Fall to; we must flay the creature. Belike we can sell that part of the hide we take not home ourselves."

"How propose ye to get the hide back to Liptai? It must weigh in the hundreds."

"We shall hitch the dragon's tail to our two nags and lead them, dragging it behind. 'Twill be a weary swink; but we must needs recover as much as we can, to recoup our losses."

An hour later, blood-spattered from head to foot, they were struggling with the ponderous hide when a man in forester's garb, with a large gilt medallion upon his breast, rode up and dismounted. He was a big, rugged-looking man with a rat-trap mouth.

"Who slew this beast, good my sirs?" he inquired.

Jillo spoke: "My noble master, the squire Eudoric Dambertson here. He is the hero who hath brought this accursed beast to book."

"Be that sooth?" said the man to Eudoric.

"Well, ah," said Eudoric. "I cannot claim much credit for the deed—"

"But ye were the slayer, yea? Then, sir, ye are under arrest."

"What? But wherefore?"

"Ye shall see." From his garments, the stranger produced a length of cord with knots at intervals. With this device he measured the dragon from nose to tail. Then he stood up.

"To answer your questions, on three grounds: imprimis, for slaying a dragon out of its lawful season; secundus, for slaying a dragon below the minimum size permitted; and tertius, for slaying a female dragon, a beast protected the year round."

"You say that this be a female?"

"Aye; 'tis as plain as the nose on your face."

"How does one tell, with dragons?"

"Know, knave, that the male hath small horns behind the eyes, the which this specimen patently lacks."

"Who are you, anyway?" demanded Eudoric.

"Senior Game Warden Voytsik of Prath, at your service. My credentials." The man fingered his medallion. "Now, pray, show me your licenses."

"Licenses?" said Eudoric blankly.

"Hunting licenses! Understand ye not plain Pathenian?"

"None told us that such were required, sir," said Jillo.

"Ignorance of the law is no pretext; ye should have asked. That makes four counts of illegality."

Eudoric said: "But why—why in the name of the God and Goddess—"

"Pray, swear not by your false heretical deities!"

"Well, why should you Pathenians wish to preserve these monstrous reptiles?"

"Imprimis, because their hides and other parts have commercial value, which would perish were the entire race exterminated. Secundus, because they maintain the balance of nature by devouring the giant snails, which otherwise would issue forth nightly from the forest in such numbers as to strip bare our crops, orchards, and gardens and reduce our folk to hunger. And tertius, because their presence embellishes the landscape, thus luring foreigners to visit our land and spend their gold therein. Doth that explanation satisfy you?"

Eudoric had a fleeting thought of assaulting the warden, to render him harmless while he and Jillo salvaged their prize. Even as he thought, three more tough-looking fellows, clad like Voytsik and armed with crossbows, rode out of the trees and formed up behind their leader.

"Now come along, ye two," said Voytsik.

"Whither?" asked Eudoric.

"Back to Liptai. On the morrow, we shall take the stage to Velitchovo, where your case will be tried."

"Your pardon, sir; we take the what?"

"The stagecoach."

"What's that, good my sir?"

"By the only God, ye twain must come from a barbarous land indeed! Ye shall see. Now come along, lest we be benighted in the woods."

II

The Smiling Sorcerer

The stagecoach made its rounds between Liptai and Velitchovo thrice a fortnight. While Jillo sat out the journey caked with dried blood and sunk in gloom, the equally blood-soaked Eudoric kept his mind off his filthy, stinking state by studying the passing countryside. When possible, he queried the driver about his occupation. pay, hours, fares, the cost of the vehicle, and so on. At last the man tired of his odorous questioner and brusquely ordered him to sit on the dickey seat projecting from the rear of the vehicle, where his fragrance would less offend the other passengers.

As they neared the capital, the driver whipped his team to a gallop. They rattled along the highroad beside the muddy river Pshora until the stream made a bend. Then they thundered across it on the planks of a bridge.

Velitchovo was an impressive city, with a cobble-stoned main street leading to the onion-domed, red-black-and-golden cathedral of the One God. In a

massively-timbered municipal palace, a bewhiskered
magistrate asked: "Which of you two aliens truly
slew the beast?"

"The younger, hight Eudoric," said Voytsik.

"Nay, Your Honor, 'twas I!" said Jillo.

"That is not what he said when we came upon
them red-handed from their crime," said Voytsik.
"This lean fellow plainly averred that his companion
had done the deed, and the other denied it not."

"I can explain that," said Jillo. "I am the servant of
the most worshipful squire, Eudoric Dambertson of
Arduen. We set forth to slay the creature, thinking
this a noble and heroic deed that should redound to
our glory on earth and our credit in Heaven. Whereas
we both took part in the act, the fatal stroke was
delivered by your humble servant here. Howsomever,
wishing like a good servant for all the glory to go to
my master, I gave him the utter credit, not knowing
that this should be counted as blame."

"What say ye to that, Master Eudoric?" asked the
judge.

"Jillo's account is essentially true," said Eudoric.
"I must confess, all the same, that my failure to slay
the beast was due to mischance and not to want of
intent."

"Methinks they utter a pack of lies to confuse the
court," said Voytsik. "I have told Your Honor of the
circumstances of their arrest, whence ye may judge
how matters stand."

The judge put his fingertips together. "Master
Eudoric," he said, "ye may plead innocent, or as
incurring sole guilt, or as guilty jointly with your
servant. I do not think that ye can escape some guilt,
since Goodman Jillo, being your servant, acted under your orders. Ye are therefore responsible for his
acts and at the very least a fautor of dragocide."

"What happens if I plead innocent?" asked Eudoric.

"Why, in that case, an ye can find an attorney, ye

shall be tried in due course. Bail can plainly not be allowed to foreign travelers, who can so easily slip from the grip of the law."

"In other words, I needs must stay in jail until my case come up. How long will that take?"

"Since our calendar be crowded, 'twill be at least a year and a half. Whereas, an ye plead guilty, all is settled in a trice."

"Then I plead sole guilt," said Eudoric.

"But, dear Master—" wailed Jillo.

"Hold thy tongue, Jillo! I know what I do." Turning to the judge, Eudoric added: "Furthermore, Your Honor, I do solemnly declare Jillo to be completely innocent, imprimis: because as the court said, he acted under my orders; and secundus: because his action was aimed, not at any gain of's own, but at saving his master from the monster's maw, as any good and faithful servant would do."

The judge chuckled. "An old head on young shoulders, I perceive. Well, Master Eudoric, I find you guilty on all four counts and amerce you the wonted fine, which be one hundred marks on each count."

"Four hundred marks!" exclaimed Eudoric. "Our total combined resources, at this moment, amount to fourteen marks and thirty-seven pence, plus some items of property left with Master Kasmar in Liptai."

"So, ye shall serve out the corresponding prison term, which comes to one mark a day—unless ye can find someone to pay the balance for you. Take him away, jailer."

"But, Your Honor!" cried Jillo. "What shall I do without my noble master? When shall I see him again?"

"Ye may visit him any day during visiting hours. It were well if ye brought him somewhat to eat, for our prison fare be not of the daintiest."

At the first available visiting hour, Jillo pleaded to be allowed to share Eudoric's sentence. He wailed:

"Oh, the disgrace of it, that the scion of the noble house of Arduen be mewed up like a common peasant or mechanic! I had a thousand times rather serve your sentence myself—"

"Be not a bigger fool than thou canst help!" snapped Eudoric. "I took sole blame so that you should be free to run mine errands; whereas, had I shared my guilt with you, we had both been clapped up here. Take this letter to Doctor Raspiudus, seek him out, and acquaint him with our plight. If he be in sooth a true friend of our own Doctor Baldonius, belike he'll come to our rescue."

Doctor Raspiudus was short and fat, with a bushy white beard to his waist. "Ah, dear old Baldonius!" he cried in good Helladic. "I mind me of when we were lads together at the Arcane College of Saalingen University! Doth he still string verses together?"

"Aye, betimes he does," said Eudoric.

"Now, young man, I daresay that your chiefest desire is to escape this foul hole, is't not?"

"That, *and* to recover our three remaining animals and other possessions left behind in Liptai, *and* to depart the land with the two square yards of dragon hide that I've promised to Doctor Baldonius, with enough money to see us home."

"Methinks all these matters were easily arranged, young sir. I need only your power of attorney, to enable me to go to Liptai, recover the objects in question, and return hither to pay your fine and release you. Your firearm is, I fear, lost to you, having been confiscated by the law."

" 'Twere of little use without a new supply of the magical powder," said Eudoric. "Your plan sounds splendid; but, sir, what do you get out of this?"

The enchanter rubbed his hands together. "Why, the pleasure of favoring an old friend—and also a chance to acquire most of a dragon's hide for mine own purposes. I know somewhat of Baldonius' experiments. An he can do thus-and-so with two yards of dragon, I can surely do more with a score."

"How will you obtain this dragon hide?"

"By now the foresters will have skinned the beast and salvaged the other parts of monetary worth, all of which will be put up at auction for the benefit of the kingdom. And I shall bid them in." Raspiudus chuckled. "When the other bidders know against whom they shillaber, I misdoubt they'll force the price up very far."

"Why can't you get me out of here now and then go on to Liptai?"

Another chuckle. "My dear boy, erst I must see that all be as ye say in Liptai. After all, I have only your word that ye be in sooth the Eudoric Dambertson of whom Baldonius writes. So bide ye here in patience a few days more. I'll see that ye be sent better aliment than the slop served here. And now, pray, your authorization. Here are pen and ink."

To keep from starvation, Jillo got a job as a paver's helper and made hasty visits to the jail during his lunch hour. When a fortnight had passed without a word from Doctor Raspiudus, Eudoric told Jillo to go to the wizard's home for an explanation.

"They turned me away at the door," reported Jillo. "They told me that the learned doctor had never heard of us."

As the import of this news sank in, Eudoric cursed and beat the wall in his rage. "That filthy, treacherous he-witch! He gets me to sign that power of attorney; then, when he has my property in his greasy paws, he conveniently forgets about us! By the God and Goddess, if I ever catch him—"

"Here, here, what's all this noise?" said the jailer. "Ye disturb the other prisoners."

When Jillo explained the cause of his master's

outrage, the jailer laughed. "Why, everyone knows that Raspiudus be the worst skinflint and treacher in Velitchovo! Had ye asked me, I'd have warned you."

"Why has none of his victims slain him in revenge?" queried Eudoric.

"We are a law-abiding folk, sir. We do not permit private persons to indulge their feuds on their own, and we have some *most* ingenious penalties for homicide."

"Mean ye," said Jillo, "that amongst you Pathenians, a gentleman may not avenge an insult by the gage of battle?"

"Of course not! *We* are not bloodthirsty barbarians."

"Ye mean there are no true gentlemen amongst you," sniffed Jillo.

"Then, Master Tiolkhof," said Eudoric, calming himself by force of will, "am I stuck here for a year and more?"

"Aye, but ye may get time off for good behavior at the end—three or four days, belike."

When the jailer had gone, Jillo said: "When ye be free, Master, ye must needs uphold your honor by challenging this runagate to the trial of battle, to the death."

Eudoric shook his head. "Heard you not what Tiolkhof said? These folk deem duelling barbarous and boil the duellists in oil, or something equally entertaining. Anyway, Raspiudus could beg off on grounds of age. We must, instead, use what wits the Holy Couple gave us. I wish now that I'd sent you back to Liptai to fetch our belongings and never meddled with this roly-poly sorcerer."

"True, dear Master, but how could ye know? I should probably have bungled the task in any case, what of my ignorance of the tongue and all."

After another fortnight, King Vladmor of Pathenia died. When his son Yogor ascended the throne, he declared a general amnesty for all offenses lesser than murder. Thus Eudoric found himself out in the street again, but without horse, armor, weapons, or money beyond a few marks.

That night in their mean little cubicle, Eudoric said: "Jillo, we must needs somehow get into Raspiudus' house. As we saw today, 'tis a big demesne with high, stout wall around it."

"An ye could get a store of that black powder, we could blast a breach in the wall."

"But we have no such stuff or means of getting it, unless we raid the royal armory, which is beyond our powers."

"Then how about climbing a tree near the wall and letting ourselves down by ropes inside from a convenient branch?"

"A promising plan, *if* there were such an overhanging tree. But there isn't, as you saw as well as I when we scouted the place. Let me think. Raspiudus must have supplies borne into his stronghold from time to time. I misdoubt his wizardry be potent enough to conjure foodstuffs out of the air."

"Mean ye that we should seek entrance as, say, a brace of chicken farmers with eggs to sell?"

"Just so. But nay, that won't do. Raspiudus is no fool. Knowing of this amnesty that enlarged me, he'll be on the watch for such a trick. At least, so should I be in his room, and I credit him with no less wit than mine own. . . . I have it! What visitor would be likely to call upon him now, one whom he would not have seen for many a year but whom he would hasten to welcome?"

"That I know not, sir."

Eudoric said: "Who would wonder what had become of us and, detecting our troubles in his magical scry-glass, would follow upon our track by uncanny means?"

"Oh, ye mean Doctor Baldonius!"

"Aye; my whiskers have grown nigh as long as his since last I shaved. And we're much of a size."

"But I never heard that your old tutor could fly about on an enchanted broomstick, as some of the mightiest magicians are said to do."

"Belike he can't, but that is something Doctor Raspiudus would not know."

"Mean ye," said Jillo, "that ye've a mind to play Doctor Baldonius? Or to have me play him? The latter would never do—"

"I know, good my Jillo. You lack the learned patter proper to wizards and other philosophers."

"Won't Raspiudus recognize you, sir? As ye say, he's a shrewd old villain."

"He's seen me but once, in that dark, dank cell, and that for a mere quarter-hour. Methinks I can disguise myself well enough to befool him—unless you have a better notion."

"Alack, I have none! Then what part shall I play?"

"I had thought of going in alone—"

"Nay, sir; dismiss the thought! Me, let my master risk his mortal body and immortal soul in a witch's lair without my being there to help him—"

"If you help me the way you did by touching off that firearm whilst our dragon was out of range—"

"Ah, but who threw the torch and saved us in the end? Besides, a man of the good doctor's standing would not travel about without an attendant or servant. What disguise shall I wear?"

"Since Raspiudus knows you not, there's no need for any. You shall be Baldonius' servant as you are mine."

"Ye forget, sir," said Jillo, "that if Raspiudus know me not, his gatekeepers might. Forsooth, they're like to recall me because of the noisy protests I made when they barred me out."

"Hm. Well, you're too old for a page, too lank for

a bodyguard, and too unlearned for a wizard's assistant. I have it! You shall go as my concubine!"

"Oh, Heaven above, sir, not that! I am a normal man! I should never live it down!"

Eudoric smiled. "Then each of us shall have a hold on the other. If you'll hold your tongue on events wherein I have appeared in less than heroic light, I will keep mum about your disguise."

To the massive gate before Raspiudus' house came Eudoric, with a patch over one eye and his beard, uncut for a month, bleached white. A white wig cascaded down from under his hat. He presented a note, in a plausible imitation of Baldonius' hand, to the gatekeeper:

Doctor Baldonius of Treveria presents his compliments to his old friend and colleague Doctor Raspiudus of Velitchovo, and begs the favor of an audience, to discuss the apparent disappearance of two young protegés of his.

A pace behind, stooping to disguise his stature, slouched a rouged and powdered Jillo in woman's dress. If Jillo was a homely man, he made a hideous woman, at least as far as his face could be discerned beneath the head cloth. Nor was his beauty enhanced by the dress, whch Eudoric had stitched together out of tacky cloth. The garment looked like what it was: the work of a rank amateur at dressmaking.

"My master begs you to enter," said the gatekeeper.

"Why, dear old Baldonius!" cried Raspiudus, rubbing his hands together. "Ye've not changed a mite since those glad, mad days at Saalingen! Do ye still string verses?"

"Betimes. Ye've withstood the ravages of time well yourself, Raspiudus," said Eudoric in an imitation of Baldonius' voice. He added:

"As fly the years, the geese fly north in spring;
   Ah, would the years, like geese, return awing!"

Raspiudus roared with laughter, patting his paunch.
"The same old Baldonius! Made ye that verse but
now?"

Eudoric made a deprecatory motion. "I am a mere
poetaster; but, had not the higher wisdom claimed
my allegiance, I might have made some small mark
in poesy."

"What befell your poor eye?"

"My own carelessness in leaving open a corner of a
pentacle. The demon got in a swipe of's claws ere I
could banish him. But now, good Raspiudus, I have
a matter to discuss, whereof I told you in my note—"

"Yea, yea, time enow for that. Be ye weary from
the road? Need ye baths? Aliment? Drink?"

"Not yet, old friend. We have but now come from
Velitchovo's best hostelry."

"Then let me show you my house and grounds.
Your lady—?"

"She'll stay with me. She speaks nought but
Locanian and fears being separated from me amongst
strangers. A mere swineherd's chick, but a faithful
creature. At my age, that is of more moment than a
pretty face."

Presently, Eudoric was looking at his and Jillo's
palfreys and their sumpter mule in Raspiudus' stables. Eudoric made a few hesitant efforts, as if he
were Baldonius seeking his young friends, to inquire
after their disappearance. Each time, Raspiudus
smoothly turned the question aside, promising en-
lightenment later.

An hour later, Raspiudus was showing off his magical sanctum. With obvious interest, Eudoric examined a number of squares of dragon hide spread out
on a workbench. He asked:

"Be this the integument of one of those Pathenian dragons, whereof I have heard?"

"Certes, good Baldonius. Are they extinct in your part of the world?"

"Aye. 'Twas for that reason that I sent my friend and former pupil to fetch me some of this hide for use in my work. How doth one cure this hide?"

"With salt and—*unh!*"

Raspiudus collapsed, Eudoric having struck him on the head with a short bludgeon that he whisked out of his voluminous sleeves.

"Bind and gag him and roll him behind the bench!" said Eudoric.

"Were it not better to cut his throat, sir?" asked Jillo.

"Nay. The jailer told us that they have ingenious ways of punishing homicide, and I have no wish to prove them by experiment."

While Jillo bound the unconscious Raspiudus with a length of rope from beneath his dress, Eudoric chose two pieces of dragon hide, each about a yard square. He rolled them into a bundle and lashed them with another length of rope. As an afterthought, he helped himself to the contents of Raspiudus' bulging purse. Then he hoisted the roll of hide to his shoulder and issued from the laboratory, calling to the nearest stable boy.

"Doctor Raspiudus," he said, "asks that ye saddle up those two nags." He pointed. "Good saddles, mind ye! Are the animals well shod?"

"Hasten, sir," muttered Jillo. "Every instant we hang about here. . . ."

"Hold thy peace! The appearance of haste were the surest way to arouse suspicion." Eudoric raised his voice. "Another heave on the girth, fellow! I am not minded to have mine aged bones shattered by a tumble into the roadway."

Jillo whispered: "Can't we recover the mule and your armor to boot?"

Eudoric shook his head. "Too risky," he murmured. "Be glad if we get away with skins intact."

When the horses had been saddled to his satisfaction, he said: "Lend me some of your strength in mounting, youngster." He groaned as he swung awkwardly into the saddle. "A murrain on thy master, to send me off on this footling errand—me, who haven't sat a horse in years! Now hand me that accursed roll of hide. I thank thee, youth; here's a little for thy trouble. Run ahead and tell the gatekeeper to have his portal well open. I fear that, if this beast pull up of a sudden, I shall go flying over its head!"

A few minutes later, when they had turned a corner and were out of sight of Raspiudus' house, Eudoric said: "Now trot!"

"If I could but get out of this damned gown. . . ." muttered Jillo. "I can't ride decently in it."

"Wait till we're out of the city gate."

When Jillo had shed the offending garment, Eudoric said: "Now ride, man, as never before in your life!"

They pounded off on the Liptai road. Looking back, Jillo gave a screech. "There's a thing flying after us! It looks like a giant bat!"

"One of Raspiudus' sendings," said Eudoric. "I knew he'd get loose. Use your spurs! Can we but gain the bridge. . . ."

They fled at a mad gallop. The sending came closer and closer, until Eudoric thought he could feel the wind of its wings.

Then their hooves thundered across the bridge over the Pshora.

"Those things will not cross running water," said Eudoric, looking back. "Slow down, Jillo. These nags must bear us many a league, and we must not founder them at the outset."

*   *   *

". . . so here we are," Eudoric told Doctor Baldonius. "Ye've seen your family, lad?"

"Certes. They thrive, praise the Divine Pair. Where's Lusina?"

"Well—ah—ahem—the fact is that she be not here."

"Oh? Then where?"

"Ye put me to shame, Eudoric. I promised you her hand in return for the two yards of dragon hide. Well, ye've fetched me the hide, at no small effort and risk, but I cannot fulfill my side of the bargain."

"Wherefore?"

"Alas! My undutiful daughter ran off with a strolling player last summer, whilst ye were chasing dragons, or *vice versa*. I'm right truly sorry. . . ."

Eudoric frowned silently for an instant, then said: "Fret not, esteemed Doctor. I shall recover from the wound—provided that you salve it by making up my losses in more materialistic fashion."

Baldonius raised bushy gray eyebrows. "So? Ye seem not so griefstricken as I should have expected, to judge from the lover's sighs and tears wherewith ye parted from the jade last spring. Now ye'll accept money instead?"

"Aye sir. I truly loved the lass and still do, albeit I confess that my insensate passion had somewhat cooled during our long separation. Was it likewise with her? What said she of me?"

"Aye, her sentiments did indeed change. I would not outrage your feelings—"

Eudoric waved a deprecatory hand. "Continue, pray. I have been somewhat toughened by the months in the rude, rough world, and I am interested."

"Well, I told her she was being foolish to the point of idiocy; that ye were a shrewd lad who, an ye survived the dragon hunt, would go far, but her words were: 'That is just the trouble, Father. He is too shrewd to be very lovable.' "

"Hmph," grunted Eudoric. "What looks to one

acquaintance like a virtue appears to another as a vice. 'Tis all in the point of view. One might say: I am a man of enterprise, thou art an opportunist, he is a conniving exploiter." Eudoric released a small sigh. "Well, if she prefer the fools of this world, I wish her joy of them. As a man of honor, I would have wedded Lusina had she wished. As things stand, trouble is saved all around."

"To you, belike; though I misdoubt my headstrong lass will find the life of an actor's woman a bed of violets.

> "Who'd wed on a whim is soon filled to the brim
> With worry and doubt, till he longs for an out.
> So if ye would wive, beware of the gyve
> Of an ill-chosen mate; 'tis a harrowing fate.

"But enough of that. What sum had ye in mind?"

"Enough to cover the cost of my good destrier Morgrim and my panoply of plate, together with lance and sword, plus a few other chattels and incidental expenses of travel. Fifteen hundred marks should cover the lot."

"Fif-teen-*hundred!* Whew! I could never afford— nor are these moldy patches of dragon hide worth a fraction of the sum."

Eudoric sighed and rose. "You know what you can afford, good my sage." He picked up the roll of dragon hide. "Your colleague Doctor Calporio, wizard to the Count of Treveria, expressed a keen interest in the material. In fact, he offered me more than I have asked of you, but I thought it only honorable to give you the first opportunity."

"What!" cried Baldonius. "That mountebank, that charlatan, that faker? Misusing the hide and not deriving a tenth of the magical benefits from it that I should? Sit down, Eudoric; we will discuss these things."

An hour's haggling got Eudoric his fifteen hundred marks. Baldonius said: "Well, praise the Divine Couple that's over. And now, beloved pupil, what are your plans?"

"Would ye believe it, Doctor Baldonius," said Jillo, "that my poor deluded master's about to disgrace his lineage and betray his class by a base commercial enterprise?"

"Forsooth, Jillo? What's this?"

"He means my proposed stagecoach line," said Eudoric.

"Good Heaven, what's that?"

"My plan to run a carriage—ye know, like that thing the Emperor rides about Solambrium in, but of vastly improved design—weekly from Zurgau to Kromnitch, taking all who can pay the fare, as is done in Pathenia. We can't let the heathen Easterlings get ahead of us."

"What an extraordinary idea! Need ye a partner?"

"Thanks, but nay. Baron Emmerhard has already thrown in with me. He's promised me my knighthood in exchange for the partnership."

"Nobility hath been extinguished!" wailed Jillo.

Eudoric grinned. "Jillo is more loyal to the class whence I have sprung than I am. Emmerhard said much the same sort of thing, but I convinced him that any enterprise involving horses were a fit pursuit for a gentleman. Jillo, you can spell me at driving the coach, which will make you a gentleman, too!"

Jillo sighed. "Alas, the true spirit of knighthood is dying in this degenerate age. Woe is me, that I should live to see the end of chivalry! How much did ye think to pay me, sir?"

III

The Count's Coronet

When King Valdhelm II of Locania died, his heir, King Valdhelm III, bade all his nobles to his coronation in the royal city of Kromnitch. This was also the county seat of the King's feudatory, Count Petz of Treveria. One of Petz's liege men was Baron Emmerhard of Zurgau, among whose vassals was Sir Dambert Eudoricson of Arduen.

After the royal command arrived, Sir Dambert and his family met before dinner to discuss their plans. Eudoric joined them late and dirty.

"Eudoric!" cried the Lady Aniset. " 'Tis the third time of late that thou hast tracked mud into the castle. What's got into thee?"

"Mother!" exclaimed the young man. "If you'd had my troubles—"

"Thy carriage-wagon?" asked Sir Dambert.

"Aye. The thing overset on a turn and spilt me into the mud. Lucky I wasn't slain, besides which, the vehicle has suffered scathes that'll take a fortnight to remedy. I fear the fabrication of such a

37

device be beyond our local wainwrights. I should have thought on that ere I entered into this compact with Baron Emmerhard."

"Belike," observed Eudoric's middle brother Olf, "your coach be too high and narrow."

"Aye, but there's no easy remedy. If I make the tread wider, the cursed thing can't pass the narrow straits on the Zurgau-Kromnitch road, for which traffic the wain's especially designed. If I make the wheels smaller, they'll give the passengers a fine bouncing."

Eudoric's sister asked: "Why go you not back to Pathenia, where this art be better understood, and buy a carriage-wain already made?"

" 'Tis an arduous two-months' journey, and the road over the Asciburgis is a mere track, impassable to wheeled traffic."

"Then," said Eudoric's younger brother Sidmund, "why not hire a brace of Pathenian wainwrights to come hither and work for us?"

"They would not depart their own land unless compelled by force."

"Then compel them!" snorted Sir Dambert. "By the Divine Pair, are we of gentle blood or are we not? Where's thy knightly mettle? Eh?"

Eudoric smiled. "Father, you know not the Pathenians' persnickety ideas of the rights of their citizens. 'Twould but get me mewed up in prison again, with none to go bail for me."

"The Emperor hath an one," said Sir Dambert thoughtfully. "This carriage must needs have been made by local wainwrights."

"Aye, I've seen it," said Eudoric. " 'Tis but a farmer's wagon with a fancy gilded body on top. Gives the passengers a fearful shaking; can't turn sharply-angled corners. My coach, contrarywise, suspends the body from springs and leather straps, to soften the jouncing, and can turn in its own length. I marked these virtues of the Pathenian coach when I rode in it, when Jillo and I were on our way to Velitchovo."

Sir Dambert sighed. "A fantastical land, this Pathenia, where dragons have the law's protection and villeins assert their rights against their betters. But let's to this question of the coronation. Wilt thou come, Eudoric? 'Twould pleasure me to have thee by me, but the choice is thine."

"Your pardon, Father," replied Eudoric, "but I plan to tarry here. Not being knighted, I'm not included in the royal command. Someone should remain to keep an eye on our demesne, lest that caitiff Rainmar raid us. I must, moreover, ride my wainwrights with a needle-spined spur, lest Baron Emmerhard seize the pretext to flout our compact."

"Doth he cool towards thee, then?" asked Dambert, frowning.

"Aye. 'Twas all firmly fixed: he to pay for the building of the coach and, upon its completion, to knight me and give me Gerzilda in marriage, in requital for a partnership in my coach line. Now he holds back the money and sidles around his promises like a crab on the strand. Meanwhile, my wainwrights grow loud in demands for arrears in their pay—"

"Part of thy trouble," said Dambert, "lies at the door of Emmerhard's lord. Petz of Treveria is a man of antique fancies, who likes not the grant of golden spurs for aught but deeds of dought upon the battlefield. Quotha, there's been too much purchase of honors and titles by baseborn tradesmen—"

"My spurs will be for the dragonslaying, not for carriage building."

"But, son, thy dragonslaying was done, not in the Empire before witnesses, but in a distant, heathen land. So Petz and Emmerhard have nought but thy word—"

"What ails my word?" began Eudoric angrily.

"Oh, I believe thee; so do we all. But these others know thee not as we do."

At an inn of Kromnitch, Baron Emmerhard admired his scarlet-and-ermine reflection in a pier glass. He ran a comb through his graying beard, slapped a sandstorm of dandruff from his robe, and said to his wife:

"Not bad for a man of mine age, my dear. Now, prithee, the coronet!"

The Baroness Trudwig turned to Emmerhard's body servant. "My lord's coronet, Sigric! 'Tis in the trunk with the scarlet stripes."

"Forgive me, Your Ladyship," said the valet, "but 'tis not there."

"How now?" said Emmerhard. "Let me see. . . . Thou are right, varlet! Then where is the accursed bauble?"

"I know not, my lord," said Sigric. "Mona and Albrechta and I have already searched the twenty-three trunks and coffers. I know not how to tell you, sir, but I fear me it hath been left behind in Castle Zurgau—"

"*What!*" roared Emmerhard, hopping and stamping. "Thou dolt! Ass! Noodlehead!" He aimed a punch at Sigric but was careful, even in his rage, to move slowly enough to give Sigric time to duck. Good valets were not easily come by.

A half-hour later, the contents of the twenty-three traveling chests of Baron Emmerhard and his family were spread around their suite, but there was no sign of Emmerhard's coronet. The baron sat in a chair with his face in his hands, while his wife and four daughters tried to comfort him.

"Nay, nay," he groaned. "By the God and Goddess, I cannot take my place in line without my regalia. 'Twere a slight to the fledgling King. I should never live it down. I'll send a message to young

Valdhelm, that I'm taken with a sudden tisic and like to die o't."

"Could not a hard-riding courier gallop back to Zurgau to fetch the thing hither in time?" asked the Lady Trudwig.

"Nay, with the fleetest steeds in relays, he could not return ere the morrow, and the coronation's at high noon today."

Gerzilda, the tall, willowy, blond eldest daughter, spoke up: "Father! Don't you call to mind that my lord Petz be abed with the gout? He hath been excused from the ceremony."

"Well?"

"Why can ye not borrow Treveria's coronet?"

"Nay, 'tis a count's coronet. It hath more spikes and knobs than that of a mere baron."

"None would notice. If any do, ye can explain the circumstance and pass it off with a jest. And I shall die if I cannot attend in my new gown. . . ."

Baron Emmerhard grumbled some more, but at length his womenfolk brought him round.

"Well," he said at last, "let's forth, stopping at Count Petz's on the way. Since his house be on t'other side of the city, this divigation will force us to miss the burning of the heretics; but that can't be helped."

Because of the gathering of the nobility, the narrow, winding streets of Kromnitch were more crowded than usual, despite a persistent drizzle. The chairs bearing Baron Emmerhard and his family were stopped a score of times as the chairmen bearing them slipped and staggered over the muddy cobbles. It took the party over an hour to reach Count Petz's mansion.

Knowing his master's vassals by sight, the door-keeper promptly opened the portal for the Zurgau family. He told Emmerhard: "My lord is with his physician, sir; but I'll send a message."

"A pox!" cried Emmerhard. "This brooks no delay. Petz knows me well enough. Stay here, ladies; I'll go up myself."

"But, my lord—" began the doorkeeper.

"My good man, take thine etiquette and stuff it. I'm in a very swivet of a hurry. Show me to your master's chambers or call me one who will."

When Baron Emmerhard, preceded by a frightened servant, burst into Count Petz's bedchamber, they found the huge old Count of Treveria sprawled on his bed, and a gray-bearded, bespectacled little man pottering around a tripod and muttering. A mixture of burning powders perfumed the air with a rainbow of aromatic smokes. The physician chanted: "*Abrasaxa, Shenouth—*"

"Petzi!" cried Emmerhard, heedless. "Pardon the intrusion, but I must have your help instanter!"

"Oh, Emmeri!" growled Petz, heaving his great bulk up and rearranging his vast white beard atop the covers. "Why in the name of the Divine Pair did ye interrupt Calporio's spell against my gout? Now he must needs start over."

"A grievous thing indeed, my lords," clucked the little man. " 'Tis the second such interruption. I might as well go back to bleeding."

"Which will doubtless finish off my liege lord altogether," said Emmerhard. "Doctor Baldonius tells me that bleeding's a useless, discredited—"

"Baldonius!" snorted Doctor Calporio. "I will not try Your Lordship's patience with my opinion of his servants, but if that mountebank—"

"Hold thy tongue, sirrah; we've no time for disceptation. Petzi, my trouble is this. . . ." Emmerhard rattled off his tale of the forgotten coronet.

"Certes, ye shall have mine," said Petz. He spoke to the servant who had ushered Emmerhard in.

"Harmund! Give the baron my coronet to wear at the coronation. Yarely; he hath but little time."

"A thousand thanks, Petzi!" roared Emmerhard, turning with a wave to follow Harmund out. "Let me know when I can do aught for you."

Harmund led Emmerhard to Count Petz's strong room. After comings and goings with key rings—for the door could be opened only by turning two keys in the lock at once—they entered the room. When a massive chest was unlocked and the lid thrown back, two coronets lay revealed, each in its padded, satin-lined box. Harmund hesitated, saying:

"My lord said not which to give you, sir. Shall I go back to ask—"

"Nay, nay, no time. Besides, 'twould grossly upset his little wizard, were his spell to be thrice interrupted. The crown on the left looks the worse for wear; let's try it! I would fain not expose my old friend's best headpiece to the risk of dent or downfall."

The old coronet proved a size too large. "Murrain!" said Emmerhard. "This thing rides upon mine ears."

"I'll fix it, my lord," said Harmund. A strip of parchment stuck with flour paste to the inside of the lining made the coronet fit passably well; and the baron, beaming with relief, rushed off to join his women.

As Emmerhard had anticipated, they were too late to view the burning of the heretics, three unrepentant monotheists from Pathenia. They reached the Great Temple of the Divine Pair just in time to take their places for the coronation. Emmerhard, torn between haste and the wish to move in a stately, dignified manner, was the last man to reach the barons' rank. He ventured a glance down the knights' rank, behind the barons, and nodded briefly as Sir Dambert greeted him with a small, discreet wave.

While Emmerhard was lining up with the other

barons of the Empire, Doctor Calporio sought out the chest in Count Petz's strong room, wherein lay the remaining coronet. "Harmund!" shrieked Calporio.

"Aye, Doctor?" Rattling keys, the servant hastened into the storeroom.

"Why gavest thou the baron the old coronet?"

"He chose it himself, sir; none forbade—"

"Knowst not that I've been using the bauble for a mighty magical work? That it be charged with puissant sorcerous powers? Ah, demons of the Pit, with what ninnyhammers am I surrounded!"

Calporio dashed out with his purple robe flapping and, back in Count Petz's bedchamber, told his employer of this untoward development.

"Carry not on so, good my Doctor," said the count. "From what ye told me, the wearer must needs do certain things and make a wish, ere the demon imprisoned in the gem will act. Is't not so?"

"Aye, but—"

"Since Emmerhard knows not the formula, he cannot activate the demon. So let us calmly await his return of the object."

Calporio did not look convinced.

Baron Emmerhard stood in the Great Temple, in a row with his fellow barons, while the ceremony ground on. It had already lasted two hours, and ahead lay at least two hours more of hymns and sermons and speeches and ritual acts of allegiance to the King. Valdhelm III, resplendent in blue and gold, had just made his appearance before the altar.

The new king was a nondescript young man, pleasant enough but not, it would seem, very bright. Rumor had it that at times he fancied himself a watering pot. The effective rule of the kingdom would doubtless devolve into the hands of a cabal of ruthless, power-hungry magnates like the Duke of Tencteria, who had been acting as adviser to the crown prince. Emmerhard looked upon the future with gloom.

For the present, the baron's feelings were of suffocating boredom. Even the most glittering tableaux lose their glamor with time; and for Emmerhard, the coronation had long since passed that point. He was evidently not the only one so afflicted. Out of the corner of his eye he had seen Baron Randver of Sidinia sneak a quick gulp of water-of-life from a flask concealed in the sleeve of his robe.

Furthermore, the baron's feet hurt. The Emperor and his family were seated in the front pew, and behind them sat several kings of the Empire. Everyone else, however, had to stand. Moreover, the parchment strip inside the coronet began to cut painfully into Baron Emmerhard's forehead.

King Valdhelm was involved in a lengthy series of answers to questions from the Supreme Pontiff of the Holy Universal Dualistic Church, when Emmerhard's nose began to itch.

All eyes were fixed upon the King. Some, Emmerhard suspected, feared and some hoped that the young simpleton would get his responses mixed up, thus casting doubt upon the validity of the ceremony, or at least cause political embarrassment and get the reign off to an ill-omened start.

Making sure that no one was watching him, Baron Emmerhard gave his nose a furtive scratch. At the same time he thought, silently moving his lips: "I wish I were home!"

And *floomp!* he found himself alone in a forest.

The baron's first impulse was to flee shouting in mad terror, but he mastered himself. After all, he reflected, he was a mature man of worldly experience, who had survived riots, battles, and assassination attempts. Now he studied his surroundings.

Nothing but greenery could be seen in any direction. Judging by the fresh springtime foliage, he might well be somewhere in his own well-forested barony of Zurgau, although he could not say just where.

In youth, Emmerhard had often hunted in the woods of the county of Treveria; but during the last decade he had hardly hunted at all. At first an injury had discouraged this activity; later he had become too involved with the economic side of his barony to resume the sport. Now he had forgotten most of the topographic details of his forested demesne.

Still, he reasoned that if he walked downhill, he would surely come to a stream. This would lead him to the River Lupa, which flowed past the village of Zurgau. He thought of climbing a tree to get his bearings but decided against it, lest he ruin his coronation clothes. Besides, the pale-green leaves were too thick to enable him to see far, even from aloft.

He was plainly the victim of magic; some spell had whisked him from the coronation to this distant spot. He wondered whether any had noticed his disappearance and whether some foe had done this to shame him. If magic had brought him hither, magic was needed to take him back.

Before setting out on a hike, for which his coronation costume was ludicrously unsuited, Emmerhard raised his voice in a bellow:

"Hola! Hola, there! Help!"

On the third attempt, he heard a faint reply: "Who calls?"

"Help! Help!" repeated Emmerhard.

"I come," said the voice.

Emmerhard heard the sound of hooves, muffled by turf. Soon a horse came in sight, the rider swaying and ducking as he avoided branches.

"Eudoric!" cried Emmerhard. For the rider was indeed his stocky, square-jawed prospective son-in-law. Caring little for appearances, Eudoric wore rough, stained forester's garb. A pair of bulging canvas saddlebags hung from the horse's withers.

"By the guardians of Hell!" cried the baron. "How camest thou here so timely?"

"I've been visiting with my former tutor, the learned Doctor Baldonius," said Eudoric. "By the God and Goddess, my lord, what do you here in your court regalia? A horse on a housetop were no more incongruous."

"I know! I know!" cried Emmerhard, kneading his knuckles. "Saidst thou we be nigh unto Baldonius' house? Pray lead me to him, forthwith! Magic brought me hither, in the blink of an eye but now; and magic shall take me back. Hasten Eudoric, so that I may return ere the coronation be over or my absence marked!"

Eudoric studied the baron with narrowed eyes. "A moment, good my lord. Meseems there be a question or two to be answered first."

"What questions, sirrah?"

"Imprimis, there's my oft-promised knighthood. You know of my dragonslaying in Pathenia, not to mention my serving a month in their stinking jail for the breach of their game laws. So now, where's my title?"

"Dost mean that thou would abandon me in the trackless wildwood, an I comply not with thy demands?"

Eudoric grinned. "You grasp the import of my words, my lord, albeit I should have framed my request more tactfully. Secundus, you've promised me Gerzilda's hand; and when I've pressed you of late, you've put me off, as if you were minded to renege on our bargain."

"The final word shall be the lass's own. I'm no petty tyrant, to give my ewe lambs to husbands against their will."

Eudoric waved a hand. "That aspect frets me not. And lastly, there's the money I owe the wainwrights, which you've promised me and then withheld—"

"Thy damned coach-wagon hath been a-building for months, with no end in sight. Am I to pour my silver down a bottomless well?"

The argument raged for another quarter-hour, while Baron Emmerhard grew ever more agitated. At last he burst out:

"Oh, very well, thou scoundrel! I'll yield to thy extortionate demands because I must. Now show me the way to Baldonius' house!"

"Not that I mistrust your word," drawled Eudoric, "but I shall be able better to guide you when your undertakings are writ on parchment."

"Impudent knave!" shouted the baron, waving clenched fists. "What shall we write upon in this wilderness? Bark?"

Eudoric brought out of one saddlebag several sheets of parchment and a quill and stoppered inkhorn. "Here, by good hap, are the latest drawings of plans for our coach. The backs will serve nicely."

"Hast pen and ink, too, thou young devil?"

"Certes. A gentleman of business like me must ever be prepared. First we'll set down my patent of knighthood. I'll serve as scribe if you wish, my lord."

"Write clearly, then. Remember, I read not badly."

Another quarter-hour passed while Eudoric painstakingly composed three documents binding Baron Emmerhard to fulfill his promises. The documents signed, Eudoric seated the wrathful baron upon his horse's rump and clucked the beast to a trot.

Doctor Baldonius weighed the coronet, peered at it through a lens, and pressed an ear against the gold. Then he shook his head.

"Typical of Calporio's incompetency," he said. "The demon was entrapped in the great emerald for but a single usage. When my lord scratched his nose and murmured a wish to be back in his own demesne, the demon whisked him hither and then fled back to its own plane. Now the coronet bears no more magic than any other headpiece."

"Why didn't the sprite deposit me at Castle Zurgau instead of in the woods?" asked Emmerhard.

"The spell had been tailored to the needs of Count Petz. All the demon knew of you was that ye were the Lord of Zurgau; so it dropped you at random in the barony. Or else it was the simple inaccuracy that one expects of a pilot model. 'Twas a stroke of luck that ye encountered Sir Eudoric."

"Luck, say ye? Humph!"

Doctor Baldonius' smile showed briefly through his long gray beard. "I said not what kind of luck it was, my lord. Would ye enact the ritual of knighting now, ye twain?"

A moment later, Eudoric grinned wryly as he felt his sore shoulder. "My father-in-law-to-be has had his revenge. He dubbed me nigh hard enough to break my collar bone."

"No more than thou meritest, whelp," growled Emmerhard. "Now, Doctor, canst send me back to Kromnitch ere the damned ceremony be over?"

"There is a spell," mused the wizard, "but 'twill cost you a thousand marks—"

"Hoy! Art mad, old man?"

"Nay, my lord. This cantrip calls for my rarest ingredients and leaves me fordone for a sennight. Time presses; shall we begin?"

A puff of displaced air announced the return of Baron Emmerhard to the Great Temple of Kromnitch, just as the Supreme Pontiff lowered the royal crown, its great gems winking in the lamplight, on to the head of the kneeling Valdhelm. Since all eyes were fixed on the twinkling, many-hued gems, the only one to notice Emmerhard's materialization was the person standing directly behind him, in the front rank of the knights.

Sir Fredlin Yorgenson of Aviona, far to the north, blinked and stared in disbelief at the baron's suddenly visible back. When Emmerhard disappeared, over an hour before, Sir Fredlin assumed that he had dropped off to sleep on his feet and that he had only dreamed of a man who had stood before him. Now Fredlin was sure that he had not dozed; but he decided never to cast doubt upon his sanity by telling of this phenomenon.

That eventide, Baron Emmerhard sat in his suite at the inn, fuming. "A pox on that young extortioner!" he barked. "I ought to have snatched the damned parchments out of his hands and destroyed them. But, by the time I bethought me of that, Baldonius had already witnessed them, and the whelp had returned them to his scrip. Besides, he's a well-thewed youth, and I'm not so young as whilom."

"Why not see our counselor-at-law, Doctor Rupman?" asked Gerzilda. "Surely he could find a way out of these legal gyves that Dambert's son has tricked you into."

"Nay, nay, puss," said Emmerhard. "Rupman's legal fees would exceed all that I owe Eudoric under my bond. And, forsooth, when I look at the matter with the eye of reason, that's the only one of the three instruments that truly hurts. 'Tis nought to me if Eudoric Dambertson strut about with 'sir' before his name. And whether he wed thee or not is, in fine, a matter for thy choice."

"If Eudoric's coach enterprise succeed, we may recover our coin," added Baroness Trudwig.

"A big 'if,' my dear," grumped Emmerhard. "I've lost faith in the scheme, what of the long delays. Nor am I fully convinced that such a partnership be meet for a nobleman, despite Eudoric's argument that anything to do with horses be a gentlemanly pursuit *ipso facto*. Still, 'tis not impossible."

"What said Count Petz when thou didst return his coronet?"

"He thought it a splendid joke, albeit that little grasshopper of a wizard, Calporio, was vexed at the expenditure of his costly enchantment on such a sleeveless errand. But Petzi, between roars of laughter, said he was thankful that the spell had first been tested on his faithful vassal—me—'stead of on's fat and gouty self. A murrain on all magical mummeries! Now, my dears, ye'd best get on with your robing and primping, lest we be late for the royal feast and the coronation ball."

Feeling very tall and noble in his gilded spurs, Sir Eudoric handed the reins to Jillo and swung down from the driver's seat of his coach in the courtyard of Castle Zurgau. Baron Emmerhard sourly regarded the gleaming paint, as yet unmuddied and unmarred.

"Well, my lord?" said Eudoric.

Emmerhard jerked a thumb. "Thou shalt find her in the flower garden."

Eudoric left the coach in charge of Jillo. In the flower garden he came upon Gerzilda. "Darling!" he cried, spreading his arms.

"Darling me no darlings, sirrah!" she said, backing away.

"Why, what's the matter? Are you not my betrothed?"

"Nay, nor never shall be. Think you I'd wed a man who so entreated my poor father?"

"But, Gerzilda, it was the only way I could—"

"Talk all you please, but 'twill make no difference. Go! Your presence is hateful to me."

Eudoric went. In the courtyard, he and Baron Emmerhard traded looks. Eudoric said: "Knew you what she'd say?"

"Aye. Blame me not; 'twas her idea entirely."

Eudoric thought. "Has her head been turned by the attentions of the fops in Kromnitch?"

Emmerhard shrugged. "All I can say to that is, she cut a swath at the grand ball, with several young noblemen dancing attendance upon her. Some have requested permission to call upon her here.

"Now, if I may offer advice, *Sir* Eudoric, meseems a young fellow like thee, who cares little for distinctions of rank and hath the outlook of a tradesman, were happier with some tradesman's daughter."

"Oh? I'll think on't." Eudoric's melancholy visage brightened. He swung into the driver's seat, took the reins from Jillo, and waved cheerfully to Baron Emmerhard as he guided the vehicle out of the castle gates and towards the town of Zurgau, to pick up his first passengers for Kromnitch.

After all, he thought, while he was sorry to lose Gerzilda—a fine girl, whom he could have loved—that was not the only factor. For one thing, she was taller than he; for another, she had hinted at plans for making Eudoric over into her idea of a stylish, sophisticated young gentleman of leisure. And, while there were plenty of girls in the world, nothing could equal a good, trusty source of steady income.

IV

The Sensuous Spider

The gilding had not yet begun to wear off Eudoric's spurs when he sat in Castle Zurgau with his father and Baron Emmerhard. They spoke of the recent holdup of Eudoric's stagecoach by a band of masked robbers as it made its weekly journey from Zurgau to Kromnitch. After taking the passengers' money and pretties, the bandits had waved the coach on its way.

"From what ye tell me," said Eudoric's partner Emmerhard, " 'Tis certain that this be Rainmar's doing. Ordinary outlaws would have slain the people and burnt the carriage to vent their spleen. But Baron Rainmar's a thrifty thief, not fain to kill the duck that lays the emerald eggs."

"That decided, sir," said Eudoric, "what's to do? I'm not more timorous than most; but I'm not fain to gallop up to Castle Hessel, ring my lance against his portal, and dare Rainmar to come forth and fight it out."

"Aye, certes, thou hast right," puffed Sir Dambert. "By the God and the Goddess, he'd hang thee in-

53

stanter, heedless of the punctilios of chivalry. Time was when we'd saddle up, to raid and waste his robbers' hold in vengeance—"

"But no more," interrupted the baron, "now that the crown hath gathered so much power unto itself. Even Rainmar dare not openly raid his neighbors, as was his former wont. So, to sweeten's pudding, he doth these fribbling banditries."

"Well," said Eudoric, "couldn't you gentlemen lend me men-at-arms to escort my coach, where the road passes nigh unto Rainmar's domain? There were ten or twelve in his gang; so a dozen sturdy guards should suffice and a score be a plenty."

Baron Emmerhard shook his head. "The King hath called upon me for a draft of men, to help the Emperor quell the rebels in Aviona. Praise the Divine pair, he commanded not mine aging self to take the field in person. And the rest of my menfolk I shall need for the haying."

"The men of Aviona must be daft, to fight at the height of the harvest," observed Sir Dambert.

"Nay," said Emmerhard, "they live farther north and so have already finished their field work."

"How about you, Father?" asked Eudoric.

Sir Dambert shook his head. "Aye, certes, would that I could help thee; but 'tis the same with me. I lack enough men to guard the castle as 'tis. I dare not strip it of all protection, lest Rainmar essay a sudden descent in spite of royal bans. Moreover and besides, Rainmar hath a plenty of men, the which he feeds on the usufruct of's robberies. An we put on ten guards, he'll come at thee with a score; an we put on twenty, he'll summon up two score, eh?"

"A fine basket of grapes," snorted Eudoric, "when a harmless, law-abiding gentleman can't make an honest living. Let me think. . . . I recall the saying of the soldier of fortune, Karal of Gintz: 'If thou canst not vanquish them, unite them with thyself.' "

Gruffly, Dambert laughed. "Tell me not, son, that thou think of turning reaver likewise!"

"Nay, nay. Methought a call upon the lord of Hessel and a friendly discussion might yield results. At least, it's better than driving the coach to Kromnitch empty of passengers, they being daunted by fear of another ambuscado."

Emmerhard said: "Have a care that he clap thee not up in's dungeon for ransom."

"Has he not a daughter?" asked Eudoric. "Meseems I have heard of such an one."

"Aye," said Emmerhard. "A truly nubile daughter, whom Rainmar would dearly love to marry off. Trouble is, none of his noble neighbors will countenance a union with this caitiff rascal. So Rainmar faces the choice of, imprimis, leaving poor Maragda an unwed spinster; secundus, of wedding her to one of his scurvy knaves of low degree; or tertius, of reforming his evil ways."

"Well, sir," said Eudoric to the baron, "since your own lovely daughter jaculated me forth, I have been casting about."

"Eudoric!" cried Sir Dambert. "Thou shalt not marry into that clan of banditti! I forbid it!"

"Easy, Father. I have no intention of wedding the lass, at least so long as Rainmar pursue his larcenous course. But think: if Rainmar accept me as a suitor, he'd be less fain to rob his prospective son-in-law's coach, would he not? With a call at Castle Hessel from time to time, we should be able to keep the pot on the boil until the Emperor settle his score with Aviona and our men-at-arms come home. Then we can do as we list."

Dambert gloomily shook his head. "Oh, thou art clever, son; cleverer than becomes a knight, forsooth. Thine estate of knighthood entails obligations—"

"Chide not the lad," said Baron Emmerhard. "In these degenerate days, when a stroke of the pen oft outweighs a slash of the sword, we need all the wit we can muster."

Days later, Baron Rainmar of Hessel, a huge, red-bearded, broken-nosed man, stared suspiciously at his caller. Behind him, men-at-arms handled pikes and fingered crossbows.

"State thy business," he barked.

Eudoric allowed a smile to cross his normally serious face. Although a little shaken by the row of Rainmar's victims—hanged, impaled, or beheaded—beside the front gate, he hid his feelings. He said:

" 'Tis merely a friendly visit, my lord; my first to your hold. I must avow my admiration for its strength."

"It serves as a shield 'twixt me and mine envious neighbors—but is this all thou came for? I can scarce believe—"

Trying to look like a bashful lover, Eudoric said: "Truth to tell, I have heard of your daughter, whose beauty, they say, outshines that of the Goddess herself. Being unwed, methought a closer look might lead to better things."

Rainmar grunted. "Well, sit down, sit down. Ye may go," he told his cutthroats. "Witkin! Tell the Lady Maragda that her presence is desired. Now then, Sir Eudoric, I've heard some tales of thee: that thou have adventured in distant lands; that thou be hand in glove with mine old enemy Emmerhard; and that, despite thy gilded spurs, thou seek to gain wealth by a base, unknightly enterprise: to wit, running a carriage-wagon from Zurgau to Kromnitch. What sayest thou? Katilda! Wine!"

"As to the first point," said Eudoric, "it's true that I've journeyed to Pathenia. 'Twas there I learnt of this system of carrying men and goods from hence to thither, at regular intervals, for an established fare. For the second, Baron Emmerhard is my partner in the business. Who his friends and foes be amongst the nobility is no concern of mine. And for the third, I hold that no trade founded on horses can be construed as base. Didn't the word 'knight' once mean simply 'one who rides a horse'?"

"A doctor of law or theology art thou in spirit," growled Rainmar, "for all thy purported knighthood. Ah, Maragda, my dear! Here's a neighbor's scion, hight Sir Eudoric Dambertson, come to make our acquaintance."

The tall, red-haired young woman curtseyed as Eudoric rose and bowed. When she was seated, the conversation wandered off into weather, crops, the latest plague, an outbreak of witchcraft, and imperial politics. In parting, Eudoric received a guarded invitation to call again.

When at last he cantered away on Daisy, Eudoric drew a long breath. At least, the robber lord had neither hanged him nor held him for ransom.

As autumn advanced and nights grew cold, Eudoric found himself calling more and more often at Castle Hessel. As he had predicted, the attacks on his coach had ceased. Moreover, he had come to like Rainmar's daughter Maragda. He was not, Eudoric sternly told himself, authentically in love. He had been through that delightful and perilous state before, but the outcome had never been happy. Now he viewed such matters in a colder, more critical light. Calculation and expediency counted at least as much as the fleshly urges of a normal man in his twenties.

He noted, for instance, that Maragda's generous build and exuberant health predicted healthy offspring. If, he thought, he could but find some means to persuade or coerce Baron Rainmar into giving up his career of rapine. . . .

On Eudoric's sixth call, however, Rainmar said bluntly: "A word, Sir Eudoric, ere I allow thee a sight of my chick. What are thine intentions towards her?"

"I had thought," said Eudoric carefully, "that, if she be willing, I should—as soon as mine own affairs render me able and worthy—enter a formal suit for her hand."

"Methought as much," growled Rainmar. "Thou hast things in thy favor, for all that thou art connected with the sniveling Emmerhard. But thou hast also some in disfavor, which must needs be settled."

Eudoric raised his eyebrows. "To which of my many faults do you refer, my lord?"

"This new knighthood, for ensample. I'm told 'twas not for any knightly deed, but for base monetary return—that thou didst, in fine, bribe Emmerhard with the offer of a partnership."

"No bribe, my lord. The two were quite distinct. I had the knowledge to launch our enterprise; Emmerhard, the gold. So we pooled the twain. For the other, I had done a deed of dought in slaying a dragon in Pathenia; although, because of distance, I could not trot out witnesses to the act. Ask the learned Doctor Baldonius whether the two square yards of hide I fetched him from the East be not the integument of an authentic dragon." Eudoric refrained from mentioning that, first, Jillo Godmarson had actually killed the beast; and second, Eudoric had promptly been thrown in jail for breach of the Pathenian game laws.

"That may be." Rainmar ran thick fingers through his beard, in which a few threads of silver appeared amid the copper. "But I'm not quite satisfied. Dost thou adhere strictly to the code of knighthood: to be loyal to thy suzerain, protect the female kind, and so forth?"

"To the best of mine ability," said Eudoric.

"Hm. Well, now, I have a task for thee, which will test thy mettle. Accomplish it, and Maragda shall be thine. Knowest thou the deadly wood of Dimshaw, in the farthest reaches of my demesne?"

"Who does not?"

"Hast heard of the great spider, whom we call Fraka, that haunts it?"

"Yea, and how she has slain the men who blundered into her web. What—?" With sinking heart, Eudoric realized what was coming next.

"In fine," said Rainmar, "thy task is to slay this monster."

Eudoric gulped, acutely aware of the obligation of knighthood to show no fear, no matter how one felt. "Why don't you simply burn that part of Dimshaw where Fraka dwells?"

"That were to waste good timber, which I mean to cut to sell to the Emperor's shipwrights. Besides, in a dry spell such as we now undergo, such a fire might get out of hand and devastate the barony. Nay, this is a task for one fearless hero—to wit, thyself."

"How shall I do this deed, sir?" said Eudoric, feeling anything but fearless.

"That's thine affair. Thou shalt, howsomever, do it in true knightly fashion. No magical sleights or base commercial tricks! I demand a proper stand-up fight, in accord with the ethic of chivalry. Mine own past may not have been utterly sinless," (which Eudoric thought the understatement of the century) "but my lass shall wed none but the purest and most unsullied gentleman of the realm."

Eudoric hastened to the forest dwelling of Doctor Baldonius, who got out his huge, iron-bound encyclopedia and turned the pages of crackling parchment.

"Here we be," he said. " 'Arachnida. . . . The class is remarkable for the variety of its methods of copulation and fertilization. Among the Scorpiones, copulation takes place front to front by apposition of the genital orifices of the two sexes, located forward on the underside of the cephalothorax. In the Opiniones. . . .' Let's omit those. 'In most of the Araneae, the terminal segments of the palpi of the male are modified into intromittent organs—' "

"Very interesting," said Eudoric, "but I would fain kill this creature, not make love to it."

"I shall come to that," said Baldonius. " 'The females of most species of spiders readily seize and eat the smaller specimens of their kind. To avoid being thus devoured, spiders male have instinctive patterns of behavior to inhibit the cannibalistic tendencies of the females, at least until after copulation. Some perform courtship dances, displaying colored tufts on one pair of appendages.' "

"Forsooth, must I dance a fandango before Fraka, whilst waving a feather duster at her?"

"Nay. Be patient but a little longer. 'Among the web-spinning spiders, recognition is effected by jerks on the female's web, according to a code specific to the species.'

"Now let me think. Meseems I recall a little treatise on the codes of jerks of different arachnids, by Doctor Bobras, mine old fellow student at Saalingen. Ah, here it is!"

Baldonius pulled a scroll from a cabinet of pigeon-holes, which held a score of books in this antiquated format. He unrolled it and scanned. "Here we be. 'Among the Gigantaraneae, the code is one long pull, two short jerks, one long pull, and two short jerks, followed by a pause before repeating.' "

"You mean," said Eudoric, "a kind of dum-deedee-dum-deedee rhythm?"

"Exactly; in poetical terms, a double dactyl, if mine ancient colleague be correct. If threatened by Fraka, ye may be able to halt her advance by jerking her web in that manner."

"Even though I look not at all like a male spider?

At least, the code is not something complicated, which one might forget in the stress of the moment. But suppose I get a leg caught in the sticky web? From what I hear, it's the devil's own task to cut oneself loose."

"The cure for that, my boy, is fire. These webs quickly yield to flame."

"But if I must needs strike sparks into tinder with my igniter, whilst the Lady Fraka advances upon me—"

"Carry a lanthorn, with spare candles. If caught, lift the lid and apply the candle flame to the web. Fear not this great bug; *omne ignotum pro magnifico est.*"

"If a sudden gust blow out my flame, I shall be in no very rosy predicament," Eudoric mused. "What puzzles me is, how these creatures make a living. One can see how an insect, having but little wit, can blunder into a spider's web. But one would think that beings of a higher order, such as birds, hares, and swine, would speedily learn to avoid entangling strands."

Baldonius shrugged. "This I know not; but Bobras says that a spider can live for many months without aliment."

"And how is the race of these vermin propagated? Fraka is the only spider of her kind in the circumjacent demesnes. Albeit long-lived, she'll not live forever, even if I fail to terminate her existence. Whence would come her normal mate?"

"Methinks from the wilderness of Bricken, west of Rainmar's dominions. There, they say, dwell many uncanny creatures, which have vanished from more cultivated lands. Whether Fraka migrated thence to Dimshaw, or whether she already dwelt in Dimshaw when the intervening lands were cleared for farming, I know not."

"Has she ever been seen outside of Dimshaw?"

"I think not. Once a spider of this family hath built its web, it strays not thence. If in your quest ye learn aught of the habits of the Gigantaraneae, be sure to let me know. I can get a small monograph out of it, *saltem.*"

"And," said Eudoric, "if I fail, be sure that I get a nice tombstone, *in absentia.*"

Leaving Jillo to hold the horses, Eudoric plunged into Dimshaw on foot. He wore half armor and hip boots, with a crossbow slung across his back. The crossbow was of the simple stirrup type, cocked by putting one's foot in the stirrup and pulling back the string with both hands. It was more powerful than a longbow and also quicker to reload than a heavy steel siege crossbow, which required a winch or at least a cocking lever. While all of this gear made Eudoric slow and clumsy, he thought it would give him a better chance of escaping Fraka's fangs.

In one hand he carried a boar spear and a small storm lantern. The lantern's flame was hardly visible in the low, autumnal sunshine, which slanted through the bare branches and gnarled trunks of ancient trees. In the other hand he bore his cutlasslike hunting falchion, with which from time to time he blazed a tree to insure the finding of his homeward way. This forethought was typical of Eudoric's methodical habits.

Eudoric spent the day in prowling Dimshaw without success. At nightfall, he and Jillo returned to the village of Hessel West.

With the dawn, they were back in Dimshaw Wood. Eudoric had been plodding among massive oaken trunks for an hour when something caught his foot. He almost fell but saved himself by a thrust of the butt of the spear. He looked down but could see nothing. Nevertheless, his left boot was firmly fixed in place.

He struck with his falchion. The blade encountered some yielding, springy substance, to which it stuck fast. Pulling and twisting failed to tear it loose.

Eudoric thrust the point of his spear into the earth and set down the lantern. The falchion, which he had released, remained in mid-air, swaying gently. A rising breeze, which rustled the thick carpet of dead leaves, made the sword wobble more widely.

When he looked closely, Eudoric made out faint silvery gleams in the air. If he moved his head, these gleams, he discovered, formed a continuous streak. This streak began at the roots of an ancient oak beside him and rose slantwise into the branches above. The streak was tangent to the skin of his left boot and to the blade of the falchion.

Now Eudoric realized something that he had not known: Fraka's web was almost invisible. In full sunlight, one could see faint reflections from its surfaces; in dim light, one could probably not see it at all.

This explained how Fraka could make a living from the beasts and birds of Dimshaw. Be they never so clever, they could not avoid the strands of a web that they could not see. Hence the forest was large enough to furnish game for a single predator of Fraka's kind.

Looking up along the strand of web on which he was caught and moving his head, Eudoric made out more shimmering gleams among the branches and saw that he was at the edge of a monstrous web, covering several acres. Then he saw something else.

A large, black, hairy object, moving briskly among the strands of the web, was fast approaching.

Eudoric had a moment of panic. Fraka, he saw, had a body as big as a cask and eight hairy legs, each longer than a man is tall. As she came closer, it transpired that the strand of web on which he was caught was not the only one in that neighborhood. Several others slanted down to the ground nearby. If he had avoided the one he had struck, he would have blundered into another strand.

In his panic, he sought to free himself from the web at all costs. Snatching up the lantern, he lifted the lid to apply its little flame to the strand that prisoned him. At that moment, however, the breeze —as he had feared it might—freshened and blew out the flame.

Lowering herself on the nearby strands that slanted down to the ground, Fraka came close enough for Eudoric to see the fangs that tipped her foremost pair of mandibles. A foot long each, they resembled the ends of a pair of bull's horns: dark, shiny, curved, and needle-pointed. Her four forward eyes gleamed like great, round, dark jewels.

Eudoric thought of trying to struggle out of his boot. Without help, however, this would take more minutes than Fraka would need to reach him. He wondered if he could unstrap his crossbow, charge it, and get off one quarrel before Fraka reached him. If he failed to kill with the first shot, he would be doomed, tethered as he was. And where in that bulbous body lay the vital organs? Perhaps a lusty thrust of the boar spear between the mandibles. . . .

While these thoughts flashed through his mind, Eudoric fumbled for his igniter. The urge to get free of the web overrode all else.

He brought out the little copper device, consisting of a tinder box with an open compartment on top and a little hammer bearing a piece of flint in its jaws. His hands shaking, Eudoric pulled out the little drawer containing the tinder. With forced deliberation, he put several pinches of tinder into the tray. Shielding the igniter with his free hand, he snapped the hammer.

The igniter missed fire. Fraka was now almost within reach of his spear, and another stride would bring her foremost legs upon him. Her eight eyes— four in front, two on top, and one on either side—

gleamed like onyx, and her mouth parts worked hungrily.

Then Eudoric remembered the signal code. Frantically, he seized the hilt of his falchion and gave a series of tugs—long-short-short, long-short-short.

Fraka hesitated, her forelimbs poised above Eudoric. The knight repeated the jerks, again and again.

Instead of pouncing on Eudoric, Fraka reared back on her after legs and spread the four forelimbs, as if offering him her nether side. He noticed that the spider's underside was buff-colored, and the hairs on the belly were short and silvery instead of long and black like those on the rest of her body.

As Eudoric repeated the signal, Fraka remained immobile in her spread-eagled pose. On her underside, just below the narrow waist, Eudoric saw what he supposed to be her genital opening, moving and working as if in lustful anticipation.

Eudoric's mind raced, wondering how long he could make Fraka remain in her attitude of "Take me, I am yours!" Any time, the spider might get it into her cephalothorax that he was not, after all, her true love. Then she would eat him, as spiders of more usual size devoured flies.

He might pick up the spear, which stood upright in the turf, and plunge it into her; but that would probably break the spell that held her. If he failed to kill with the first thrust, she would finish him in her death throes.

Fraka's forelimbs twitched, as if she were coming out of her nuptial trance. Eudoric jerked the falchion, and the spider once more froze in position.

Stooping, Eudoric again shielded the igniter with his hand. Watching Fraka, he cautiously held the device below the strand of web that touched his boot. Then he waited for a lull in the breeze.

The wind took a long time to die. Eudoric had to jerk the web again to immobilize the arachnid. As he did so, a sudden puff of wind blew all the tinder out of the tray of the igniter.

Cursing under his breath, Eudoric reloaded the tray. At last came another lull. Quickly, Eudoric snapped the hammer. The sparks spat into the tinder, which briefly blazed up.

For a few precious seconds, the flame engulfed the web, which hissed and began to burn. Yellow flames ran up and down the strand, which parted like a snapping fiddle string. The falchion fell to the ground, and Eudoric found his leg free.

The knight snatched his spear and lurched back beyond Fraka's reach as the spider came abruptly out of her trance. When a flame ran up the burning strand to one of her legs, she whipped around with surprising agility and rapidly climbed the strands by which she had descended.

Dropping his spear, Eudoric unslung his crossbow, cocked and loaded the weapon, and aimed. The after end of Fraka's bulbous abdomen would have been an easy shot. But Eudoric did not shoot.

Fraka continued her scramble, growing smaller. The flame ran on up the burning strand to its junction with another. It became two flames, eating away the web in divergent directions; then three and four and six.

Fraka continued her flight until she was a mere dot in a distant tree. Some of the flames in the nearer parts of the web fizzled out. Others spread; then they, too, died. A goodly part of the web had been destroyed.

Eudoric unloaded, unbent, and shouldered his crossbow. Guided by his tree-trunk blazes, he made his way back to the edge of the wood.

Baron Rainmar's mouth fell open. "Thou—allowed-est—this—monster—to escape unscathed? No jest?"

he gasped. "In the name of the God and Goddess, why? What demon of stupidity possessed thee?"

Eudoric smiled. "Well, sir, ere I set out, you lectured me on knightly conduct. You commanded me to adhere most punctiliously to the rules thereof. One such rule is to protect the female kind; another is not to betray one who has given the knight her love.

"I'm no spider of the family Gigantaraneae, as Your Lordship knows. Yet it was patent that, as a consequence of my tugging on her web, Dame Fraka saw in me her destined lover. She's not the sort of mate with whom I'd willingly consort; yet the fact that she was a female, who in her peculiar way did care for me, kept me from slaying her.

"Forsooth, 'tis not a matter of much pith and moment. Fraka confines herself to Dimshaw Wood. If you'd guard your folk from her, forbid them to enter the wood. She does none harm where she abides."

Rainmar struggled with his emotions. He tugged at two fistfuls of red beard. "Thou—thou—idiot! Ass! Fool! Witling! Incondite knave! I'll teach thee to play japes with me! Guards! Seize me this runagate! We shall see what ransom—"

"Better not, my lord," said Eudoric, pointing at Rainmar's middle the crossbow, which, to furnish color to his tale, he had cocked and loaded while narrating his adventure. "Hands off your weapons, sirrah! Order your men out of sight. Now shall you accompany me until I'm safely on my way. Remember, at this range the square-headed bolt can punch through armor plate as through that new writing stuff called paper."

With Eudoric's weapon trained on his kidneys, Rainmar preceded Eudoric out the front door, under the portcullis, and across the drawbridge to the greensward where Jillo held the horses. An instant later,

Eudoric and Jillo were galloping away, while a fuming Rainmar screamed orders for pursuit.

The next time a band of masked robbers stopped the Zurgau-Kromnitch coach, a score of stout men-at-arms, lent by Sir Dambert and Baron Emmerhard for the occasion, rushed upon the attackers. The brigands lost five of their number, one to Eudoric's sword. Another lived long enough to confess, under torture, to having been sent by Baron Rainmar.

Eudoric filed a civil suit in the imperial courts against the robber baron. The law's delays being what they were, the suit was still winding its way through the maze of courts long after Eudoric, Rainmar, and all the others mentioned in this tale were in their graves.

At Castle Hessel, Maragda wept.

V

The Virgins
And The Unicorn

When Eudoric's stagecoach line was running smoothly, its proprietor thought of expansion. He would extend the line from Kromnitch to Sogambrium, the capital of the New Napolitanian Empire. He would order a second coach. He would hire a scrivener to relieve him of bookkeeping. . . .

The initial step would be to inspect the Sogambrian end of the route. So in Zurgau and Kromnitch he posted notices that, on a certain day, he would, instead of turning around at Kromnitch to return to Zurgau, continue on to Sogambrium, carrying those who wished to pay the extra fare.

Eudoric got a letter of introduction from his silent partner, Baron Emmerhard of Zurgau. The letter presented Eudoric to the Emperor's brother, the Archduke Rolgang.

"For a gift," said Emmerhard, fingering his graying beard, "I'll send one of my best hounds. Nought is done at court without presents."

"Very kind of you, sir," said Eudoric.

"Not so kind as all that. Be sure to debit the cost of the bitch to operating expenses."

"At what value?"

"Klea should fetch at least fifty marks—"

"Fifty! Good my lord, that's absurd. I can pick up—"

"Be not impertinent with me, puppy! Thou knowest nought of dogs. . . ."

After an argument, Eudoric got Klea's value down to thirty marks, which he still thought much too high. A few days later, he set out with a cage, containing Klea, lashed to the back of the coach. In seven days the vehicle, with Eudoric's helper Jillo driving, rolled into Sogambrium.

Save once as an infant, Eudoric had never seen the imperial capital. By comparison, Kromnitch was but a small town and Zurgau, a village. The slated gables of the capital seemed to stretch away forever, like frozen waves of the sea.

The hordes who seethed through the flumelike streets gave Eudoric pause. They paraded fashions never seen in rural parts. Men flaunted shoes with long, pointed toes, attached by laces to the wearer's legs below the knee; women wore yard-high conical hats. Everyone seemed in a hurry. Eudoric had trouble understanding the metropolitan dialect. The Sogambrians slurred their words, dropped whole syllables, and seldom used the old-fashioned familiar "thou" and "thee."

Having taken quarters at an inn of middling grade, Eudoric left Jillo to care for the coach and team. Leading Klea, he made his way through a gray drizzle to the archducal palace. He tried on one hand to take in all the sights but, on the other, not conspicuously to stare, gape, and crane his neck like a bumpkin.

The palace, sheathed in stonework carved in fantastic curlicues, in the ornate modern style, rose adjacent to the Cathedral of the Divine Pair. Eudoric had had enough to do with the court of his own sovran, King Valdhelm III of Locania, to know what to expect at the palace: endless delays, to be shortened only by generous tipping of flunkeys. Thanks to this strategy, Eudoric got his audience with the Archduke on the second day.

"A bonny beast," said Rolgang, stroking Klea's head. Clad in gold-and-purple Serican silks, the Archduke was a fat man with beady, piercing eyes. "Tell me, Sir Eudoric, about this coach-wagon enterprise."

Eudoric told of encountering regular coach service, unknown in the Empire, on his journey to Pathenia. He recounted bringing the concept back to his home in Arduen, Barony of Zurgau, County of Treveria, Kingdom of Locania, and of having a coach of Pathenian style constructed by local wainwrights.

"This bears thinking on," said the Archduke. "I can foresee some effects adverse to good government. Miscreants could use your coach to flee from justice. Bankrupts could leave the site of their indebtedness and set up in business elsewhere. Subversive agitators could travel 'bout, spreading discontent and rousing the rabble 'gainst their betters."

"On the other hand, Your Highness," said Eudoric, "if the business prosper, you may be able to tax it some day."

The beady eyes lit up. "Aha, young sir! Ye've a shrewd instinct for the jugular vein! With that consideration in mind, I'm sure His Imperial Majesty will impose no obstacle to your enterprise. I'll tell you. His Imperial Majesty holds a levée at ten tomorrow. Be there with this pass, and I'll present you to my 'perial brother."

Leaving the palace pleased by this unexpected stroke of fortune, Eudoric considered buying a fine new suit, although his thrifty nature winced at the idea of spending capital on another such garment before his present best had begun to show wear. He cheered up at the thought that he might well make a better impression as an honest rustic, clean and decent if not stylish, than as an inept imitation of a metropolitan dandy.

Next morning Eudoric, in plain russet and black, stood in line with a hundred other gentry of the Empire. Emperor Thorar IX and his brother passed slowly down the line, while an official introduced each man:

"Your Imperial Majesty, let me present Baron Gutholf of Drin, who fought in the Imperial forces to put down the late rebellion in Aviona. Now he doth busy himself with the reconstruction of his holding, dyking and draining a new polder."

"Good, my lord of Drin!" said the Emperor. "We must needs show our deluded subjects, stirred to rebellion by base-born agitators, that we love 'em in spite of all." Thorar was tall, thin, and stooped, with a gray goatee, an obvious hair piece, and a creaky voice. He was clad all in black, against which blazed a couple of jeweled decorations.

"Your Imperial Majesty," said the usher, "this is Sir Eudoric Dambertson of Arduen. He hath instituted the coach line from Zurgau to Kromnitch."

" 'Tis he of whom I told you," said the Archduke.

"Ah, Sir Eudoric!" creaked the Emperor. "We know of your enterprise. We'll see you anon on this matter. But—are ye not that Eudoric who slew a dragon in Pathenia and later fought the monstrous spider in the forest of Dimshaw?"

Eudoric simpered with affected modesty. "Indeed, 'twas I, Your Imperial Majesty, albeit I came through more by good hap than by good management." He did not add that Jillo had killed the dragon, largely by accident; and that Eudoric, when he had the giant spider Fraka under his crossbow, had let her go on a sentimental whim.

"Stuff, my boy!" said the Emperor. "Good luck comes to those prepared to make the most of it. Since ye've shown such adroitness with strange beasts, we have a task for you." The Emperor turned to the Archduke. "Have ye a half-hour to spare after this, Rolgang?"

"Aye, sire."

"Well, bring the lad to the Chamber of Privy Audience, pray. And tell Heinmar to dig Sir Eudoric's dossier out of the file."

The Emperor passed on.

In the Chamber of Privy Audience, Eudoric found the Emperor, the Archduke, the Minister of Public Works, the Emperor's secretary, and two bodyguards in silver cuirasses and crested helms. The Emperor was turning the pages of a slender folder.

"Sit down, Sir Eudoric," said Thorar. "This bids fair to take time, and we'd not needlessly inflict sore knees 'pon loyal subjects. Ye are unwed, we see, albeit nearing thirty. Why is this?"

Eudoric thought the old boy might give the appearance of doddering, but there was nothing wrong with his wits. He said: "I have been betrothed, Your Imperial Majesty, but chance has each time snatched away my promised bride. That I am single is not from lack of inclination towards the other sex."

"Hm. We must needs 'mend this condition. Rolgang, is that youngest daughter of yours promised yet?"

"Nay, sire."

The Emperor turned back. "Sir Eudoric, the gist is this. Next month, the Grand Cham of the Pantorozians comes on a visit of state, bringing a young dragon to add to the 'perial menagerie. As ye may've heard, our zoölogical collection is, after the welfare of the Empire, our greatest passion. But, for the honor of the Empire, we can't let this heathen Easterling outdo us in generosity.

"Dragons are extinct in the Empire, unless a few still lurk in the wilder wastes. We're told, howsomever, that west of Hessel, in your region, lies the wilderness of Bricken, where dwell many curious beasts. Amongst these is a unicorn."

Eudoric raised his eyebrows. "Your Imperial Majesty wants a unicorn to give to this Pantorozian?"

"Aye, sir; ye've put the bolt in the gold. How 'bout it?"

"Why—ah—sensible though I be of the honor, Your Imperial Majesty, I know not whether I could manage it. As I told you, my previous escapes were more by luck than by skill or might. Besides, my coach line, requiring constant attention to detail, takes all my time—"

"Oh, stuff, my boy! Ye crave a just wage for your labor, as do we all, however we bluebloods affect to be above base thoughts of material gain. Eh, Rolgang?"

The Emperor winked. Eudoric found this ruler's genial cynicism refreshing after the elaborate pretence of the country gentry among whom he lived to care nothing for vulgar money. Thorar continued:

"Well, at the moment we have no vacant baronies or counties to bestow, but my brother hath a nubile daughter. She's not the fairest of the fair—"

"Petrilla's a *good* girl!" the Archduke broke in.

"None denies it, none denies it. Neither doth anyone propose her for the Crown of Beauty at tournaments. Well, Sir Eudoric, how about it? One unicorn for the hand of Petrilla Rolgangsdaughter?"

Eudoric took his time about answering. "The young lady would have to give her free consent. May I have the honor of meeting her?"

"Certes. Rolgang, arrange it, if you please."

While Eudoric had been in love several times, the

outcomes of these passions had given him a cynical, practical view of the battle of the sexes. He had never found fat girls attractive, and Petrilla was fat—not grossly so yet, but give her a few years. She was dark, dumpy, blunt of feature, and given to giggles.

Sighing, Eudoric totted up the advantages and disadvantages of being joined with this unglamorous if supremely well-connected young woman. For a career of courtier and magnate, the virtues of being the Archduke's son-in-law overbore all else. After all, Petrilla seemed healthy and good-natured. If she proved too intolerable a bore, he could doubtless find consolation elsewhere.

Back in Arduen, Eudoric sought out Doctor Baldonius, who again got out his huge encyclopedia, unlocked its iron clasps, and turned page after page of crackling parchment.

"Unicorn," he said. "Ah, here we are. 'The unicorn, *Dinohyus helicornus*, is the last surviving member of the family Entelodontidae. The spirally twisted horn, rising from the animal's forehead, is actually not one horn. This would be impossible because of the frontal suture, along the mid-line of the forehead. It is, instead, a pair of horns twisted into a single spike. The legend that the beast can be rendered mild and tractable by a human virgin appears to have a basis in fact. According to the story. . . .' But ye know the tale, Eudoric."

"Aye," said Eudoric. "You get a virgin—if you can find one—and have her sit under a tree in a wood frequented by unicorns. The beast will come up and lay its head in her lap, and the hunters can rush out and spear the quarry with inpunity. How could that be?"

Baldonius: "My colleague Doctor Firmin hath published a monograph—let me look—ah, here 'tis." Baldonius pulled a dusty scroll from his cabinet of

pigeonholes. "His theory, whereon he hath worked
since we were students at Saalingen together, is that
the unicorn is unwontedly sensitive to odors. With
that great snout, it could well be. Firmin deduces
that a virgin hath a smell different from that of a
non-virgin human female, and that this effluvium nul-
lifies the brute's ferocious instincts. *Fieri potest.*"

"Very well," said Eudoric. "Assuming I can find
me a virgin willing to take a part in this experiment,
what next? It's one thing to rush upon the comatose
beast and plunge a spear into its vitals and quite
another to catch it alive and unharmed and get it to
Sogambrium."

"Alas! I fear I have no experience in such things.
As a vegetarian, I have avoided all matters of chase
and venery. I use the latter word in its hunting
sense; albeit the other meaning were also apt for an
abstemious widower like myself."

"Then who could advise me in this matter?"

Baldonius pondered, then smiled through his silvery waterfall of beard. "There's an unlikely expert
dwelling nigh unto Baron Rainmar's demesne, namely
and to wit: my cousin Svanhalla."

"The witch of Hesselbourn?"

"The same, but don't let her hear you call her
that. A witch, she insists, is a practitioner, of either
sex, of black, illegal goëtics, whereas she's a respect-
able she-wizard or enchantress, whose magics are all
benificent and lawful. Mine encyclopedia traces the
derivation of these words—"

"Never mind," said Eudoric hastily, as Baldonius
began to turn the pages. "I've not met her, but I've
heard. She's a cranky old puzzel, they say. What
would she know of the techniques of hunting?"

"She knows surprising things. 'Twas always said in
the fraternity, if ye wish some utterly useless bit of
odd information, which nobody on earth could rightly
be expected to have—say, for ensample, what Count

Holmer the pretender had for breakfast the day they cut off his head—go ask Svanhalla. I'll give you a letter to her. I haven't seen her for years, for fear of her raspy tongue."

"So now ye be a knight?" said Svanhalla, sitting with Eudoric in the gloom of her hut. "Not by any feats of chivalry, ta-rah! ta-rah! But by shrewdly taking advantage of what luck hath brought you, heh? I know the tale of how ye slew that Pathenian dragon—how ye missed clean with the Serican thunder tube and ran for your life, and how Jillo by chance touched off the sack of fire-powder just as the beast waddled over it."

Silently cursing Jillo's loose tongue, Eudoric kept his temper. "Had I been twice as brave and thrice as adept with the thunder weapon, Madam, 'twould have availed us nought had luck been against us. We should have made but toothsome morsels for the reptile. But let's to business. Baldonius says that you can advise me on the capture of unicorns in Bricken."

"I mought, if ye made it worth me while."

"How much?"

After a haggle, Eudoric and Svanhalla agreed on a fee of sixty marks, half down and the rest when the unicorn was secured. Eudoric paid.

"First," said the witch of Hesselbourn, "ye must needs find a virgin, of above fifteen years. If the tales I hear be true, that may take some doing in Arduen, what with you and your lecherous brethren."

"Madam! I have not carnally known any local lass for nigh a year—"

"Aye, aye, I ken. When the lust becomes too great to endure, ye fare to the whores of Kromnitch. Ye should be respectably wived by now, but the girls all think you a cold-blooded opportunist. Therein, they're not altogether wrong; for, whilst ye love women, ye love your gold even more, heh!"

"You needn't rub it in," said Eurodic. "Besides, I seek advice on hunting, not on love."

"Strange, when your brother Olf doth cut a veritable swath amid the maids of Arduen. Not that I blame the lad overmuch. He's good-looking, and too many peasant maids think to catch a lordling with their coyntes for bait. They hope, if not for lawful wedlock, at least for affluent concubinage. So they all but shout: 'Come, take me, fair sir!' 'Tis a rotten, degenerate age we live in."

"Since you know so much about affairs in Arduen, who, then, *is* still a virgin?"

"For that, I must needs consult my familiar." She issued further instructions on the mechanics of capture, ending: "Come back on the morrow. Meanwhile go to Frotz the rope-maker to order your net and Karlvag the wainwright for your wheeled cage. Be sure they be big and strong enough, else ye may have less luck than ye had with the dragon, heh!"

When Eudoric returned to Svanhalla's house, he found her talking to a bat the size of an eagle. This creature hung upside down from her rafters, along with smoked hams, bags of onions, and other edibles. When Eudoric jumped back, the witch cackled.

"Fear not Nigmalkin, brave and mighty hero! She's as sweetly loving a little demon as ye shall find in the kingdom, heh. Moreover, she tells me what ye be fain to know."

"And that is?"

"Know that in all of Arduen there be but one wench to fill your bill. True, there be other virgins in fact, but none suitable. Cresseta Almundsdaughter is ill and like to die; Greda Paersdaughter's father is a religious fanatic who won't let her out of his sight; and so on."

"Then who is available?"

"Bertrud, daughter of Ulfred the Unwashed."

"Oh, gods! She takes after her sire; one can detect her down-wind at half a mile. Is that the best you can do, Svanhalla?"

"So it is. Take it or leave it. After all, a proud, fierce adventurer like yourself shouldn't mind a few small stinks, now should he?"

Eudoric sighed. "Well, I shall imagine myself back in that prison cell in Pathenia. It stank even worse. I'll get word to Ulfred and his lass."

Dawn, a fortnight later, saw Eudoric riding with Jillo's younger brother, a simple farm hand named Theovic Godmarson, to the home of Ulfred the Un-washed. Since Ulfred had been told by a fortune-teller that he would die of a tisic caught while bathing, the goodman had forsworn all external contact with water. His only child had adopted the paternal habit.

Yet Bertrud Ulfredsdaughter would, if cleaned up, have been a handsome girl. As Eudoric noted when he swung her up to ride pillion on Theovic's mount, some would even deem her beautiful.

Eudoric and his helper took a roundabout path from Arduen to the wilderness of Bricken, in order to avoid the demesne of his old foe Baron Rainmar. Eventually they overtook Jillo, driving an oversized farm wagon to which was affixed a monstrous cage.

At the edge of Bricken Forest, Eudoric left Jillo and the vehicle, for beyond this point there were no passable roads. Loading the tackle and supplies on his horse's back, Eudoric led his mount into the leafy gloom, while Theovic and Bertrud trailed behind.

After an hour of searching among the trees, watch-ing cautiously to avoid the nearly-invisible webs of the giant spiders, Eudoric chose a spot near an efflu-ent of the Lupa. Here grew a grand old beech, with boughs near the ground for easy climbing. Here they pitched their camp.

Rigging the net took the rest of the day. Eudoric

and Theovic, with Bertrud's help, attached the net by slip knots to the higher branches of the beech and to two other trees, so that one pull on the release lanyard would bring the whole thing down. Leaden weights along the edges of the net assured that, when it fell, it would envelop the prey.

The net was heavy and the day, hot. By the time they had completed their task, Eudoric and Theovic were soaked in sweat. They threw themselves down on the soft leaf mold and lay for a time listening to the buzz and chirp of insects.

"I'm for a bath," said Eudoric. "You, too, Theovic? Bertrud, if you go round yonder bend in the stream, you'll find a pool where the stream is gentle and you can wash in privacy. 'Twould do you no scathe."

"Me, wash?" said the girl. "'Tis an unwholesome habit. An ye'd risk your death of cold, 'tis your affair."

During the night, Eudoric heard the snort of a unicorn. The next morning, therefore, he caused Bertrud to sit at the base of the beech, while he and Theovic climbed the tree and waited. Peering through the bronze-green leaves, Eudoric held the lanyard that would release the net. Betrud languidly waved away the cloud of flies that seemed to be her permanent escort.

When it arrived, in the afternoon, the unicorn did not look much like the dainty creatures, half horse and half gazelle, shown on tapestries in the Emperor's palace. Its body and limbs were like those of a buffalo, six feet tall at the shoulder hump, while its huge, warty head bore some resemblance to that of a gigantic boar. The twisted horn arose from its forehead above the eyes.

The unicorn approached the massive beech, beneath which Bertrud sat. The beast moved cautiously, one step at a time. When it was almost under the net, it halted, sniffing with flaring nostrils and baring huge canines more suitable to a beast of prey than a hoofed plant-eater.

The unicorn sniffed some more. Then it threw up its head and uttered a colossal grunt, as loud as a lion's roar but more guttural. It rolled its eyes and pawed the earth with cloven hooves.

"Bertrud!" Eudoric called. "It's going to charge! Climb the tree, quickly!"

As the unicorn bounded forward, the girl, who had watched it with growing dismay on her soil-caked face, scrambled to her feet and swarmed up into the low branches. The beast skidded to a halt, glaring about with bloodshot eyes.

Eudoric pulled the lanyard; but as the net began to fall, the unicorn sprang forward again, swerved to miss the tree, and continued on. One of the leaden weights struck the unicorn's rump as the net descended.

With a frightful bellow, the unicorn whirled, champing its tusks. Seeing no foe, it galloped off into the forest. The crashing and the drumming died away.

When the unicorn-hunters were back on the ground, Eudoric said: "That settles it! Baldonius said these creatures be sensitive to odors. You, my dear Bertrud, have odor for six. Theovic, you shall go to Hessel manor to buy a cake of soap and a large sponge. Here's money."

"Wouldn't ye rather go and leave me to guard the lass, me lord?" said Theovic with a cunning gleam in his pale-blue eyes.

"Nay. Were I recognized, Rainmar would have his bully-boys after us; so keep a close mouth whilst there. Go, and with luck you'll be back for dinner."

Sighing, Theovic saddled his horse and trotted off. With a trembling lip, Bertrud asked: "What—what will ye do to me, sir? Am I to be beaten or raped?"

"Nonsense, wench! I won't hurt a hair of your

head. Think not that, because I have a 'Sir' before my name, I go about bullying my father's people."

"What will ye do, then?"

"You shall see."

"Ye mean to wash me, that's what! I'll not endure it! I'll run away into the wildwood—"

"With unicorns and other uncanny beasts lurking about? Methinks not."

"I'll show thee! I go—"

She started off at random. When Eudoric imitated the grunt of the unicorn, Bertrud shrieked, ran back, and threw her arms around Eudoric's neck. Eudoric firmly unpeeled her, saying:

"When you're nice and clean and the unicorn's caught, then, if you're fain to play such games, we shall see."

Theovic returned at sunset with a bundle. "Here's your soap and all, me lord. Jillo asked after you, and I told him things were going well."

Since Bertrud was busy cooking their supper, Eudoric let the bath go until morning. Then, stripped to his breech clout and with gleeful help from Theovic, he pushed and hauled Bertrud, struggling and weeping, down to the stream. They pulled off her skirt and blouse and forced her, shrieking, into the water.

"Gods, that's cold!" she cried. " 'Twill spell the death of me!"

" 'Tis the best we have, my lady," said Eudoric, scrubbing vigorously. "By the Divine Pair, you have layers of dirt over layers of dirt! Hold still, damn your arse! . . . Hand me the comb, Theovic. I'd get some tangles out of this hair ere washing it. . . . All right, I can manage the rest. It's time you fed the horses."

Looking disappointed, Theovic started back towards the camp. Eudoric continued soaping, scrubbing, and ducking his victim, who by now was too cowed to complain.

"Now," he said, "does that feel so dreadful?"

"I—I know not, sir. 'Tis a feeling I never have had before. But I'm cold; let me warm myself against you. My, bean't ye the strong fellow, though?"

"You're no weakling yourself," said Eudoric, "after the struggle we had to get you into the water."

" I work hard. There's none to do the chores but me, since me mother ran away with that pedlar. What thews!"

She felt his biceps, inching closer until their bodies touched. Eudoric felt his blood stir.

"Now, now, my dear," he said, "*after* the brute's captured, not before." When she continued her explorations, he barked: "I said nay!" and pushed her away.

He pushed harder than he intended, so that she fell backwards and got another ducking. When she scrambled up, her expression had changed.

"So!" she said. "The high and mighty knight won't look at a poor peasant lass! Too grand for aught but them perfumed, painted whores of the courts! Ye may take them all to Hell with you, for all of me!"

She strode out of the pool, picked up her garments, and vanished towards the camp.

Eudoric looked after her with a troubled smile. He devoted himself to his own ablutions until the smell of breakfast reminded him of the passage of time.

He and Theovic rigged the net again. The unicorn came around noon. As before, it seemed about to approach the seated Bertrud but then went into a frenzy of rage. Again, Bertrud had to scramble up the tree to safety.

This time, the unicorn did not even wait for Eudoric to pull the lanyard. It blundered off into the forest at once.

Eudoric sighed. "At least, we shan't have to haul that damned net up into the trees again. But what could have gone wrong this time? . . ." He caught a faint smirk on Theovic's face. "Oho, so thither lies the wind, eh? Whilst I was bathing this morn, you were futtering our frail, so she's no more a virgin!"

Theovic and Bertrud giggled.

"I'll show you two witlings!" howled Eudoric.

He whipped out his hunting flachion and started for the pair. Although he meant only to spank them with the flat, they fled with shrieks of mortal terror. Eudoric ran after them, brandishing the short, curved sword, until he tripped on a root and fell sprawling. When he had pulled himself together again, Theovic and Bertrud were out of sight.

On the borders of the wilderness, Eudoric told Jillo: "When that idiot brother of yours comes in, tell him, if he wants his pay, to return to finish his task. Nay, I won't hurt him, for all his loonery. I should have foreseen what would happen. Now I must needs leave these nags with you whilst I ride Daisy back to Svanhalla's hut."

When Eudoric came again to the cabin of the witch of Hesselbourn, Svanhalla cackled. "Ah, well, ye did your best. But, when the devil of carnal desire reaves a youth or a maid, it takes one of monkish humor to withstand it. That's something neither of those twain possesses."

"All very true, madam," said Eudoric, "but what next? Where shall I find another virgin, sound of wind and limb?"

"I'll send me familiar, Nigmalkin, out to scout the neighboring holdings. Baron Rainmar's daughter Maragda's a filly unridden, but she's to wed in a month. Besides, I misdoubt ye'd find her suitable."

"I should say not! Rainmar would hang me if he could lay hands on me. But. . . . Harken, Madam Svanhalla, would not *you* qualify for the part?"

The witch's bony jaw sagged. "Now that, Sir Eudoric, is something I should never have hit upon.

Aye, for all these years—an hundred and more—I have forsworn such carnal delights in pursuit of the highest grades of magical wisdom. For a price, mayhap. . . . But how would ye get an ancient bag of bones like me to yonder wildwood? I'm spry enough around this little cabin, but not for long tramps or horseback riding."

"We'll get you a horse litter," said Eudoric. "Bide you here, and I shall soon be back."

Thus it came to pass that, half a month later, the aged witch of Hesselbourn sat at the foot of the same beech tree on which Eudoric had rigged his net. After a day's wait, the unicorn approached, sniffed, then knelt in front of Svanhalla and laid its porcine head in her bony lap.

Eudoric pulled the lanyard. The net fell. As Svanhalla scrambled to safety, the unicorn surged up, shaking its head and snorting. Its efforts to free itself got it only more entangled. Eudoric dropped down from the branches, unslung the hunting horn from his back, and blew a blast to summon Jillo.

Eudoric, Jillo, and the forgiven Theovic rolled the beast, exhausted but still struggling, onto an ox hide. Avoiding thrashing hooves and foaming jaws, they lashed it down. Then the hide was hitched to three horses, which towed the ungainly bundle along the trail to the place where they had left the wheeled cage.

It took most of the next day to get the animal into the cage. Once it almost got away from them, and a soaking thunderstorm made their task no easier. But at last the brute was securely locked in.

Eudoric and his helpers shoved armfuls of freshcut grain stalks through the bars. The unicorn, which had not eaten in two days, fell to.

The Archduke Rolgang said: "Sir Eudoric, ye've done well. The Emperor is pleased—nay, delighted.

In sooth, he so admires your buffalo-pig that he's decided to keep the monster in his own menagerie, 'stead o' sending it off to the Cham of the Panto-rozians."

"I am gratified, Your Highness," said Eudoric. "But meseems there was another matter, touching your daughter Petrilla, was there not?"

The fat Archduke coughed behind his hand. "Well, now, as to that, ye put me in a position of embarrass-ment. Ye see, the damsel's no longer to be had, alas, no matter how noble and virtuous her suitor."

"Not dead?" cried Eudoric.

"Nay; quite otherwise. I'd have saved her for you, but my duty to the Empire overbore my private scruples."

"Will you have the goodness to explain, my lord?"

"Aye, certes. The Grand Cham paid his visit, as planned. No sooner, howsomever, had he set eyes 'pon Petrilla than he was smitten with a romantical passion. Nor was she 'verse."

"Ye see, laddie, she's long complained that no gallant gentleman of the Empire could ever love a squatty, swarthy, full-bodied lass like her. But here comes the mighty Cham Gzik, master of hordes of fur-capped nomads. He, too, is a short, stout, swart, bowlegged wight. So 'twas love at first sight."

"I thought," said Eudoric, "she and I had ex-changed mutual promises—not publicly, but—"

"I reminded her of that, also. But, if ye'll pardon my saying so, that was a hard-faced commercial deal, with no more sentiment than a turnip hath blood."

"And she's—"

"Gone off with the Grand Cham to his home on the boundless steppes, to be his seventeenth—or mayhap eighteenth, I forget which—wife. Not the husband I'd have chosen for her, being a heathen and already multiply wived; but she'd made up her mind. That's why my 'perial brother did not deem it necessary to send the Cham your unicorn, since Lord Gzik had already received from us an unthridden pearl of great price.

"But, even if Petrilla be no longer at hand, my brother and I mean not to let your service go unrewarded. Stand up, Sir Eudoric! In the name of His Imperial Majesty, I hereby present you with the Grand Cross of the Order of the Unicorn, with oak leaves and diamonds."

"Ouch!" said Eudoric. "Your Highness, is it necessary to pin the medal to my skin as well as my coat?"

"Oh, your pardon, Sir Eudoric." The Archduke fumbled with fat fingers and finally got the clasp locked. "There ye are, laddie! Take a look in the mirror."

"It looks splendid. Pray convey to His Imperial Majesty my undying thanks and gratitude."

Privately, Eudoric fumed. The medal was pretty; but he was no metropolitan courtier, swanking at imperial balls in shining raiment. On his plain rustic garb, the bauble looked silly. While he could let Petrilla go without uncontrollable grief, he thought that, if they were going to reward him, a neat life pension would have been more to the point, or at least the repayment of his expenses in unicorn-hunting. Of course, if times got hard and the order were neither lost nor stolen, he could pawn or sell it. . . .

He said nothing of all this, however, endeavoring to look astonished, awed, proud, and grateful all at the same time. Rolgang added:

"And now, laddie, there's the little matter we spake of aforetime. Ye are authorized to extend your coach line to Sogambrium, and beyond, if ye can manage. By a decree of His Imperial Majesty, howsomever, all fares collected for such scheduled carriage shall henceforth be subject to a tax of fifty per centum, payable monthly. . . ."

VI

The Sporting Sovran

In the gloom of his tree-shadowed house in the forest, Doctor Baldonius pushed his spectacles up his falconine nose and contemplated Eudoric, who sat before him. "Ye'd fain know why ye, a likely fellow past thirty, of knightly rank and a capable man of affairs, be still unloved and unwed?"

"You've put your shaft in the gold, learned sir," said Eudoric. " 'Tis plain that in this demesne I've bungled. In Franconia, whither my business takes me, I may discover a lass who more esteems my virtues, however small, and is less critical of my faults, however vast. But I count not upon this happy upshot. Meanwhile, what's the answer? To put it curtly, what's the matter with me?"

Baldonius combed his gray cascade of beard with age-knobbed fingers. "Ye'll not take offense if I speak you plain?"

Eudoric's serious countenance wrinkled into an infrequent grin. "Wherefore? You've known me since erst I was sent to you to learn my letters."

"And whacked your small arse when ye put frogs in my hat. But, *lucide exponere,* whereas ye be a good man of your hands and your head, *et cetera,* ye want a very lovable nature. Ye be too coldly calculating, say the maids."

Eudoric sighed. "I feared as much. What's the remedy? Wanton foolery, like unto that ass Landwin of Kromnitch? I long ago learned that clowning was not my calling; my buffooneries offended many and tickled none."

Baldonius reached down his huge encyclopedia, unsnapped the iron clasps, and thumbed through the crackling sand-yellow pages. "When all else fail, consult the wisdom of Aristocles of Spheron, the master of them that know. Ah! Here we be! 'Human beings most readily love others of their species who, alpha, do services for them; beta, flatter them; gamma, refrain from reproaching them for errors; and delta, cultivate good nature and ease of manner.' *Ecce!* Canst comply with that formula, Eudoric?"

Although Eudoric's face had grown as long as an olifant's nose, he squared his broad shoulders. "I'll try; I am not yet quite a dotard. Ere I go, where's your lovely daughter, my whilom betrothed? I heard she'd come home."

"Lusina is out back, hiding. She hath besought me not to divulge her whereabouts to any, especially to you. Such is her shame at having run off with that dastardly vagabond."

"What fetched her back?"

"The actor lown got drunk and beat her, so she lost the child she carried. I lament my unborn grandchild." It was the old scholar-wizard's turn to sigh. "Its absence doth simplify life; but I'd liefer have a bastard heir than none."

"Tell her, pray, that I cherish no hard feelings; a grudge makes a starveling diet. In sooth, I am fain to resume our old acquaintance. That, howsomever, must await my return from Franconia. You'll lend me Forthred for my squire? Mine own has formed a passion to join the priesthood."

"Aye. Ye will find him no more foolish and flighty than most apprentices. But beware of his blundering efforts to cast wizardly spells! Because he hath mastered an incantation for finding lost articles, he thinks himself ready to turn Baron Rainmar into a butter churn."

"My thanks," said Eudoric. "Pray, bid him wait upon me early tomorrow, at the castle."

"Who'll command your stagecoaches?"

"I'm leaving my assistant Jillo to direct the coachmen and my brother Olf to keep the books. Farewell!"

"A pleasant journey, and beware of Rainmar's ruffians!"

A month later, Eudoric and Forthred, sweating in the summer's heat, drew rein at the eastern gate of Letitia, the mighty-walled capital of Franconia. Eudoric, in plain pine-green forester's garb, rode his dappled-gray palfrey Daisy. He had never replaced the destrier Morgrim, which he had lost years before on his dragon hunt in Pathenia. Since then, he had not been mustered for any war of the New Napolitanian Empire; and having little taste for jousting, Eudoric saw no reason to keep so much of his capital tied up in a huge, voracious steed, too massive for peaceful pursuits.

Forthred was a skinny blond youth with the protruding front teeth of a rodent. He rode a common hackney and led two spare horses and a sumpter mule. Among the burdens borne by the mule was a knobby, canvas-wrapped bundle, within which Eudoric's armor lay nested. One never knew when it might be needed.

Eudoric showed his identification to the guards. There was a letter from his father, Sir Dambert of

Arduen—a letter written for Dambert by the castle chaplain. There was a note on good parchment from his father's suzerain, Baron Emmerhard of Zurgau, who was Eudoric's silent partner in the stagecoach line. A third epistle, bearing a gilded coronet at the top, came from Emmerhard's overlord, Count Petz of Treveria.

Since Eudoric knew but little of the Franconian tongue and the guards not a word of Eudoric's native Locanian, a delay ensued while they hunted up an officer fluent in Helladic, the international language. While one guard searched for this officer, another busied himself sealing Eudoric's sword into its scabbard by means of a peace wire.

Eudoric had attended the Imperial Court at Sogambrium and the royal Locanian court at Kromnitch. He was, therefore, unsurprised at the delay in getting permission to see the King, and at the tips extorted by flunkeys before they would even put him on the waiting list. Another month went by before he obtained his audience. During this time, he worked away at the Franconian tongue, dragooning Forthred into tedious word drills.

At last, an official presented a pass to the King's next levée. Eudoric stood in line with foppish Franconian gentlemen, on the tesselated white-and-purple marble of the candle-lit ballroom in King Clothar's palace. The candles were unnecessary, since a brilliant morning sunshine streamed through the tall windows; but Clothar was given to ostentatious display. The candles twinkled; the sun gleamed on cloth-of-gold, cloth-of-silver, and brilliant silks from distant Serica. Incense candles obscured but did not eradicate the odor of the gentlemen, who were not famed for personal cleanliness.

In contrast to all this splendor, the Franconian peasantry, Eudoric had observed along the way, had seemed a singularly downtrodden, miserable lot. He recalled that, a generation before, they had revolted and been put down with merciless rigor.

A blare of golden trumpets announced the King. Clothar was a tall, blond, well-built man of approximately Eudoric's age, with nondescript features enhanced by a mustache and goatee meticulously waxed to three long points, and artificially curled hair down to his shoulders in the Franconian manner. He wore a crimson doublet in the latest style, with twenty-odd silver buttons down the front. The buttonhole had been invented a few-score years before; so the well-born, who had theretofore fastened their garments with pins, laces, and toggles, now embraced the fad of buttons, the more the better.

The heels of the King's high boots resounded on the gleaming marble as he passed along the line, presenting his ring-laden hand to be kissed. An usher read off names from a strip of parchment:

". . . .and next, Your Majesty, is Sir Ganelot of Charomois, who gained the prize at the tourney of Avral. . . ."

"Enough!" said King Clothar suddenly. "We shall be late for our hunt." Holding his hand up with the palm turned outward, he raised his voice: "The rest of you, deem yourselves received. Our thanks for your courtesy. You may refresh yourselves ere departing."

The King strode out, followed by a scuttle of servitors and leaving the usher standing agape with the list in his hand. As the gentlemen began to mill about and chatter, scullions brought in trays of food and bottles of wine, which they set on tables at one end of the ballroom.

Eudoric spooned black caviar on a delicate biscuit and, in his stumbling Franconian, asked his neighbor: "Excuse, sir, but is—are all levées so short as this? I am foreigner."

"This was a long one," said the Franconian, scratching an insect bite. From the breast of his doublet a jeweled order flashed in the sunshine. "Know, good my sir, that His Majesty is a splendid sportsman. If 'tis not hunting, it's jousting, or billiards, or bowls, or tennis, or the Three True Gods know what." Although the man's mouth remained solemn, his eyes revealed a trace of twinkle.

"Then how, pray, do one—does one get one's business with him done?"

"Take up your affair with Master Brulard yonder." He indicated a pudgy, bald, little plain-clad man talking to a glittering noble.

"Who is him—I mean, that man?"

"The King's minister."

"Would you have goodness to present me? I have business."

The man cocked his head with a smile. "A gift for a gift, saith the wise Aristocles. Dost take my meaning?"

"What is—ah—customary here?"

"One golden noble should suffice. 'Twill go to a worthy charity, fear not."

Privately, Eudoric fumed. In the Empire, men of rank were known to solicit bribes, but not so blatantly, nor by amounts that would severely dent the funds he had brought from home. The "worthy charity," Eudoric was sure, would be the man before him. He dug into his wallet.

"Not so crass, young fellow!" murmured the man. "Let us shake hands on it." Eudoric palmed the coin and slipped it into the man's hand under cover of a handshake. The man caused the coin to vanish as by a conjuring trick. "And now, my dear young sir, what is your appellation?"

"Eudoric Dambertson of Arduen, knight," replied Eudoric. "And, sir, may I know your name?"

"Burgenne," said the man. "Come along! May I present my young friend, Sir Eudoric Dambertson?

This is master Brulard, Secretary of State to His Majesty. Give him a moment, Brulard; he seems to have some business in mind."

"I will, Your Grace," said Brulard. "What's toward, Sir Eudoric?"

As he bowed, Eudoric realized with a shock that the person whom he had bribed to introduce him was the Duke of Burgenne, the second most powerful noble in the kingdom. The Franconian nobility, he thought, must be the most grasping lot of aristocrats on earth. "Permit me, Your Excellency. Does —do you know about the novel form of transportation called stagecoaches? . . ."

When Eudoric had made his pitch, Secretary Brulard said: "I shall take counsel with His Majesty and inform you of his decision. Come to my chamber of office in the palace two days hence."

Eudoric politely took his leave of the minister and endeavored to mingle with others at the levée; this, however, with only indifferent success. He hoped to strike up some acquaintance that he could eventually parlay into introductions to nubile young women, since the levée was a strictly male event. To ennoble his search for a mate, he had sworn off commerce with whores and light women. Hence his lusts were beginning to fever him.

The Franconian popinjays, however, were not impressed by Eudoric's plain if decent suit of russet and black, nor by his thick Locanian accent. They were not even beguiled by the Grand Cross of the Order of the Unicorn, with oak leaves and diamonds, which Eudoric had received from the Emperor's brother. Eudoric rarely wore the costly bauble but had trotted it out for this occasion. Most of the nobles flaunted several decorations each, many of which far outblazed Eudoric's. The medal wearers he found polite enough when he accosted them; but they quickly turned their attention elsewhither.

At last, when the others had begun to drift away, Eudoric came upon a youth who had taken too much wine. This young man stared glassily. "Sh-Sir Eudoric Dambertson, didst say? I hight the Cavalier Thwars. P-pleased to know you, sir. A foreigner, be ye not? Some say all foreigners be caitiff rogues, but I am above such boorish prejudice. Some, methinks, are almost true human beings."

"Sir Thwars," began Eudoric cautiously, "pray enlighten me. Another gentleman tell me—ah—that this was a long levée as such thing go. Those at Kromnitch be—are much longer. Why this?"

The youth snorted. "What expect ye under His do-nought Majesty? All his time doth go to games and sports—ahorse, afoot, or abed—leaving none for the business of state. So a baseborn rascal like Master Brulard yonder becomes the veritable ruler of the realm. When the King's unco sister was here, she at least forced the royal nose to the grindstone of public business. Methinks 'twas resentment of her stern governance that led him to dispatch her to the Far West; but now—"

"Shut thy gob, thou ninny!" snarled a gray-thatched nobleman, turning to glare at the speaker. "Wouldst bring trouble upon us all?"

"But, Father—" began Sir Thwars.

"Hold thy flapping tongue! Any fool can see thou'st had too much."

"Oh, very well," grumbled Thwars. "Sir Eudoric, dost attend the duel this afternoon?"

"What duel?"

"Sir Pancar hath challenged Baron Odilo to a fight to the death, with axes afoot. 'Tis strictly unlawful; but who of gentle blood cares for that? I'll escort you to the secret field of honor—"

"Come along, thou noddy!" snapped the father. "An thou remain here, surely shalt thou bring destruction upon us! Your pardon, foreign sir!"

With a nod to Eudoric, the father seized the arm of his son and hauled him, feebly protesting, towards the exit. Eudoric wolfed a slice of fowl, another of bread, and a swig of wine. Then he, too, departed.

In the room that he shared with Forthred, Eudoric lit the three-branched brass candelabrum and opened his book on Franconian grammar. To Forthred he said: "Now say in Franconian: 'I fetched water from the well; I am fetching water from the well; I shall fetch water from the well.' "

Wearing a martyred look, Forthred scratched his head as he fumbled for the words. Then, as he started to speak, a heavy knock resounded. A voice cried:

"Open in the name of the King!"

Master and pupil traded startled looks. Eudoric reached for his scabbarded sword and began to loosen the peace wire, whispering: "Open it, Forthred; but only a crack till we see who it is."

Forthred complied. He began: "Meseems 'tis the King's guard—" when the door flew wide, throwing the apprentice halfway across the room before he recovered his balance. Four mailed men in surcoats of crimson and white, bearing the royal escutcheon, shouldered in. The first said:

"Sir Eudoric Dambertson, ye are summoned to the palace. Come at once!"

"What am I supposed—" began Eudoric. The guardsman snapped: "No questions! Come instanter. Nay, leave your sword."

"Guard our possessions," Eudoric muttered to Forthred as he was led away. In the street, the soldiers positioned themselves in a square surrounding him. One retrieved the lantern on a pole that he had left against the wall.

At least, thought Eudoric as he tramped gloomily through the nighted alleys with his silent escort, he would not be set upon by robbers, who made solitary

nocturnal walking in Letitia an invitation to murder.
He wondered how he could have fallen afoul of
Franconian officialdom. Had he not been scrupu-
lously careful to avoid discussions of religion or politics? Had some unknown foe laid a false accusation
against him? Still, a government hard-pressed for
money, as most governments chronically were, might
seize a passing stranger in hope of squeezing a ransom out of his foreign kith and kin.

With visions of the noose, the block, and the stake
pursuing one another through his somber mind,
Eudoric was ushered into the palace. He presently
found himself in a chamber aglow with a score of
candles. Seated beyond a massive desk were Secretary of State Brulard and King Clothar, flanked by a
pair of bodyguards. The four who had escorted Eudoric
went to their places beside the two arched doorways
and stiffened to immobility.

"Your Majesty!" said Eudoric, touching a knee to
the floor. Although he burned with eagerness to
know the reason for his summons, he kept his peace.

"Ah, Sir Eudonius!" said the King. "Wert not at
the levée this morn?"

"I was, my lord."

"Methought we saw you, even though we were
compelled to depart ere we had converse with you.
Brulard informs us you have a proposal that touches
upon our kingdom's welfare."

Relaxing, Eudoric allowed himself a small smile.
"I have, my lord," he said, adding to Brulard: "Shall
I repeat what I said this morning?" Receiving assent,
he plunged into his sales pitch.

When he had finished, the King pursed his full
lips and nodded. " 'Tis a plausible scheme, Sir Edric.
We shall give it our accord—*if* and provided that you
first do us a certain service."

"What are—what is that, my lord?"

"Know that we have an unwed sister, hight Yolanda.

Woman though she be, she hath the mind of a man in matters of statecraft. Some months agone, we sent her with an escort westward, to King Gwennon of Armoria, with whom we have certain differences. These Yolanda sought to resolve. Although the maid was an ambassador of the greatest kingdom the world hath ever seen, we learn that the losel hath clapped her up in durance vile. Such an affront is not to be born!

"And so, Sir Doricus, your task lies plain before you. Get you to Armoria and return with our sister, and you shall have our permission to prolongate your coach line hither. If you do not, then your petition shall be rejected out of hand."

After an appalled hesitation, Eudoric said: "But, my lords! Why me? I know little enough of Franconia, let alone the lands along the Western Ocean. Why not one of your own warriors?"

"As the world's most chivalrous, mighty, and brave," said the King, "the gentlemen of our court are too far-famed."

"Or, perchance," interjected Brulard with a cynically raised eyebrow, "they are less fearless than they vaunt themselves to be."

"Enough, Brulard!" said the King. "Mind thy place. To answer your question, Sir Eutheric, the presence of our renowned cavaliers would instant suspicion excite. So we must needs delegate the task to some auspicious foreigner, to wit: yourself."

Eudoric asked: "Would not the Armorians be even more suspicious of my appearance amongst them?"

"You can tell them you scout the land for a stage-coach route, as you do now in Franconia."

Eudoric looked narrowly at the King. "If, Your Majesty, your realm be the whole world's mightiest, why cannot you march your army into Armoria?"

Frowning, the King turned to his minister. "Explain it, Brulard."

"The difficulty, Sir Eudoric," said the Secretary,

"is that, imprimis, King Gwennon hath a prow army of's own; he were no easy nut to crack. Secundus, he is in an alliance with the Empire of Celtica, which rules not only the Celtic isles beyond that strait we call the Sleeve, but also the lands along the ocean south of Armoria. Tertius, the demesne of the Duke of Dorelia lies athwart the path that our army should follow perforce.

"Relations with Dorelia have been uneasy of late. I'll not ensnare you in a net of details. Suffice it to say that we would fain not drive Dorelia to open rebellion—at least, not until our forces more assuredly overmatch his."

Duke Sigibert of Dorelia, Eudoric knew, was the most powerful noble in Franconia. While nominally subject to King Clothar, he was in fact an almost independent sovran, who kept his quasi-autonomy by playing off his powerful neighbors, the kings of Franconia, Celtica, and Armoria, one against the other.

"Besides the which," the King added, "Gwennon holds our sister hostage and might well slay her ere we could rescue her."

"Your Majesty," ventured Eudoric. "I must ask: What is—what are a—the difficulties betwixt Your Royal Highness and the King of Armoria? Why has he imprisoned your sister? I cannot do aught, going into this royal dispute in a blindfold."

The King sighed and looked appealingly at Brulard, who took up the discourse. "It began, Sir Eudoric, with a dispute over perry."

"Excuse, pray. What is perry?"

"A drink they make in Armoria; pear cider, in fact. Know ye what cider be?"

"Aye, sir. But wherefore. . . ."

"To replenish our coffers and quiet the plaints of our vintners, who claimed that imports of perry spoilt their trade in wine, we enacted a tariff on such imports and in so doing roused the wrath of King Gwennon. When we refused his insolent demand to abolish this just and reasonable tariff, Gwennon declared an embargo on importation of wine. So the Armorians, whose climate is too cold and wet to be suitable for the growing of grapes, are compelled to comfort themselves with beer and perry, which is fine for those who relish the stuff. Thereupon, naturally, we imposed an embargo upon all perry from Armoria."

"But what have—has that to do with His Majesty's sister?"

Brulard shrugged. "We know not the details. The princess was sent to sound out King Gwennon on a treaty concerning imports of wine and perry. In addition, Gwennon had previously invited Yolanda, who is something of a seer, to take a post as the King's occult adviser. Ere she departed on her mission, the princess averred that she would think deeply on that monarch's offer.

"We know not how things went awry with the mission. Thrice we have written Gwennon, demanding satisfaction; but no reply have we had—not even one from Gwennon's jester, who, 'tis said, doth truly rule the kingdom as Gwennon's minister. A valorous knight of our court, Sir Clivain, volunteered to go to her rescue; but he had scarce set foot in Armoria when the King's men seized him and offered him the choice of leaving the kingdom instanter or being hanged."

The last thing Eudoric wished to do was to set off on a wild-goose chase in pursuit of an unknown woman, when he should be promoting his proper business. Were it not better to slip away quietly back to his home and be satisfied with what he had? On the other hand. . . .

"Your Majesty," he inquired, "said you not that your sister was unwed?"

"Aye, Sir Ruderic."

"I pray, tell me about this lady. If I undertake quest, my lord, shall need all information I can get."

The king bit his lip in thought. "Our sister is three years our junior and a woman of eminent gifts and royal bearing. As for her person, behold!" He unbuttoned some of the silver buttons at his throat and displayed a miniature suspended on a golden chain. Hoisting the chain over his head, he passed the miniature to Eudoric.

The picture, set in an oval frame of gold and surrounded by sparkling diamonds, showed a beautiful, strong-featured, brown-haired woman; but Eudoric could not make out much detail from the miniature. Besides, he felt sure that the painter had depicted the lady, not necessarily as she was, but as she wished to appear.

Still for one who, like Eudoric, was actively seeking a wife, a chance to place a king's attractive sister under obligation was not to be scorned, although he thought a woman nearer his rank in the feudal hierarchy would prove a more suitable mate than a royal. While Eudoric hesitated, Brulard spoke:

"And by the bye, Sir Eudoric, think not that we make a leap in the dark by nominating you. We have investigated your history and know somewhat of your deeds of dought in distant lands. Ye are indeed the rational choice."

Eudoric sighed. He had the uneasy sense that events were rushing along too fast to control. So much for the name of a hero! It would do no good to protest that his repute was founded more on luck than on prowess. Although this was true, the Franconians would merely accuse him of false modesty. He said:

"Very well, my lords. I will undertake mission."

Brulard looked at the King, saying: "Ere we strike

hands upon the bargain, were it not prudent to have Tsudai inspect him for sincerity?"

Clothar sniffed. "That old he-witch! An unbelieving mountebank from some far, uncivilized land, where doubtless men have tails beneath their trews."

"Sire, remember the good advice he gave us in the matter of Dorelia's—"

"Oh, do as you list." To a guard, the King said: "See if Doctor Tsudai be in his cabinet. If so, bid him hither."

Awaiting the return of the guard, Eudoric said: "Your Majesty, if I take up quest, I shall need money."

Brulard smiled. "Knowing your repute for astuteness in such matters, we anticipated your request. Let us assume that, at current prices, one mark per month—"

A knock announced the return of the guard, who snapped to attention beside the opened door. After him came a man who, to Eudoric's eyes, appeared fantastically exotic. He was small and elderly, with a mere wisp of mustache and whiskers. His features were flat, and his yellowish skin was beseamed by a multitude of tiny wrinkles. A shimmering robe of emerald green, embroidered with golden dragons, embellished his spare form. On his sparse gray hair rested a small, round, black cap, surmounted by a great crimson jewel. Brulard said:

"Sir Eudoric, behold Doctor Tsudai the Serican. We rely upon his arcane powers to warn us of gins and snares, as did His Majesty's sister ere she went to Armoria. Doctor Tsudai, this is Sir Eudoric Dambertson of Arduen, somewhere in the barbarous Empire."

Doctor Tsudai inserted both hands into his voluminous sleeves and bowed low, first to the King, then to Brulard, and lastly to Eudoric. He said:

"How can this humble one serve Your Omnipotence?" While the sage's Franconian was fluent if not altogether grammatical, his accent was even stronger than Eudoric's; and he employed curious turns of phrase, which Eudoric supposed to be literal translations from his natal tongue.

Brulard answered for his less articulate sovran: "We propose to entrust Sir Eudoric, for a consideration, with a task that be imbued with difficulty and danger. We are fain to know how far he may be trusted beyond the reach of our authority."

The Serican bowed again. "May this person seat Sir Eudoric and myself at yon small table?"

The King waved a jeweled hand. "Shog along."

Guards drew up two chairs. From a flowing sleeve, Tsudai produced a foot-long ebony rod, from which he opened out three hinged brass feet at one end and three brackets at the other, and set the stand on the table. From his other sleeve the seer produced a crystal ball and carefully placed it on the brackets.

When Tsudai and Eudoric were seated opposite each other, the former brought his eyes up close to the crystal, as if he were looking through it. Staring back, all that Eudoric saw was a blur, with now and then a glimpse, as Tsudai shifted position, of a slanting brown eye grotesquely magnified.

After a period of silence, the Serican sat back, saying: "To best of my negligible knowledge, I perceive no abodements. Whereas Sir Eudoric hath little of those fanciful notions of honor, for which your Franconian gentlemen lose battles and cheerfully butcher one another, he is punctilious in matter of trust and obligation. Whereas he is no quarreler, if conflict be forced upon him, he will valiantly defend. He sees further ahead than most. Despite his title, his character bespeaks the qualities of an upright tradesman. Your pardon, Sir Eudoric; this worm means no offense. But His Majesty hath demanded a scrupulous answer."

"No offense taken," said Eudoric with a rare grin.

"Better an honest tradesman than a noble nitwit, dead in some footling quarrel."

"Huh!" grunted the King. "The world is going to the dogs, with false religions sprouting like weeds despite burnings; agitators spreading subversive doctrines by that reprehensible new device, the printing press; and noblemen demeaning themselves by earning vulgar money. These evils waft across the Helvetians from those accursed republics in Tyrrhenia. One day we must liberate the Tyrrhenians from republican turbulence by imposing our just and orderly rule upon them.

"Dost know that one madman, whom we hanged but last week, in sooth proposed that the *nobility* be taxed like the common rabble? Did one of our titled subjects attaint himself in an enterprise like unto yours, Sir Ericson, he would have his spurs hacked off and his sword broken over his head. Since the nobles of the Empire are less fastidious, it would seem, you'll do as manager of this coach line—provided you meet your end of the bargain. You have our leave, Doctor Tsudai."

As the Serican bowed himself out, Eudoric, suppressing his anger at the royal sneer, turned to the King's minister. "And now the matter we began on when your wizard came in. . . ."

"Ah, yea," said Brulard. "Let us assume that, at current prices, one golden mark per month should suffice to maintain you and your man and beasts along the road. . . ."

VII

Svor The Stroller

Half an hour later, Eudoric in turn bowed himself out of Brulard's chamber of office. The minister said: "Come back hither at the time erst appointed, Sir Eudoric—two days hence—and ye shall have your coin."

"Good-night and good luck, Sir Eudovix!" said King Clothar heartily, awakening from his torpor. The King had yawned through the lengthy bargaining between Eudoric and Brulard and almost fallen asleep, but he roused himself to bid a gracious farewell.

A guard escorted Eudoric through the halls and out the gates of the palace. At the exit Eudoric, suddenly conscious of the fact that his sword was back in the rented room with Forthred, asked: "Wilt guide me home? I fear getting lost in this warren of alleys. I can pay." He did not voice his real concern—the fear of being, in his unarmed state, set upon by footpads.

"Nay; duty forbids," said the soldier. "It's easy

enough. Three streets that way, left one, right one, half a block and there ye be. The Three True Gods give you good night!" The guardsman vanished.

Eudoric started upon his route with an uneasy feeling of being watched. A crescent moon was setting, leaving the streets in Acheronian darkness. We do things better in the Empire, thought Eudoric. Emperor Thorar had decreed street lighting at night in Sogambrium, and King Valdhelm had followed suit in Kromnitch. To be sure, the lighting was from cressets affixed to the walls of buildings at the principal crossings, and the municipal servants supposed to replenish the firewood often neglected to keep the fires alight; but even this feeble ruby flicker was better than a moonless night's funereal gloom.

As his eyes adjusted, Eudoric became aware of motion ahead in the otherwise deserted street. He was following someone or something at the very limit of vision. Since the figure got no closer, Eudoric inferred that at least the person did not mean to pause to waylay him. Still, he would have been happier with his sword, or even with his dagger or a stout walking stick.

The unknown one ahead, Eudoric thought, must be at the crossing where Eudoric had been told to turn left. Suddenly there were more shadowy figures in motion. Someone shouted a phrase in an unfamiliar tongue.

Eudoric lengthened his stride and soon perceived that one shadow, he thought the person whom he had been following, was ringed by three additional shadows. As Eudoric approached, he perceived that the three newcomers were armed with one sword and two daggers, while the wayfarer kept his attackers at bay by whirling a curious weapon. This consisted of two batons or short clubs connected by a length of chain. The defender held one of these billets of wood and whirled the other in loops and figure-eights. As Eudoric neared, the swinging club hit one attacker with a hollow sound and sent him staggering back howling. Again the defender shouted the unknown phrase.

Unarmed as he was, Eudoric had a fleeting urge to slip into his alley and let the incident take care of itself. But the whim was gone in a flash. While he might not take to heart all the arrogant Franconian code of knighthood, such flight, he felt, would be unworthy of his knightly station.

Coming up behind the swordsman, Eudoric threw himself at the fellow's legs and clutched them tightly. He had once seen this form of attack employed by a group of pilgrims from Celtica, who played a game with a leather-covered bladder, which they threw, kicked, carried about the field, and wrested from one another.

The swordsman had scarcely turned his head when Eudoric hurled him prone. Bounding to his feet, Eudoric stamped with all his force on the man's sword hand. Snatching up the weapon, he sent a quick thrust into the fallen one's body and faced the remaining attackers. These twain backed away, took to their heels, and vanished into the darkness, while the man whom Eudoric had sworded heaved himself slowly to his feet and staggered off, holding his side and groaning.

"Should have kill him," said the small man whom Eudoric had rescued. Eudoric recognized the sing-song accent as that of the Serican sage, Doctor Tsudai.

"To slay a wounded man is hardly—well. . . ."

Tsudai shook his head. "Ye Westerners are all sentimentalists at heart. Ye understand not. If he recover and learn who stuck him, he'll seek to way-lay you for vengeance. Furthermore, had we his corse, we might find upon it evidence of him who set whose bravos upon this person."

"Who might hire these cullions?"

"This one makes no accusation without evidence. Still, it is known that the Duke of Dorelia bears this insect no love, for having exposed his plot to murder King Clothar."

"And I've been hired to pass through the Duchy of Dorelia!" said Eudoric with a grunt. "By the Divine Pair, let's hope none of those fellows saw me well enough to know me again."

The Serican spread his hands. "Ye are young knight from the Empire, who would extend coach line hither, so-not-so?"

"Aye, sir. May I lead you to my room, to rest and refresh yourself?"

"Nay, thank you. From Secretary's chamber, this despicable one returned to own cabinet, gathered belongings, and set out for his humble home. In the excitement of attack, this stupid one called for help in his own language."

"If you are a wizard, why not summon your demon and set him upon those knaves?"

"Tried but forgot it was the demon's day of recreation. Penalty of age is forgetfulness. Wouldst come to my slatternly dwelling? Shall feel more at ease with a swordsman by side. Then, belike, ye might deign to meet repulsive wife and degenerate children."

"I shall be honored," said Eudoric, suppressing a smile at the Serican's extravagant self-deprecation.

Tsudai's wife proved not at all repulsive, and the children seemed remarkably bright, clean, and well-behaved. Eudoric tried to pump Tsudai about Princess Yolanda. But the seer said he had settled in Letitia only after the King's sister had departed. Further questions about Yolanda, Tsudai turned aside with elaborate politeness. He brought the conversation around to Serican business practices, a topic that his guest found completely absorbing.

"For a private enterprise like yours," said Tsudai, "we have a device called *hong*. Suppose three men wish to start a business, but each one has different sum to invest. So they print, let us say, twelve certificates, each for ownership of one-twelfth of the hong. Say, one buy five shares, one four, one three. When business make profit, the profit is shared in proportion to holdings, and votes by shareholders for mandarins of company are likewise weighted."

Eudoric listened keenly. "What if the company go bankrupt?"

"Then the owners of shares may lose their shares, given to creditors; but are not otherwise liable. Makes sale of shares much easier."

"In other words, such a company acts as a human being, with the same powers, restrictions, and liabilities?"

"Yea; one may call it an artificial person."

"I see possibilities," said Eudoric, "but our laws would need revision. Now, Doctor, canst forecast my future?"

"Only in most general way, honorable sir. This disgusting worm can read something of character in my crystal and draw inferences. For ensample, if ye be an inveterate gambler, ye will surely end in want; if ye be a constant quarreler, chances are overpowering that ye will die by violence. But precisely when and how, I know not.

"When this one looked through crystal, he saw that ye had set out from home in hope of wiving, your previous courtships having gone awry. I marked how your interest quickened at talk of the King's sister."

"What think you of my chances—not perforce with the King's sister, but with womankind in general? How happy shall I be if I ever do find a mate?"

"As to that, ye shall probably attain your goal, albeit with toils and troubles. At least, when ye do wive, she may be sure of your fidelity."

"How know you that?" asked Eudoric.

Tsudai chuckled. "Because ye lack the charm and surface gallantries that oft beguile women, wherefore they'll give you scant encouragement to stray. Few lusty young men would count this quality a virtue; but it will natheless save a mort of grief. Your chosen one may find you less enchanting company than a hero of romance; but she can ever rely upon you. And that, with advancing years, becomes the thickest strand in marital tie." He rose. "Sir Eudoric, this creature owes you his worthless life. When in dire strait, be free to seek my ineffectual aid."

Tsudai sent Eudoric off with two bottles of Franconia's finest vintage wrapped in his cloak. Slightly the worse for wine, Eudoric weaved his way back to his room. He tried to compensate for his tipsiness by gripping the robber's sword and darting suspicious glances into every dark recess. But nothing happened.

While traversing the lands of the Duke of Dorelia, Eudoric tried to be quietly inconspicuous and to move in the casual, leisurely manner of one to whom the journey was a timeworn tale. He expected at every step to be stopped by the men of the Duke, eager to lay their hands on a hireling of the Duke's inimical suzerain, King Clothar. Eudoric rehearsed the speeches that he would make to convince his captors that he was nothing more than a stagecoach owner looking for means of expansion. He ruthlessly practised Forthred in local manners and customs, so that the apprentice should not draw unwanted attention by flagrantly foreign behavior.

As things turned out, Eudoric's careful precautions proved superfluous. Nobody questioned them. Indeed, nobody showed any interest in a pair of quiet, orderly, taciturn travelers.

At the Armorian border, a customs inspector went through Eudoric's baggage until he came to the re-

maining bottle of golden Franconian wine, the gift of
Tsudai the Serican. Eudoric had saved this bottle so
that he and Forthred could celebrate reaching
Armoria. The inspector blew a whistle, and two mailed
customs men-at-arms bustled up. The inspector cried
in Armorian:

"Arrest these men! They seek to smuggle a forbid-
den fluid into the land!"

"Eh?" said Eudoric. "Oh, you mean that bottle of
wine." He spoke Helladic, which the inspector understood. "I had forgotten your law—"

"Ignorance of the law is no excuse!" barked the
inspector. "Take them to prison—"

"Now see here!" blustered Eudoric. "I am no mere
vagabond, but a leiger from His Majesty the King of
Franconia to His Majesty the King of Armoria—"

"Ha! A likely story! Where is your escort? Where
are your credentials? Your letters under the royal
seal?"

"I was sent forth with only the passport you hold,
lest the Duke of Dorelia get wind of the plan. 'Tis
said that the Duke fears that my mission might lead
to renascent amity betwixt the two monarchs, thus
depriving him of a diplomatic advantage."

The inspector shook his head. "I have nought to
do with matters of statecraft. Take them away, men,
whilst I seek counsel."

Eudoric and Forthred found themselves in a ver-
minous cell in a nearby building, lit only by overcast
daylight through a small, high, barred window. While
Eudoric examined the door, the walls, and the window for weak spots, Forthred said in the gloom:

"Sir Eudoric, I never thought you such a glib liar.
My master warned me that ye were a man of tough
standards, exact and demanding, but nought of this
singular endowment."

"There's no spur to invention that vies with necessity," grunted Eudoric. "And keep your voice down."

"Suppose these Armorians demand to know what sort of mission we be on? What'll ye answer?"

"I'm thinking up a story."

The next day the travelers, scratching flea bites, were brought back to the customs post. With the inspector was a gray-bearded man wearing a scarlet gown and the tall black hat of a justice of the peace. The graybeard asked Eudoric:

"Now then, sir, what is this secret mission ye claim to serve?"

"King Clothar wishes to end this footling dispute over wine and perry. He has sent me to negotiate a treaty of mutual approval of your two kingdoms' respective beverages. I brought that bottle as a nominal gift to His Majesty King Gwennon, to—ah—soften his ire."

"What terms are ye authorized to offer?"

Eudoric smiled. "My lord, as a man of the bench, learned in the law, you would not truly expect me to reveal my terms in advance of negotiation. Let us say that I hope to get an agreement that shall leave both monarchs equally pleased—or equally displeased, as the case may be."

The justice frowned. "Meseems King Clothar sent his sister on a similar mission within the past twelve-month. If she could not achieve that aim, wherefore thinks he that an unknown foreigner could succeed?"

Thinking fast, Eudoric said: "On the contrary, my lord, it was altogether a logical decision."

"How so? From far-flying rumor, that royal noodle-head hath never a thought in his sconce beyond trouncing a courtier at some silly game or futtering a willing wench."

"Well then, let us say that it was logical of King Clothar's minister, Master Brulard. The King's sister would surely incite suspicion on the part of the

Armorians, being both intimate kin to Clothar and active, I am told, in the occult arts. She must have attempted some magical sleight, if it be true that she be immured."

"Hmm." The justice paused to study his collocutor. "I heard that she had been accused of witchery and named as the monster's bride. Proceed, Sir Eudoric."

"So it seemed to Minister Brulard that a stranger like me, having no ties in either land, would command more confidence as a fair-minded intermediary to arbitrate this dispute."

The justice chewed a wandering whisker, then said: "Sir Eudoric, meseems ye be either an excellent choice for arbitrator, or the most plausible liar that hath come this way during my term of office. My judgment is that ye be sent on to Ysness, but with an escort, to make sure that ye be he who ye say ye be. If it transpire that ye be not. . . ." The justice drew an ominous finger across his throat.

"My lord," said Eudoric, "what is this about the Princess Yolanda's being given to a monster?"

"Ah, that is on account of the curse of Svor the Stroller."

"Who? What curse?"

"Know ye not? The tale is old and well-worn in Armoria. Svor the Stroller was a mountebank from a land even farther away than yours—a country hight Pathenia."

"I have been there," said Eudoric.

"Have ye indeed? Is it true that Pathenians devour their own firstborn?"

"Not that I ever heard; meseems they rear their families in much the same way as other folk. But tell me more about this curse."

"This Svor had a traveling show, with a few performers and some foreign wonders for yokels to gape at. One of these was his monster, a kind of sea dragon, the which he kept in a tank of water and dragged with him about the land. This monster was but a child of its race, not much longer than a man, and the tank confined it straitly. Svor averred he had raised it from an egg and fed it only meagerly, lest it grow too large to be contained.

"He had trained the beast to perform certain tricks, giving commands in Pathenian and rewarding it with little fishes. With him it was as tame as a dog. When he called: 'Here, Dru—Druzhok!' (at least, that is what I think he named the creature) it would rear up out of its tank to be stroked and to nuzzle its master. Never have I beheld a cleverer beast; it seemed to understand every word that Svor spake.

"Somehow, Svor fell afoul of the King's jester, Master Corentin, who, far from being a fool, hath magical powers of's own. One day they met on the beach at Ysness, and the quarrel brake out openly. Both cast spells; but Corentin's proved the stronger, causing Svor to burn alive where he stood.

"Ere he died, Svor shrieked a curse upon the land: that his monster should escape to the sea, wax immense, and yearly return to ravage the shores of Armoria, unless it were given a maiden each year to devour.

"When the King's men rushed to Svor's caravan to see how the monster betid, they found that Druzhok indeed had crawled out of its tank, departed its wagon, waddled down to the shore, and swum away. The rest of the mountebank's company, who seemed to be harmless folk, were let go with a warning.

"For six years, no ills from the curse materialized. Then the monster, grown to the size of one of the smaller whales, appeared along the coast, destroying fishing craft and snatching unwary bathers. King Gwennon commanded that the justices name the female criminal then in custody as the one most richly deserving of death, and they brought forth a woman who'd poisoned her children and man. So she was duly chained to a rock on the shore near Ysness.

"The monster tore her loose from her chains, engulfed her, and vanished. Next year it appeared again, but this time the victim, another murdering woman, already cowered in place. So the creature enjoyed its repast and departed without effecting further harm.

"And so things have gone ever since. Princess Yolanda will be the seventh victim—or belike the eighth. As ye see, the monster seemingly cares but little for the personal conduct of its victims, so long as they be tasty."

Eudoric frowned in thought. "When is the next such sacrifice?"

The justice paused to think. "In ten or twelve days, meseems. If your escort hasten, ye should arrive in the capital in time this fête to witness. It were well to reach the place early, because enterprising fellows set up benches along the shore and let sitting space to spectators."

"An arresting spectacle, no doubt," said Eudoric dryly. "Has none essayed to slay the monster?"

"Aye; the King hath offered a recompense for such a hero. When the third maiden was to be devoured, one bold knight, Sir Tugen, climbed out upon the rock with sword in hand. But the monster knocked him into the deep with a flip of's flipper.

"It would doubtless have devoured Sir Tugen as well as the woman, but that he was wearing armor. Having attempted a bite or two, it left the man and took the victim, chained as before. That served the knight but ill, for he was drowned by the weight of his plate. After the monster departed, the armored corse was fished fom the sea, bearing dents from Druzhok's teeth. Why, Sir Eudoric, didst think of attempting that feat yourself?"

"Having only now heard of this singular rite," said

Eudoric cautiously, "I am not prepared to answer. How soon can we start for Ysness?"

The green and rolling countryside of Armoria jounced past as Eudoric, Forthred, and their escort jogged steadily westward. Now and then the open landscape was broken by a patch of forest or by a hill that rose in a hump above the plain. Atop of many such hills, Eudoric noted graying prominences that seemed from afar to be a regular shape. Blurred by the hazy Armorian air, these protuberances appeared to be made of huge slabs of stone leaning against one another. Eudoric asked Sreng, the officer of the squad, about these eminences.

"Tombs of our ancient kings," replied Sreng shortly. He rode a little in advance of Eudoric, with Eudoric's reins in his fist.

When they skirted another megalithic tomb more closely, Eudoric said: "Those look like mighty stones for men to have hauled up such a slope."

Sreng retorted: "Know, O foreigner, that our wizards could magic yon stones into their present place, were they an hundred times as massy."

"Wizards!" snorted Kibhauc, Sreng's lieutenant. "More like 'twas the magic of chieftains' whips, laid across the backs of tribesmen whilst they hauled the stones with leathern ropes."

"Oh, shut thy gob!" said Sreng. "Ye be ever carping and doubting. 'Twere not beyond belief that ye doubt the blessed gods themselves and have gone over to that accursed Triunitarian cult that's spread by missioners from Franconia, so as to weaken our national unity and bring us under Letitia's dominion."

"Find me a wizard who can by magic loft any weight above ten pounds, and I shall be happy to believe. What think ye, Sir Eudoric?"

Eudoric smiled faintly. "My friends, I have traveled through divers lands; and I have found it prudent never to dispute the beliefs of the dwellers therein. How far from Ysness are we?"

"A few hours should see us thither," said Sreng, "if this weather hold, which looks unlikely."

A lowering sky grew darker; thunder rumbled from the black-bottomed clouds. Eudoric said: "There's the largest of your royal tombs so far. Could we not seek to shelter ourselves within?"

Sreng gasped. "Invade King Balan's tomb? Ye must be moonstricken! No man who enters one of these tombs comes out alive."

"What befalls him?"

"How should I know, since none hath returned to tell the tale? Nay, we'll make do with such shelter as yon copse provides."

Sreng led the group into the designated woodland. They were still rigging a lean-to of branches with cloaks and blankets spread out upon them when the rain began. A steady downpour kept them huddled beneath this imperfect shelter for the rest of that day and half the next. They munched black bread, cheese, dried beef, and onions; dozed; cast knucklebones; boasted of heroic feats of carousing and fornication; and listened to Eudoric's tales of travel, while Eudoric practiced his rudimentary Armorian.

VIII

The Pastoral Palace

King Gwennon's palace was a cluster of buildings of logs with the brown bark on, save where it had peeled off in patches. The largest of these structures contained the dining hall and the throne room, as well as the private royal quarters.

Gwennon's throne was a massive armchair of wood stained black. The back and arms were carved in an intricate pattern of interlaced dragons biting one another's tails; their eyes and fangs were picked out against the sable background by gilding. The King himself proved a small, rotund, sleepy-looking, white-bearded oldster.

Eudoric quickly noted a sickly smell pervading the throne room. He soon discovered the source. This was a rack affixed to the wall, having a row of spikes on four of which were mounted human heads, pale and expressionless with half-closed eyes. Eudoric got an impression of being translated back to the earlier, ruder time that followed the fall of the old Napolitanian Empire.

Eudoric also saw whence the heads had been obtained. In addition to the usual chain-mailed swordsmen standing beside and behind the throne, one more guardsman leaned upon a broad-bladed ax. Before him stood a large, wooden, black-painted block with its top hollowed out in a shallow groove. A bucket rested on the floor in front of the block. Forthred whispered:

"Sir Eudoric, I like this place not."

"Nor I; but hold your tongue," muttered Eudoric.

Eudoric had been escorted in by the four men-at-arms who had ridden with him from the border. A green-clad usher cried: "Your Majesty, I present Sir Eudoric Dambertson of Arduen, who saith he hath a message for you from King Clothar of Franconia."

The usher motioned Eudoric forward. Eudoric dropped to one knee.

"Rise, Sir Eudoric," wheezed the King. "Here, a simple bow were enough. We set no great store by fancy manners like unto those of decadent Franconia. Nay, we—"

"Nay indeed," interrupted another, rising from a curled-up posture near the throne. A tall slender person, black of hair and pale of face, this man wore a costume of vivid checks of red, yellow, and green, with a horned headdress. Little bells on the ends of the horns tinkled when he moved. "Nay forsooth, good Sir Eudoric! In Armoria, all is feasting and fun.

> "A roamer who comes from a faraway land
> To pause and admire our silvery strand,
> An he's a good fellow, we'll wine him and dine;
> If not, we will sunder his cervical spine!"

The jester collapsed in a gale of laughter. The King smiled in a puzzled way; the men-at-arms dutifully smirked. While Eudoric was not without a sense of humor, this faculty was not his outstanding talent.

He smiled thinly, since he could see nothing very amusing in the verse, especially with the headsman standing ready for instant duty.

Eudoric assumed that the man in the fool's regalia was the jester-minister Corentin, who continued: "And now, sir, what is your business?"

Addressing the King, Eudoric went into his well-rehearsed speech about King Clothar's wish to resume amicable relations. At the climax he produced the remaining bottle of wine: ". . . .and in token thereof, His Majesty sends Your Majesty this little gift, in hopes that Your Majesty will reciprocate with a flask of your own delicious perry."

. The King leaned eagerly forward, extending a pudgy arm. Before he could grasp the bottle, the jester snatched it, saying:

"Naughty, naughty! Ye know better than to drink from aught that your faithful taster hath not sampled.

> "With poisons malign
> His Majesty's wine
> Doth featly combine;
> With toxicants crude
> Is monarchy's food
> By cunning imbued."

Corentin drew the cork and put the bottle to his mouth. He downed several swallows and handed the bottle, now half empty, to his royal master. Eudoric observed these actions with surprise; of the several rulers whom he had known, none would have tolerated such impudence on the part of a subject. Corentin continued:

"Not bad! Count to a hundred, Majesty, ere ye guzzle, to see if your faithful jester be writhing in his death throes or hath already expired. Now, Sir Eudoric! Ere we accept your bona fides, explain why King Clothar should send a lone foreigner to discuss matters of such pith and moment, in lieu of a proper envoy with escort and credentials?"

Cautiously, Eudoric said: "Brulard, the minister, apprehended that such an embassy were likely to rouse the Duke of Dorelia's suspicions and lead to my detention, or worse. Therefore my credentials, now in the custody of your customs officer, say nought of my present mission; merely that I am a harmless gentleman seeking to extend his stagecoach routes and requesting kindly treatment by the powers through whose lands I pass."

"What is a stagecoach?"

Eudoric explained. The jester cocked his head, so that his bells gave a brief tinkle, and studied his visitor. "Dost truly wish to extend this service to Armoria?"

"I must first discover whether an extension to Letitia be possible and profitable; it was for this that I set out from my homeland. I fear the roads betwixt Ysness and Letitia be mostly tracks, wide enough for a horse or mule but not for the wheels of a vehicle. Improvements were costly; so, perchance, this were a project for the future."

Corentin gave a disdainful sniff. "It sounds like an impractical device. I am sure no Armorian gentleman would ride in one unless he were too old or ill to mount his mettlesome steed."

Eudoric changed the subject. "Pray, Sir Jester, tell me of the curious sacrifice of maiden to monster, whereof I've been told. Is this true?"

"Aye; mean ye the witch Yolanda? She came hither feigning a mission like unto yours; but we soon discovered she sought to cast a spell upon His Majesty—" (Corentin glanced at the King, who had finished his bottle and fallen asleep on his throne) "—and thus to seize the rule of Armoria. Clothar no doubt dispatched his sister upon this treasonous quest and not to talk of trade in wine and perry. Therefore are we wary of compacts with King Clothar. What proof canst give that ye be not about to hatch some similar stratagem?" The jester wagged a finger as if beating time, then burst into verse:

> "In matters of state
> We trust not the great;
> They do as they choose,
> And torts they excuse
> By saying in joke:
> ' 'Tis good for our folk'!"

The pause gave Eudoric time to formulate a reply. He spread his hands. "You see that I am but one man, alone save for my squire. So I could not attack your kingdom by force, however nefarious my intentions, even had I the might of Sigvard Dragonslayer. On the other hand, I have no magical powers whatever."

"How know we that ye have no occult capabilities?"

Eudoric shrugged. "How *can* a wight prove that he have no wizardly skills? If I falsely claimed such abilities, you could demand a demonstration. But when I claim *not* to possess them. . . . well, Sir Jester, you see for yourself."

"A neat philosophical point, Sir Eudoric," said Corentin. "Let me ponder it. . . ."

"Meanwhile," said Eudoric, "pray tell me, when is the maiden to be sacrificed?"

"Three days hence. Wouldst buy a seat on one of my benches?"

"Perhaps. Has not His Majesty offered a reward for him who slays the monster?"

"Indeed he hath. Wouldst attempt that feat yourself?"

"I came not to Armoria with that thought in mind; but still, the prospect tempts me. What is this reward?"

"The traditional guerdon, as ye know, is the hand of the maiden and half of the kingdom. Alas, the realm is already bespoke by His Majesty's heir, his nephew Prince Patern; but the hand of the Princess Yolanda, the maid in question, is yours—if the twain of you survive."

"Not so swiftly!" said Eudoric with a wry grin. "How know you that I be able and willing to wed? Or that the maid and I should find each other pleasing?"

" 'Tis the lot of youthful princes and princesses to be wedded all the time to others of their rank, regardless of their personal liking. And good my sir, ye think not, I trust, that we would let the baggage go free as a masterless enchantress? Should ye both survive, ye *shall* wed, like it or not. If either balk, we will clap you up until silence and solitude do soften your obduracy.

"I confess that King Gwennon and I, his minister, find ourselves in a somewhat difficult strait. Albeit we most earnestly wish to rid ourselves of the monster, we would not wish to make a mortal foe of King Clothar, when he hath taken the primary step towards reconciliation. Yet we most particularly will not leave this dangerous, presumptuous enchantress at large within our kingdom."

"What makes you think that wedding the dame to me would render her less dire?"

"First, as a husband, ye could call upon the law if need be to keep her under discipline. Second, 'tis widely known that enjoyment of amorous intimacies doth diminish magical powers. Third and lastly, if ye slay the monster, we shall know that ye be a man of such might and valor that ye can easily master this forward wench." Corentin changed to a wheedling tone. "Besides, Sir Eudoric, methinks ye'd leap at a chance to marry into a royal house that vaunts itself the greatest in the world, notwithstanding that others dispute the claim. Why, with the adroitness ye've already displayed in your dealings with us, ye'd soon be a duke, or at least a count!"

"That is as may be," said Eudoric. "At least, if I vanquish this merdragon, you'd have your proof that I am no wizard."

"How so?"

"Who, facing a deadly peril, would eschew the use of magic to save himself, if he possessed such power?"

Corentin snorted. "Ye are too shrewd by half! If ye survive, we had better hustle you out of the kingdom forthwith, lest ye scheme it away from us! If it transpire that ye do but cozen us with crafty lies, yonder stands the cure!" He nodded towards the headsman and intoned:

> "If a varlet be hanged, the rope may break;
> If shot at with bolts, the aim may miss;
> A tempest may save him when burned at stake;
> But no man survives the ax's kiss!"

Corentin brayed one of his raucous laughs. Eudoric looked doubtful, saying: "I had no intention of wiving. Until now I have fared well enough without a wifely fardel." It was a flat lie, he knew, but he made it sound convincing.

"Dis take you!" cried Corentin. "What more wouldst have, besides the hand of a rich and mighty ruler's sister? The moon? Or Maglaun's ever-filled purse?"

"A thousand Franconian marks, or the equal in your coin, would suffice."

Corentin gave a falsetto shriek, jerking his head so that all his bells jangled. "A thousand! Art mad, like a buck hare in spring? Ye'd clean out the treasury, as would a horde of mice do in a granary. Between the princess and the fame that will accrue to you from the feat, ye need nought more. No Franconian nobleman would bargain in this base commercial vein."

Eudoric smiled. "I am no Franconian. Permit me to remind you that, if the princess be devoured, you will never get a treaty with King Clothar, no matter how beneficial to your sovran and his realm."

Corentin uttered a word in Armorian that Eudoric did not recognize but guessed to be an obscenity. The jester said: "Well then, we will offer ten golden Armorian crowns. The crown weighs a trifle less than the mark."

"Ten? Good my jester, this is one of your better jokes. Ten would scarce support our return to the Empire. Make it nine hundred, then."

"Ridiculous! I will offer twenty, and not a sesterce more."

"Then I fear I must return to Letitia empty-handed. . . ."

An hour later, they had settled for one hundred Armorian crowns. The jester said: "Ye wite, ye shall have the full amount only if the beast be slain. If ye do but send it fleeing wounded, ye shall have but the half, since we know not whether it will return anon."

"Very well, Sir Jester. And now for the means. I must have my sword, if you will kindly command these border guards to return it to me; but one weapon seems hardly adequate. In the royal arsenal, is there a dart-throwing catapult that I might borrow?"

"Catapults? Nay, sir; we manly Armorians use them not. The effete Franconians may resort to such ignoble gins mechanical; but we are true men—" (he thumped his chest) "—and rely upon our strong right arms."

"Then I hardly suppose you would have one of those Serican thunder tubes? I have seen one, a most fell weapon."

"Nay, we've never heard of such things. We could, howsomever, lend you a sturdy hunting spear."

"Better than nought," grumped Eudoric. "And now, may I see our agreement in writing?"

"Oh, very well, very well. Here one trusts the word of a gentleman. Pol! Go fetch the scrivener."

When the scrivener came in with pen, ink, and an armful of parchments, Eudoric said: "Two copies, I pray. Do you not use that new stuff called paper? They say the Sericans invented it, and it's much cheaper than parchment."

"We brave Armorians think little of newfangled things," sneered Corentin.

The scrivener scratched away, sometimes holding poised his plume while Eudoric and the jester argued over the wording of a sentence. At last Corentin stepped to the throne and roughly shook King Gwennon by the shoulder. "Wake up, Your Majesty! Here is a brace of documents for the royal seal. And now, whilst we are at it, let us set the terms of this wine-and-perry treaty. . . ."

IX

The Princess
and the Promontory

A wan yellow sun drifted up a pearly morning sky; seaward, a heavy haze hid the horizon. Middling blue-gray waves impinged upon the Rock, throwing up bursts of spray like bushes laden with silver berries. Standing ashore from the tanbark-gray Rock with the King, the jester, and a clank of guards, Eudoric said:

"My lords, two days ago I had my first sight of the ocean. From tales I have heard, I expected waves like moving hills, hurling their foam as high as treetops."

"We do get storms like that," said King Gwennon, "possibly—"

"Mainly in the winter," Corentin interrupted. "Ye are fortunate in that the weather today is mild as milk. Ah, there goes the princess with her escort!"

On the slope below, two burly men, each clutching a pale, strong-muscled arm, marched a tall woman out upon the Rock. She wore but a single silken rose-pink garment.

131

"Is she to be chained in her shift?" asked Eudoric of Corentin.

" 'Twas her wish. She gave her gown to her maid, saying she saw no reason to sacrifice a good robe to the monster's gluttony."

The woman was hauled to the crest of the Rock and thence to the farther side, where the bulge of the stone concealed her from Eudoric's view. As the guards of her escort busied themselves out of sight, Eudoric imagined how they fastened chains to the woman's limbs.

A voice broke into his thoughts. "Here's your poker," said Corentin, handing Eudoric a stout boar spear. The weapon had a hand-broad head and a crosspiece below the head, to restrain a beast already impaled upon the spearhead from forcing its way up the shaft to reach its attacker. "May the Old Gods help you. Ye'd best sit atop the Rock and rest, to gather your forces. The beast may not appear for hours."

"And try to keep your feet dry," said the King innocently, "lest ye catch your death of cold."

Laughing scornfully so that his bells tinkled, Corentin declaimed:

"Sir Morhot the Fierce was a hero of might;
He hunted down dragons and demons to fight;
He dreaded no foeman or basilisk's bite,
So long as his feet he kept dry!

He scoured the land in his quest for the right;
He rescued fair maidens, their captors to smite;
He slew every brigand and villainous wight,
But colds in the head he would fly!"

Using the spear as a staff, Eudoric picked his way down the slope to the Rock. He wondered how he, who prided himself on prudent caution and rational reasoning, nevertheless so often found himself in one fantastic predicament after another. Behind him, the notables hastened away to the front-row benches reserved for them on either side of the promontory.

On the landward side, the Rock sloped gently up from the surface of the beach, rising some fifteen feet above sea level. On the seaward side it dropped off steeply. As he began the ascent of the Rock, Eudoric could not see the Princess Yolanda, but sounds from the far side of the Rock made him pause. He heard a loud splash, followed by angry shouts. Presently the two soldiers who had brought the princess to the Rock appeared upon the summit, hastened down the slope, and trudged away, arguing furiously. One was dripping wet.

Curious, Eudoric strode up to the stony summit. On either side, shallow water washed back and forth. To left and right stretched the silvery beach, upon which scores of benches had been set; and on these benches sat hundreds of Armorians in colorful holiday finery, while sellers of cakes, sausages, and beverages circulated among the gabbling throng.

As Eudoric reached the summit, a cheer arose and swelled to a roar. Spectators waved hands, scarves, and kerchiefs in encouragement, so that to Eudoric they were but a flickering, amorphous mass.

He idly wondered, if he wounded the monster but failed to kill it, whether it would come ashore to attack the spectators. He visualized the multitude stampeding away in wild panic, screaming and trampling one another. It would, he sourly thought, serve them right; but doubtless the fickle Armorians would blame the disaster on him and slay him for it.

Where the seaward side of the Rock dropped sharply, Eudoric found himself looking down on the captive princess, who sat upon a ledge. Rusty iron chains, with a lot of slack, connected the manacles on her wrists and ankles to staples driven into the stone.

To Eudoric's startled gaze, the woman at first appeared nude. Then he realized that her clinging, filmy garment, soaked to transparency by the spray, had become all but invisible. She sat huddled, looking out to sea; as he peered more closely, he saw that she was trembling.

"God den, my lady!" he said.

The woman started. Then she raised her head. She was, he saw, quite the ineffable beauty he had seen in Clothar's miniature; if anything prettier, dark of hair and gray of eye.

"What—who are you?" she quavered.

"Permit me, my lady. I am Eudoric Dambertson of Arduen."

"Where is that? Somewhere in the Empire, to judge by your accent."

"Aye. I've undertaken to fight your monster."

"Oh." She seemed at a loss. At last she said: "May the True Triunity strengthen your arm! Did my brother send you hither?"

"For that and other purposes."

"Why has no one told me that I should have a champion? 'Twould have eased awaiting my doom." She sounded querulous.

"I know not, Princess. But methinks it better to leave such questions till later, whilst we diligently watch for the monster. Its master called it by some Pathenian name: Drugov? Druzik?"

"Druzhok," said Yolanda. "That was long before I came hither. But the Armorians well remember Svor the Stroller and his curiosities."

"I had better climb down to your ledge," said Eudoric. "Wilt hold this?" He reached down the spear. "I fain would avoid a tumble into the deep. Which gives me to think: What befell out here ere I arrived? Did one of the soldiers fall in?"

"I pushed him in. I'd have done the like to the other, too; and gleefully watched the pair drowned by their mail. But the second cuttle skipped back out of reach, my gyves having been locked; and he fished his comrade out."

Eudoric picked his way down the remaining distance, hooking his heels into the niches cut in the rock to make a rudimentary stair. As he landed on both feet on the ledge, one foot slipped seaward; but Eudoric recovered. If he had it to do over, he thought, he would not wear clumsy riding boots but would come either barefoot or in thin slippers. He had thought of donning his armor for the conflict; but the fate of the would-be monster-slayer, Sir Tugen, had dissuaded him.

"We might as well take our ease whilst waiting," he said. As Yolanda rose to hand him back his spear, he realized that the princess was substantially taller—more than a handsbreadth—than he.

Taking the spear, he lowered himself to a sitting position with his feet hanging over the edge. From where he sat, he could see the masses of spectators around the curve of the Rock to right and left. Splash from the waves soon soaked his boots. He considered taking them off but decided that the ledge was too narrow to do so safely.

For a while they sat silently, watching seaward. Eudoric strained his eyes for sight of a dorsal fin or a patch of leathery hide. Several times he saw something; but each time it proved to be merely a trick of light and shadow upon the restless waves.

Then he turned his attention to Yolanda. She was a big woman, not only tall but well-fleshed; her form, so clearly visible through the rosy silk, would arouse carnal thoughts in a statue. She was certainly the most beautiful woman he had ever known in person, even if built on a somewhat larger-than-human scale.

"I wonder if Druzhok be coming today," mused Eudoric. "If it fail to appear, do they set you free?

Do they take you from the Rock and bring you back on the morrow? Or do they leave you here for ay?"

"I know not. I am told it has always appeared on this day of the year."

"Some day it'll die, in the natural course of events," said Eudoric. "What then will the Armorians do with the woman they've chosen thus to honor?"

"You are too full of questions!" snapped Yolanda. " 'Twere better to study the waters." After a pause, she added: "Oh, I cry your pardon! I confess I am tetchy; waiting to be devoured doth not improve one's manners."

"I understand," said Eudoric. "I did but think that such light talk might take your mind off your predicament."

"So indeed it may. Continue, pray."

"Well then, tell me: The Armorians call you a witch, and others hint that you possess uncanny powers. Why can't you use these powers to free yourself and dispose of the monster?"

" 'Tis true that I've made some small study of the wizardly arts. I have, for ensample, a splendid spell for freezing a creature to immobility, as if it were turned to stone. Therewith, I could render Druzhok as stiff and harmless as if it were stuffed and mounted in the Letitian museum. But the spell requires costly apparatus, which I brought not with me from Franconia. When they arrested me, they seized my few bits of magical gear, all but the tube and powder for the Lesser Immobility. Those were on my person, which they failed to search. My rank protected me at least from that indignity."

Eudoric clucked sympathetically. "What is the Lesser Immobility?"

"Another spell, like unto the Greater Immobility, save that it be worked with a simple blowpipe and a pinch of powder. It has but a short-lived effect—say, half an hour."

"How long does the Greater Immobility endure?"

She shrugged. "I have never watched a victim of it long enough to ascertain; but the wizard who sold it to me asserted that, if well and truly performed, 'twould hold the subject fast for a decade or more. Besides, Corentin the jester is a more puissant enchanter than I. When his men-at-arms seized me, he cast a countervailing spell against my minor magics. Another spell, placed upon these chains, prevents my sundering them by my arts. If the Three True Gods ever vouchsafe me a chance to take Corentin's head. . . ." She smiled grimly.

"What had Master Corentin against you?"

"He feared that I should subvert the affections of King Gwennon to make myself Queen of Armoria, thus to overthrow the jester's mastery of the King. In a civilized land, to treat a sovran with one tenth the insolence wherewith that sneering malapert Corentin uses Gwennon would cost a subject his head. These Armorians are nought but a pack of bloody savages, beneath a film of culture as thin as this Serican silk wherein I shiver. As for Gwennon—as if I'd ever bed down with that senile lump of lard, that puppet in Corentin's hands!"

A formidable dame, thought Eudoric, not to be thwarted or crossed with impunity. He wondered whether he could somehow defer the fateful step of winning the hand of this prickly princess, at least until he knew her better.

"Speaking of matters conjugal," said Eudoric, "know you that the Armorians intend, if I defeat the monster, to wed the twain of us?"

She started visibly. "Why, the whoreson knaves! Dost mean you and me, to each other?"

"Aye."

"The fiend take them! I should have guessed they had some such zany scheme in mind. Wherefore would they foist this union upon us?"

"They have the silly notion that you were less of a danger to them wed than as a maid."

"And what if I tell them to go futter themselves?"

"They'll throw us into prison until we change our minds."

"I'll rot in their dungeons ere I yield!"

"So thought I, also. But let us not reject the plan too hastily, lest we waste away our lives. We could make it a titular marriage; on your request, I would not press my husbandly rights."

"You would find it a daunting task to press them against my will," she said ominously.

"I daresay. Then, back in Franconia, you could take legal measures to regain your single state."

She pondered Eudoric's statement. "Franconia has no divorce—but under circumstances such as these, an annulment could be had."

"Assuming that we should then wish to part," said Eudoric.

"There is that possibility. Suffer me to think."

She sat long in silence, while Eudoric scanned the seascape for a sight of the monster. After a while he asked: "You *are* single, I take it?"

"Aye; husbandless and loverless." She looked him over narrowly. "Now that I consider the matter, methinks that, failing better, you might do. You seem a man of capacity, not ill-favored, whom I might learn to love. I could fare farther and do worse. But are you of noble blood? A royal princess cannot wed a low-born upstart, be he never so brave and virtuous."

Eudoric sighed. "I am heir to a banneret knight's holding, in Locania. Is that noble enough?"

" 'Twill do; 'twill suffice. Are you, too, single?"

"Aye. Truth to tell, I embarked upon this journey in hopes of wiving."

"Are you complete in all your parts?"

"So far as I know, I am. But if we forgo our marital pleasures until we—"

"Oho, a reluctant lecher! Mean you that you're a priestly celibate, whom I shall have to teach about the bees and the flowers?"

Eudoric laughed. "Good Gods, nay!"

"Well then, have you any mistresses to be paid off and turned out? I'll not suffer my man to divide his affections, whatever some of our courtly debauchees do."

"Nay, no mistresses. I've been betrothed divers times, but fate has hitherto thwarted mine honorable intentions." Eudoric smiled. "And by the bye, my lovely enchantress, how know I that, upon our first disagreement, you'll not turn me into an earthworm?"

She laughed. "Fear not! To change the shape of a living being calls for spells far beyond my modest capacity. And, since the resulting creature must weigh as much as the being whence it came, you'd make a monstrous worm. No one ever disagrees with me anyway, save my featherpated brother.

"Now, Eudoric, since fate has dealt us this curious throw of the dice, let's make the best of it." She reached out and gave his arm a friendly squeeze. "Your offer to relinquish your rights was generous, and I thank you for it; but in this parlous strait 'twere foolish to forgo any harmless pleasures we might enjoy. I confess that I, too, have been seeking a mate. Being nearly thirty years of age, I fear a lifelong spinsterhood. I hereby swear to make you the happiest of husbands and to work no goetic magics upon your person!"

"If our marriage be one of fact as well as name, would that affect your getting an annulment—assuming you'd wish one?"

She shook her head. "For a commoner it were an obstacle; but I could afford the highest bribes the hierarchy would demand."

Eudoric studied the waves for a while; then asked: "And of our issue, should there be such, what were their standing?"

"You'll never sire a king, Eudoric. Franconian laws are strict in the succession. They'd have to run clean out of Clothar's male kinsmen, unto tenth cousins, ere they'd enthrone any child of mine. Besides, Clothar has legitimate children of's own, not to mention a swarm of little bastards. Your and my issue would receive nought but minor titles, as would you as my consort."

After another pause to scan the waters, Eudoric asked: "Speaking of magic, what *is* the strongest spell in your arsenal?"

"I have one for evoking marids. I bought it from an old Hiberian *kassaf*, who was down on his luck and wanted money for drink."

"For evoking *what?*"

"Marids; a kind of ouph that dwells in that part of the spirit world that is congruent with the Saracenic lands. It is a dangerous enterprise, for marids demand the most careful control after evocation. One must command them in the Saracenic tongue. Would that I had fetched a few marids with me from Letitia!"

"Do you speak Saracenic?" asked Eudoric.

"Enough to rule my marids."

"How would you say, in Saracenic—"

A scream from Yolanda interrupted. "Here it comes!"

A few wave crests away, a length of slick, slate-gray hide reflected the wan sun as it broke the glittering surface. Eudoric scrambled up; but the wet leather heel of one boot skidded off the damp stone of the ledge. Unbalanced, Eudoric frantically reached for something to grasp. He snatched at Yolanda, but she flinched back in panic.

Off he went with a splash, and the water closed over his head. A powerful downward stroke of his arms brought his head out of water. When his vision cleared, he perceived a smaller ledge below the narrow surface on which he had sat.

As, coughing, he pulled his arms and shoulders out of the sea, he saw his spear float away on a receding wave. It stood upright in the water, butt end upward and bobbing gently with the rhythm of the waves. Already the weapon was out of reach, although Eudoric could still have swum for it. But the monster's head arose from the sea almost with arm's length.

The fathom-long cranium tapered to a blunt muzzle. A blowhole atop its head sent out a puff of vapor. Although the flippers were still beneath the surface, the head was supported by a neck as thick as itself; the creature looked quite large enough to swallow Eudoric whole. Black corneas in white eyeballs regarded him dispassionately. Then the monster's gaze shifted back and forth between Eudoric and Yolanda, as if it were undecided which to seize.

If Eudoric let go the little ledge, he would go under again. What with the weight of sword, scabbard, and boots, he could not expect to float.

"Clumsy oaf!" screamed Yolanda.

At another time, Eudoric would have had biting words about such abuse from a woman for whom he was risking his life. Now other matters preëmpted his attention. The wedge-shaped jaws gaped, revealing scores of ivory-white fangs edging a crimson maw. The animal stank of fish.

"Druzhok!" shouted Eudoric.

The beast jerked back its head and slowly closed its empty jaws, while Eudoric desperately tried to remember what he could of the Pathenian language. "*Vniz!*" he shouted, hoping that this was the word for "down." "Druzhok! Down! Go back! Go away!"

Druzhok backed off a few feet. It remained attentively poised, as if awaiting the next command.

"Druzhok!" cried Eudoric. "Good monster! Nice monster! Go far away! Go way off thither!" He pointed westward. "Come not back, ever! Stay away from Armoria!"

Although the reptilian face was essentially expressionless, Eudoric thought he saw a brief look of hurt in the creature's eyes before the fang-provided head disappeared. He caught glimpses of slate-gray hide breaking the surface and vanishing, farther away each time. Then Druzhok was gone, save for a distant puff of vapor from its blowhole.

X

A Contested Consummation

King Gwennon's henchmen hauled a sodden Eudoric and Yolanda to the top of the Rock. Now that he had a chance to scrutinize Yolanda while they stood on the same level, Eudoric realized that she overtopped him by a good span. With her shift still clinging damply to her, she reminded him of one of those pagan goddesses worshiped in the old Napolitanian Empire before the triumph of more sophisticated theologies. To marry a six-foot beauty, of high rank and magical powers, were almost as formidable an enterprise as wedding a female deity.

The soldiers escorted the couple back to shore, where the King, the jester, the apprentice Forthred, and a gaggle of other persons waited. Two among these stood out. One wore the purple robe and mitre of a priest of the Triunitarian religion, which prevailed in Franconia. The other had thrown a cloak of wolf skin over his white linen robe, and from his head arose a furry headdress bearing the antlers of a hart.

King Gwennon seized Eudoric and kissed him on both cheeks. Eudoric found the King's breath so alcoholic that anyone near him would in time get tipsy on it. Corentin pounded his back, crying:

"In the name of the Old Gods, what did ye, Sir Eudoric? We could not see clearly, because of the bulge of the Rock. We did see the monster break the surface and open its maw to seize one of you; next, it was fleeing away as if pursued by all the fiends of the Triunitarian Hell. Did ye deal the creature a mortal hurt?"

"I merely commanded it to depart," said Eudoric, "and it went."

"By Kernun's horns! We shall enlist you as commander of the beasts, to order the wolves and bears of Armoria to leave our livestock unharmed. Now there shall be a feast, to celebrate your nuptials with the princess! Meanwhile ye shall receive words of praise from the leading men and women of our fog-bound land. This is Lord Gorbuduc, chief of the Veneti. . . ."

Eudoric soon lost track of names and faces. When the jester paused for breath, the new hero asked: "Tell me, pray: How does one wed in Armoria?"

"Amongst us it is a civil ceremony, albeit folk may hie temselves to a priest of the Old Gods, like Father Mamert here—" (he indicated the man in the horned hat) "—for a blessing. The couple exchange vows before any qualified person, such as His Majesty, or me, or any chief, magistrate, or priest. The couple then execute their duties before witnesses."

"That were no marriage amongst us Franconians," said Yolanda. "A princess of the blood cannot enter into mere concubinage. Have you no priests of the True Faith?"

"Setting aside questions of whose faith be true," said Corentin, "there stands your man: Bishop Grippo." Corentin indicated the mitre-crowned cleric.

"I insist that he perform the ceremony," said Yolanda.

"To make all secure, ye twain shall carry out the service in both forms; our Armorian way first—"

"We shall not!" exclaimed Yolanda. "The Triunitarian form must precede that of your primitive paganism."

The jester sighed. "Such a hubbub over mere mummery! How about you, Sir Eudoric? To what faith adhere ye in the Empire?"

"We Locanians subscribe to the cult of the Divine Pair—"

"That vile heresy!" growled the bishop. "As bad as the detestable monotheism of the Pathenians, which is but one step from atheism. Meseems the stake and faggot—"

"That will do, Your Holiness so-called!" barked the jester. "Ye are suffered to move amongst us to preach your creed, but not to contemn or molest the beliefs of others."

"Which will lead you all to eternal torment," grumbled the bishop, "from which horrid fate it is my duty to seek to save you."

"As I was saying," continued Eudoric, "I concern myself not with such matters. If you learned theologians differ so about the nature of the divine, who am I, a mere layman, to choose sides? So any ceremony will suffice me."

Yolanda spoke: "I, at least, insist that the bishop's ritual precede the heathen one. Since I hold the highest rank here, save for His Majesty, my wish shall prevail!"

The jester shrugged. Eudoric murmured: "As you wish, my dear."

"Then let us to it," said Corentin. "The feast were not ready till sundown. Join hands, ye twain!"

Eudoric gave a hearty sneeze. Yolanda said: "I

freeze in this wisp of damp gauze. I demand to be properly clad!"

"Time enough for that after the bishop hath twaddled his trumpery. He hath his vespers to perform. Go on, join hands! Anon, Father Mamert shall be your attestant."

The bishop, with a sour look at the jester, took a stately stance before Eudoric and Yolanda and rattled through his marriage service, ending: "I now declare that ye be husband and wife be patient with each other's faults may the Three True Gods guide you if they do ye will not submit to that heathen rite they plan for you." Bishop Grippo turned and strode briskly away.

"Lady Grania!" called the jester. "Lead Princess Yolanda forth and clothe her as befits a noble bride."

Eudoric sneezed again. King Gwennon said: "Sir Eudoric, ye should also get yourself into dry footgear. We have already warned you against the wetting of your feet!"

"He will survive," sneered the jester, adding:

"The hero so brave
Dares monster and wave
His beautiful princess from doom to save;
But after the fight
The fortuneless wight
Is felled by a cold on his nuptial night!"

The dining hall of King Gwennon's log palace held several long tables placed end to end to form a lengthy banquet board. King Gwennon sat at the head, with Eudoric on his right and, flanking him, Father Mamert. Yolanda, resplendent in an emerald gown embroidered with threads of gold, and a golden diadem on her sorrel hair, sat on the other side of the king with the jester as her dinner partner.

The pagan priest proved a loquacious old party,

who filled Eudoric's right ear with chatter: ". . . glad am I that the benighted fanatic, Grippo, be absent. He doth cast a pall upon the jolliest gathering. Why, at the Feast of Dis last year, he all but ruined the party by fussing over the beheading of Lord Brunec."

"Eh?" said Eudoric, suppressing a sneeze. He took a deep draft of perry, hoping that it would make him feel better. "What had this lord done?"

"He lost a bet."

"That seems an unduly severe penalty."

"Ah, but he had wagered his head with a rival chieftain, Lord Livertin—that red-haired cully ye see yonder near the foot of the table—and lost. He— Lord Bruce—claimed it was but in jest; but bad blood had arisin betwixt the twain. So Lord Livertin demanded satisfaction of the literal terms. Brunec appealed to the King, who referred the case to Master Corentin, who decided for Livertin. Brunec had the choice of submitting or being branded a poor sport, something an Armorian gentleman would liefer die than incur." The priest lowered his voice. " 'Tis whispered that Corentin owed Brunec money, but that is mere idle gossip. I myself *never* gossip," he added, folding his hands in a saintly pose; but at the same time he drooped one eyelid in a half-wink.

"And then?" said Eudoric.

"It was agreed that Livertin should collect his forfeit at the Feast of Dis. Brunec insisted that he be decollated in style. Clad in his finest, he lay upon his shield, borne on the shoulders of his slaves. Ever a true sportsman, Brunec hung his head off the end, to give his foe a fair cut. Livertin swung his two-handed *claidheamh mor*, and *whop!* twas over. To uphold the honor of Brunec's clan, his widow petitioned the King to be buried alive with her husband."

"And Bishop Grippo?"

"When Master Corentin caused the head to be placed on a dish to decorate the table for a feast, in honor of Brunec's sportsmanship, His so-called Holiness rose and denounced the proceeding as barbarous. Had he used such language before King Gwennon's sire, the late King Uriens, his own head had been added to the display ere he'd ceased his quacking. But some of your finical Franconian manners have begun to corrupt our simple, manly ways."

"I am not a Franconian," said Eudoric. "In my land, howsomever, such use of a person's sconce would be deemed in dubious taste."

"But to contemn the usages of another land, where one is but a tolerated guest, bespeaks even more abandoned taste. Now here is another tale, concerning the Lady Vivian—that busty woman in red yonder—and her pet boar. . . ."

Mamert rattled on throughout the repast. Eudoric wished he were alone to think things through; but he dared not rudely hush the garrulous priest, since Mamert was to preside over the second wedding ceremony. The priest might yet be needed as an ally, if Eudoric found himself unwittingly caught in the toils of some courtly intrigue. Knowing something of the ways of courts, Eudoric appreciated how easily a ruler's suspicions could cost a courtier his life. In any case he must tread warily with these people, who deemed a severed head a suitable table ornament.

On the other hand, from what he had seen of Yolanda's imperious temperament, he suspected that this wedding had been a disastrous idea. But how could he escape? He was already wed under Franconian law, and to try to pretend otherwise while traversing that powerful kingdom might land him in straits compared to which being devoured by Druzhok would seem a holiday. Another sneeze gave him an idea.

"Father Mamert," he said, "I am, as His Majesty warned me, coming down with a terrible cold in the head. I fear I may not be up to my marital duties tonight."

"Rubbish, my lad!" said the priest. "Ye'll rise to the occasion, or I'm a Triunitarian! Once the words have been said and laid is the bed, ye'll forget this trifling indisposition. Hush! Jurnach is about to recite a heroic lay in your honor."

The court bard stood up, twanged his harp, and launched into his eulogy. According to Jurnach, Eudoric had fought Druzhok with his spear until it broke; then with his sword until that, too, shattered on the monster's adamantine hide. Eudoric finally won the contest by wrestling Druzhok under water and breaking the monster's neck.

Since many of those present had a fair idea of what had actually happened, Eudoric expected them to burst into raucous laughter; but they solemnly took it all in. The thought crossed his mind to stand up and disclaim this farrago, but he dismissed the notion. If it was the Armorian custom to pretend to accept an extravaganza that made Eudoric out-hero Sigvard Dragonslayer, it would be imprudent to gainsay it.

Eudoric realized that he had drunk more perry than he had intended. Instead of clearing his wits, mazed by his gathering indisposition, it had further muddled them. He could not think clearly; in fact he could hardly think at all.

He felt that events were rushing him along towards some unknown disaster, as if a torrent were sweeping him to the brink of a waterfall. He should have taken a firmer stand about marrying Yolanda before he had a chance to know her. While he would doubtless enjoy initiating this statuesque beauty into the pleasures of carnal knowledge, and while being a royal in-law opened up vast commercial possibilities; still there was more to wedlock. . . .

* * *

The King stood up, wiped his mouth and beard, belched, and said: "We have finished. Ye may depart as ye list."

As King Gwennon waddled out, other diners rose at leisure. Eudoric felt a grasp on his arm and sensed that the jester was pulling him towards Yolanda. Father Mamert followed close behind. Without quite knowing how it came about, Eudoric found himself standing beside Yolanda before Father Mamert, who shot rapid questions at them. To all queries, the reply was a simple "Aye" in Armorian.

At last the priest intoned: "May the gods bless your marriage bed and all who repose thereon!" Then Eudoric, unsteady on his feet, was pulled and pushed out through the massive oaken door of the log palace. Two ladies of Gwennon's court, Eudoric noted, had laid hold of Yolanda's arms and led her, protesting, after him.

The two were propelled out into the torchlit courtyard, where most of the feasters were already gathered. To shouts of "Way for the bridal pair!" Eudoric and Yolanda were forced through the crowd to an open cleared space, wherein lay a large rustic bed spread with deerskins. Beside the bed stood a pair of bagpipers, one of whom gave a preliminary howl on his instrument.

"What—what's this?" mumbled Eudoric.

"The final rite!" cried Corentin, starting to unbutton Eudoric's jacket. When Mamert moved to unfasten Yolanda's emerald gown, she snatched the fabric together with one hand and slapped the priest's fumblings with the other, shrilling:

"What do you, old fool?"

"The divine pair curse you!" cried Eudoric, partly sobered. "What *is* this?"

"Why, the consummation!" said Coretin. "I told you. To render the marriage legal, ye and the wench must strip, mount the bed, and go to it, whilst the company dance about the couch and cheer you on! It were no marriage else."

"I will not!" screamed Yolanda. "Never have I heard of such a barbarous usage!"

"Balderdash, Your contumacious Highness!" snapped Corentin. "If ye knew your own history, ye'd realize that your people practiced this selfsame rite, ere the missioners of the Triunitarian faith converted them to their own persnickety creed."

"Master Jester," said Eudoric, "with the best of intentions, I fear I could never discharge my marital duties, as you call them, in public. The difference betwixt this custom and those of my native land are too great."

"Ye men of the Empire must be a feckless lot," snorted Corentin in tones of exasperation, shaking his head so that the bells of his headdress tinkled. "A manly Armorian can futter in the midst of a battle. I told you that the bridal pair must discharge their marital obligations before witnesses, or the marriage is void. Did ye not understand plain Armorian?"

"I fear I did not grasp the full import of the words," said Eudoric. "In any case I will not do it, now or ever." (He actually said the equivalent of "Id eddy case I will dot do it, dow or ever.")

"Dear, dear!" said the pagan priest. "Must we then let them go unconjoined?"

"Never!" said Corentin. "It was in the agreement, and neither His Majesty nor I will have the wench running loose with her witchly powers. She's too fell a female to chance it. Belike the threat of the headsman—"

"An empty threat, Sir Jester," said Eudoric. "If I cannot perform my husbandly part with my head in place, be certain I should be unable to do so without it."

"Perchance a stay in our darkest dungeon might soften your contumacy," snarled Corentin. "Guards!"

Several of King Gwennon's soldiers, the only armed persons present, approached. Eudoric, wishing for something on which to blow his dripping nose, braced himself.

"What makes you think," he cried, "that I could rule this headstrong—"

A yell from the farther end of the courtyard wrenched attention thither. Out of the darkness rushed a crowd of men with clubs: staves of building lumber and other improvised cudgels. At their head ran Bishop Grippo, holding up his purple robe and screaming:

"Down with the obscenity! Out with the fornicators! Frush this heathen orgy in the name of the Three True Gods!"

The mob set with vim upon the crowd in the courtyard; the thud of wood against heads and bodies punctuated cries of rage, alarm, and pain. The wedding party began to stream away, some fleeing back into the palace and some off into the darkness, with the attackers in pursuit.

Meanwhile Corentin shrieked commands to the sextet of guards in the courtyard, who formed up around Corentin, Mamert, Eudoric, and Yolanda. When two of the attackers rushed the group, the guards cut them down with their swords. The rest, recoiling before the bloodstained steel, joined in pursuit of the unarmed wedding guests. Soon the courtyard was empty, save for the guards, the quartet they guarded, two corpses, and a bagpiper who had been knocked unconscious.

In response to Corentin's commands, the six guards scattered on the tasks assigned them. From beyond the palace, Eudoric heard the sounds of a hasty mustering of soldiers: a clatter of arms and armor, the shouting of urgent commands, and the stamping and neighing of horses. Soon a mounted group could be heard as it rumbled off into the night.

"Triunitarian heads will be piled here on the morrow," muttered Corentin. "Let's hope the bishop's be amongst them. And now, my dears, we shall proceed with our interrupted ceremony. Yonder stands your nuptial couch, and Father Mamert and I shall be your witnesses. The dance, though a jolly pastime, is not required by law."

"I'll see you in Hell first!" said Yolanda.

"But my dear Princess, the departure of the noisy crowd should abate your objections. Mamert and I do promise to watch in silence, eschewing the lascivious jests that are common on such an occasion."

"It will not do, Master Jester," said Eudoric. "In Yolanda's land and in mine, only the most licentious spirits would frig in public, as it were. Now, pray, find us twain a private chamber, and we'll testify to the results upon the morrow."

Mamert pushed back his horned headpiece to scratch his balding scalp. "It were irregulous to have no true witnessing. Suppose one of the twain demand annulment on grounds of non-coition? Who shall prove non-compliance?"

Corentin gave a weary sigh. " 'Twill do; 'twill suffice. The marriage will be legal unless you or I bring an action against it, and neither of us is fain to do that. Besides, the twain will doubtless feel as bound by the Triunitarian mummery as by our wedding rite. And what care we if a brace of foreigners return to their home in a state of sin?" He beckoned a guard. "Tell the housekeeper to ready a bridal chamber. The room Duke Kiberon occupied will do. Now, ye two, come inside."

Corentin hustled Eudoric and Yolanda back into the palace, stopping at the deserted tables to pour himself a goblet of perry. He offered some to his companions, but his offer was declined. Yolanda was still tense with unspent anger, while Eudoric decided he was near enough to a drunken stupor without aggravating his condition. He asked:

"Where—where is the King?"

Corentin snorted. "Still asleep. When he's in his cups, nought less than an earthquake is needed to rouse him. I'll report the night's doings to him anon. Not that it greatly matters."

At long last, Corentin ushered the bridal couple to a room wherein a pair of chambermaids bustled about. As these glided away, giggling nervously, Corentin clapped Eudoric and Yolanda on the shoulder, declaiming:

> "When the bridegroom's in lust,
> And the maiden is fain,
> With a vigorous thrust—"

"Stop!" roared Eudoric, glowering. "Master Corentin, you've given us enough embarrassment already. Kindly omit the versifying! Good-night!"

He grasped the slender jester's shoulders, turned him about, and with a powerful push sent him staggering off, laughing madly so that his bells tintinnabulated. Then Eudoric slammed and bolted the door. As he turned to face Yolanda, she snapped:

"Husband! Wipe your nose! You're a disgusting sight!"

XI

A Jester's Jugglery

As the rising sun sent scarlet beams through the diamond panes, Eudoric, red of eye and nose, emerged from the bridal chamber and sought the dining room. He found Corentin sawing away at a slab of cold roast pork.

"God den!" said the jester. "How passed your night?"

"Better than some but worse than others," said Eudoric. "Methought my cold would unman me completely; but my lady wrought a simple spell, which somewhat abated the symptoms. So we. . . . Alas, the effect of the spell was but ephemeral; wherefore I now feel worse than ever."

"Ye stopped with the words 'So we. . . .' So we what? What befell?"

"Well, what think you? That's my affair."

"Come, come, Sir Eudoric!" Corentin leaned forward, his eyes agleam with voyeuristic eagerness. "Give me the details, I beg. I lust to know every—"

"Lust away, you evil-minded jackanapes!" barked

Eudoric. "Whence I come, a gentleman does not particularize such matters, save to his priest or his physician. You are neither."

"Oh, I cry your pardon, Sir Eudoric!" Corentin made a visible effort to wipe the prurient curiosity from his features. "I did but wish to ascertain your state of felicity. It behooves the King and me, doth it not, to insure the happiness of eminent guests?" When Eudoric merely grunted, Corentin continued: "The life of a hero, such as ye be, doth not belong to himself alone, but serves as exemplar to generations to come. So should I not ask anent the happiness of the bridal pair on this fair and sunlit morn?" He put on a charming smile.

"You may say that the groom feels relieved at having performed his duty, when for a while a successful conclusion remained in doubt. As for the bride, you must needs ask her." He looked narrowly at Corentin. "By the bye, you spake of the wench as a 'maiden.' Now, I am not that famed Hiverian, Huano, reputed to have enjoyed ten women a night for a hundred years. But neither am I an utter novice, and I avow that Yolanda be a woman of experience—*wide* experience. How about this, Sir Jester?"

Corentin swallowed. "Have one of these goose eggs. Know that, in modern Armorian, the term 'maiden' denotes a young, unwedded woman. It implies nought of her being a filly unridden, as it did in the older form of the tongue. Did she pleasure you?"

"I complain not."

Corentin laughed. "Then where's your plaint? We set no great store by virginity here."

Eudoric growled: "Simply stated, I like not having used merchandise fobbed off on me as pristine. My grievance will, howsomever, be much abated when you pay my promised hundred crowns."

The jester's eyebrows rose. "Indeed? And wherefore should we pay you such a sum?"

"You promised it as my reward for rescuing Yolanda."

"Ha! My good Sir Knight, if ye read the contract, ye'll see it saith 'for slaying the monster,' not for commanding it to levant. Since ye slew it not, the contract's null."

"By the Divine Pair!" roared Eudoric. "Of all the barefaced swindles—"

"Easy, easy," said the jester, grinning. He snapped his fingers, and four armed guards, who had been standing like statues around the room, stepped forward with hands on hilts. "My heart doth bleed for you; but the welfare of the kingdom is ever uppermost. If the contract be broken, we cannot straiten our treasury out of mere sympathy. Ye may not believe it, but Armoria's good is my capital concern. Therefore, our thanks and our praise for your worthy deed must suffice. I daresay we could hire Jurnach to compose another heroic lay about your acture."

"Heroic lays are all very fine," said Eudoric, "but gold is more useful in conducting a business. At least, it was agreed that I should receive fifty if the beast departed wounded."

"I recall the wording precise," said Corentin. "'In the event that the beast flee away wounded, so that its death be not witnessed, the said Eudoric shall receive the moiety of the abovenamed amount.' Druzhok, howsomever, departed these purlieus quite unseathed. How, then, can ye claim a reward for wounding it? If ye believe me not, I'll hale the scrivener hither with our copy of the contract." The jester finished with a malicious smile.

Eudoric frowned in thought. "When the beast departed, it gazed at me reproachfully. I am sure that its feelings, at least, were wounded."

"That signifies nought, Sir Knight; albeit ye show a

livelier wit than most of the ironclad titled loobies from the more easterly lands. We cannot summon the creature from the vasty deep and ask it: 'Hath Sir Eudoric in sooth bruised your tender soul? Poor little monster! Come hither and let us kiss your tears away!' So let the pair of you take your treaty with King Clothar and speedily hie yourselves back to Franconia. Count yourselves lucky that your heads be still affixed to the rest of you; for there be some who say ye routed Druzhok by a magical spell, after ye'd sworn ye had no such arcane powers."

"I merely spake to the monster in its Pathenian language, a tongue whereof I learned somewhat whilst in jail in Velitchovo."

Corentin's eyes waxed bright with malicious curiosity. "What offense had ye committed there?"

"Killing a dragon out of season, in ignorance of their game laws."

"My, my, ye do get around! In any case, be on your way forthwith; here we give short shrift to contentious foreigners. Without heads to see by, ye'd go astray for certain!" The jester guffawed.

Eudoric stared as murderous thoughts flitted through his brain. As if reading Eudoric's mind, Corentin added: "And think not to slay me out of hand!" He nodded towards the guardsmen. "Besides these four stout lads, my faithful demon wards me. Wouldst see?" He clapped his hands. "Matholuch, show yourself!"

The air beside Corentin's chair shimmered, and a being of roughly human size and shape took form. Instead of an ordinary skin, however, it was covered with scales having the appearance of bronze, greened with age. The center of each scale curved up to form a spine. Over most of the creature's body, the spines were no longer than a finger's breadth, but on the arms they became finger-long spikes.

The jester's mouth twisted into a sinister grin. "A

hug from Matholuch were less pleasurable than one from your princess, as the late Svor discovered."

"Methought Svor was burned alive?"

"Nay; that doth but show how rumor distorts the tale of notable events. But I've just thought of a jingle:

> "Oh, better 'tis ever to lie in the arms
> Of woman-kind lovely, enjoying her charms,
> Than wrastle my demon, whose spiny embrace
> The life of the hardiest knight doth erase!"

Corentin's gale of raucous laughter set his bells to jangling. Eudoric smiled thinly, saying: "Sea monsters and demons like man-shaped hedgehogs are not, I see, Armoria's only wonders."

"What else? Hast seen our standing stones and ancient tombs?"

"Nay; I've not had time to visit them, I refer to your sense of humor, my good jester."

"At last!" cried Corentin, throwing up his arms. "A wight who comprehends my genius! Pray join us in the courtyard at the third hour, to view the beheading of six members of last night's mob. 'Twill be a delicious sight! The cries for mercy! The spouting blood! The rolling sconces!" Corentin's expression of fiendish glee suddenly sobered. "But now, good my sir, ye must excuse me. The kingdom's business doth press upon me. Crops have failed in our southernmost province, and I must organize a shipment of edibles thither. I boast that, during my tenure, not one peasant hath starved; and I should be loath to see that record broken. Good-day!"

Back in his temporary quarters, Eudoric told Yolanda about his interview. As he spoke, her face became taut with anger. "You tottyhead! Why demanded you not the half of your gold ere venturing out upon the Rock?"

Keeping a tight grip on his temper, Eudoric replied: "Had I been clever enough to foresee the Armorians' trickery, I should not have promised to fetch you home. I could have returned to Letitia saying: Sorry, but the monster ate your royal sister ere I arrived on the scene."

Glaring, Yolanda said: "Didst demand my magical apparatus along with your lucre?"

"By the Divine Pair, how could I? When I made the contract, I knew nought of your wizardly gimcracks. But when I ask for your baggage—"

"So all that I, a royal princess, am worth to you is a sack of reeky gold!" screamed Yolanda. "I've let a worthless fortune hunter make free with my private person! Sneck up! Get out!" She threw a pillow at Eudoric.

Eudoric knocked the pillow aside and smiled mirthlessly. "Ere I go, pray tell me: Canst cook? Canst sew? Make beds? Milk a cow?"

"Nay! Why should I know the skills of a baseborn hilding?"

"Because, when I leave you in Armoria, you must needs find a way to make your living. Farewell!"

Eudoric turned away, wondering privately what he would do if, in one of her contrary fits, Yolanda did indeed refuse to return to Letitia with him. In such a case, his Franconian stagecoach line would vanish like a mirage in the Saracenic deserts.

As he strode out, Yolanda called, "Eudoric! Come back! I am sorry! I truly meant it not; suffer me to apologize. Let us not start our wedded life so ill! Come to me, love!"

Like a man in a cage with a tigress who, having just tried to devour him, was now affectionately rubbing its head against his shanks, Eudoric came. When she embraced him, he recoiled, saying: "Beware! You'll catch my cold!"

"I care not," she said, kissing him fiercely. "Since my little spell hath worn away, I'll do what I know be best for you. Off with your raiment and back to bed instanter!"

"But I must round up Forthred and prepare for our journey—"

"Tomorrow's as good as today, and I can run your errands for you. I regret that you'll miss the beheading."

"I have seen heads fall," growled Eudoric, "and find the sight no very pleasing spectacle."

"Oh, Eudoric, be not angry with me again! Forgive my hasty temper! 'Tis vile of me so to carp at him who saved my life. You're an excellent man, and it's my great good fortune that the Three True Gods sent you my way. Come, sweet!"

Eudoric let himself be bullied and cajoled back into bed. For the next three days, he had to admit that no one could have been a kinder and more assiduous nurse than this formidable female.

The throne room, as Eudoric entered, appeared the same as before, save that the heads staring sightlessly from the rack on the wall had been replaced by six new faces. These, Eudoric supposed, had belonged to the Triunitarian rioters caught by King Gwennon's troopers.

"Is your tisic better, Sir Eudoric?" wheezed King Gwennon.

"My thanks, Your Majesty. A few days' rest sufficed."

"We warned against wet feet—"

"Where is your lady fair?" interrupted Corentin the jester.

"Resting. She must store up strength for the journey; and she begs Your Majesty, and you, Sir Jester, to excuse her from the fare-thee-wells."

"That female stalwart!" muttered Corentin. "Sick or well, she could tie knots in any man."

"We regret her absence," said the King. "Albeit old, we still enjoy the sight of a well-formed woman— even though the sight be all, these days." The King sighed nostalgically.

As Forthred and a couple of scullions, under Eudoric's direction, were loading the beasts, Eudoric approached his bride. "Yolanda, my animals can bear but a fraction of your baggage. You'll have to discard most of it."

"What!" she cried. "Dost expect me, a royal princess, to travel about in my shift, as when I was chained to the Rock?"

"The beasts cannot carry so much. I've long worked with horses and mules and know whereof I speak."

"Then purchase more beasts!"

"What with? We've barely enough money, eating black bread and sleeping in our tent, to take us back to Letitia."

"Fear not on that score." From beneath her cloak she produced a large wallet, which jingled encouragingly when she shook it.

Eudoric wagged his head. "I still cannot do it, my dear. We must needs cross the lands of the hostile Duke Sigibert of Dorelia. A train of beasts, with extra grooms to manage them, would arouse unwelcome attention."

"But as things stand, I am reduced to rags and tatters! When they arrested me, they took my baggage into custody. Whilst it was in their charge, base varlets stole a half at least."

"Can't be helped," said Eudoric firmly. "Six chests would slow our progress, and speed is of the essence. Yonder lie your six chests and sacks; choose two! Your magical gear will fit one, and the other will furnish a change of clothing."

"Have I wedded a blind beggar? Should I join him in the streets with a begging bowl for alms?"

The argument raged until Eudoric barked: "Either you make your choice, or I'll make it for you! Or tarry in Armoria, if you prefer!"

"Low-born domestic tyrant!" Yolanda muttered, setting herself to opening the six containers and choosing her most valued articles. "That I, a princess of the blood, should submit to rude bullying. . . ."

"Why need you that green vase?" asked Eudoric. "It is heavy and bulky, and you can surely find another like it in Letitia."

" 'Tis part of my magical armory. Rejoice that I have resisted using it on you!" Then she seized him in a bone-cracking embrace. "Oh, dearest Eudoric, there I go again! I swear to mend my cantankerous ways."

XIII

The Crypt of a King

When Ysness faded into Armorian mists behind them, Eudoric said: "Yolanda, whence gat you that money you showed me? Did the Armorians give you back that which you brought from Franconia?"

Yolanda rode astride with her skirt hiked up to reveal peasant trews. She laughed. "Nay! I took it myself, whilst you were bidding farewell to the King and his jester."

"How did you accomplish that?"

"I told you, I still have the tube and powder for the Lesser Immobility. I went to the treasure room, uttered the cantrip, blew the powder into the guard's face, and helped myself to King Gwennon's treasury."

"Mean you the guard still stand statuelike—unless he have recovered from your spell?"

"So I ween. He may be regaining the use of his members about now."

"Good gods, woman, and you took time to argue over which clothes and hair ornaments to take, knowing that this fellow might revive any moment and

165

sound the alarm? You're out of what little mind you have!"

"Eudoric, I will not be spoken to thus! I am a royal princess—"

"Forthred!" shouted Eudoric. "Gallop!"

The three fled down the narrow road, splashing through mud puddles until all were well spattered.

A few hours later they were walking the horses to breathe them as they climbed a slope in the rolling countryside. At the crest, Eudoric halted to twist in his saddle and stare back. Surveying the distance, where the grassy green waves of the meadowlands merged with the misty gray of the sky, he said:

"Curse this foggy air! Forthred, your sight's as keen as any. See you aught on the road behind?"

Forthred squinted. "My lord, methinks I see some black specks, where the road doth meet the sky. . . . The sun doth twinkle betimes, as on a bit of steel."

"I see them now," growled Eudoric. " 'Tis time we galloped again."

"Our beasts need more rest," said Forthred in plaintive tones. "Ye'll founder them!"

"If those knaves catch us, we may rest for all eternity. Come on!"

At the next breather, Forthred looked back and said: "Sir, methinks our pursuers be closer upon us."

"You're right," said Eudoric. He studied the terrain about them. "If I mistake not, yonder hill bears King Balan's tomb, which we passed on our way hither. The Armorians fear to enter there; but I had rather chance their rumored bogles than King Gwennon's soldiery. Come on!"

They dismounted and led their animals to the top of the hill, where they studied the entrance to the tomb. This portal was framed by three huge, mossy stone slabs, two uprights topped by a lintel across them. Earth, carpeted with lush green grass, covered the burial vault, hiding all of its megalithic structure except the entrance.

"What of the beasts?" asked Forthred.

"Bring them in with us. The doorway is high enough, if we pull their heads down."

When Eudoric tried to lead his palfrey into the tomb, however, the animal snorted, reared, and nearly tore the reins out of his powerful grasp. Tugging from the front and stinging its hindquarters with a quirt failed to induce the animal to enter. It became more and more excited, rolling its eyes in terror.

"Careful, sir," said Forthred. "She'll break loose and run away."

Experiment showed that all the other animals were equally recalcitrant. At last Eudoric said: "It's no use here. We must hide them in that grove behind the hill. Let's first unload food, drink, and candles; for we know not how long our sojourn here will be."

A half-hour later saw the four horses and the mule securely tethered well inside the grove, and the three travelers huddled at the entrance to the tomb. Eudoric grunted:

"Let's pray that the beasts don't set up a racket when our pursuers go by. Come on in! Nay, no candles yet; the light might give us away. Feel your way, and watch your steps for traps or holes."

For several fathoms, the entrance passage ran straight back. Then it opened out into a circular chamber some three or four fathoms across, albeit it was hard to judge dimensions in the dark. Eudoric said: "Make yourselves comfortable whilst I watch the road."

"Comfort!" jeered Yolanda. "If sitting on a cold stone floor be your idea of comfort, I'd liefer not endure your notions of discomfort—"

"Take a horse and return to Ysness, if that be your preference," grated Eudoric.

After a short silence, she said: "I'm sorry, Eudoric

dear! I apologize. One of the House of Merovic should be able to endure discomfort without complaint." After a pause, she added: "I require privacy. How. . . ."

"Canst hold out for a while? It were rash to appear outside just yet."

For a short while Eudoric stood near the entrance, but far enough into the gloom that no one on the road below could discern him in the shadow. At length a squadron of King Gwennon's troopers came into view. They shambled past at a walk; the horses' heads hung, foam flecking their muzzles.

A soldier in the lead threw up a hand to halt the detachment. He pointed up the hillside towards the tomb and spoke. Eudoric could not hear the words, but he inferred that an argument had broken out. Arms waved; fists shook.

Several troopers dismounted. While others held their horses, two toiled up the slope, the wan sun gleaming softly from their helms and mailshirts. Eudoric retreated to the inner chamber, drawing his sword. He whispered: "Flatten yourselves against the wall around the corner and keep as quiet as the dead. The searchers have no lights, and methinks they'll not enter willingly."

The three stood motionless, scarcely breathing. Faint sounds announced the arrival of the soldiers: the swish of feet through the grass, the clink and creak of equipment, and sough of heavy breathing. A murmur of talk wafted in:

"Go on in!" "Nay, go thou first!" "Art afeared?" "Aye, verily! An the captain be so brave, let him do's own tomb search!" "Let me bespeak them, if they be within. The grass hath been trampled, as by our fugitives." "That could have been the work of a wandering cow or horse." "Hush; let me speak."

A voice was raised: "Hola! Be the runagates, the Imperial knight and the Franconian princess, within?

Come on out! Ye shall not be harmed! Ye shall be honored! The King hath sent us with sacks of gold for you! Ye shall be rich!"

After a silence, the trooper repeated his hail. Then came the dwindling sounds of retreat. When distant hooves again resounded and died away, Eudoric peeked out, to see the detachment vanishing eastward.

Eudoric reported this event to his fellow travelers, now sitting in the rotunda at the end of the passage. Rising, Yolanda said: "Oh, good! Then we can at once resume our journey."

"I fear not," said Eudoric. "We should likely run headlong into them, returning from their sleeveless chase. You, my dear, may now go out, whilst Forthred and I essay to light a candle and break out victuals."

When Yolanda returned to the tomb, Eudoric had a candle burning on the floor in the center of the rotunda. Now they could see that the circular megalithic wall was interrupted by a series of deep niches or recesses, extending clear around the circle. Some contained dimly-seen objects; others appeared to be empty.

"If I may mention it," said a subdued Yolanda, "I hunger."

"Here!" said Eudoric, handing her a slab of roast fowl and carving a slice from a loaf of dense rye bread. "I'm sorry about the lack of chairs, tables, and silverware. The scullions must all be asleep in the pantry."

She laughed lightly. "Know you, 'tis the first time I've dined thus since I was a little girl? I find it rather fun—albeit I trust we shan't have to eat in this manner for ay."

"I hope not," said Eudoric, "but we shall see. Now, about that money you filched from Gwennon's treasure room. How much gat you?"

She brought out the massive wallet and poured a

stream of gold pieces on the floor. "Share alike!" she said.

Eudoric snatched at a couple of coins that started to wheel away. Having separated the crowns, the half-crowns, and the double crowns, he began counting. At last he said: "By the Divine Pair, you have well over two hundred crowns!"

"I could have taken more, but I feared the weight would encumber our flight. Let's divide our loot."

"Give me an even hundred," said Eudoric. "That's what they promised me, and I take no more than my just desert."

She sniffed. "You *are* a tradesman at heart! No person of noble blood would bother his head with computing income and outgo to the last farthing."

"So?" said Eudoric, grinning. "Then I'll demonstrate my patrician generosity. Here, Forthred! You've been a good lad."

Eudoric scooped a fistful of coins from the pile and handed them to Forthred, who had been staring hungrily but silently at the collection. As Forthred began to stammer thanks, Yolanda said:

"Ho! Your liberality does you credit; but be sure you take the gift from your hundred crowns and not from my share. I'll keep the rest; the rogues owe me that for damages—theft of my possessions and insults to my person."

Eudoric burst out laughing. "Now who is counting to the last farthing? Forthred has faithfully served the twain of us, although his only reward has been the fortnightly stipend I alone pay him. So you can afford a bit of noble liberality yourself."

"Oh, murrain!" said Yolanda. "You should have been a lawyer. Take your hundred!"

As he counted out the coins, Eudoric asked: "What is Franconian law anent a husband's power over his wife's property?"

"Were I a common wench, considerable. As a

royal princess, howsomever, I keep control of mine. One tenth of all the moneys I receive from my estates doth go to charity—to Letitia's poorhouse, its lazaret, its madhouse, and other worthy institutions. I'll command my paymaster to prick you down for a stipend of pocket money."

"Thanks," grunted Eudoric, addressing himself to his food. When he had finished, he rose and stepped to the circular wall to examine their surroundings. He peered at the bundle in one niche.

"A long-dead body, I ween," he said. "There seem to be a dozen thereof. They must all have been here for years, or we should perceive their odor. I suppose one is King Balan and the others his royal kinsmen, or perchance soldiers and attendants sacrificed to serve him in the next world, as is done when the Grand Cham of the Pantorozians dies. But I cannot tell which be the king—"

"O ignorant one!" boomed a deep voice. "Can no one read the ancient runes in these degenerate days?"

The travelers started violently, staring about. There was no other movement in the chamber.

"I beg your pardon!" said Eudoric. "I am literate in my native Locanian and a couple of other tongues, but I have not had the privilege of studying your script. Enlighten me, pray!"

"A foreigner!" said the voice. "We suppose one must make allowances. Then know, O mortal, that we be the spirit of King Balan, condemned by a curse to spend a millennium in this tomb. Our resting place is the largest niche at the rear of the chamber, facing forth. If thou look closely, thou shalt see our name cut in the stone above the aperture. As for sacrificing attendants, thinkest thou we be barbarians?"

Eudoric, remembering the rack of human heads in King Gwennon's palace, was tempted to answer "Aye." But he forbore, not wishing to antagonize this ghost before he knew more of its powers. He said: "I am honored to meet Your Ghostliness, and I trust you take no offense at our using your tomb as a hostelry. We were pursued."

"On the contrary, good mortal, we are pleased. We have had no company for centuries, since the silly story got about that within these tombs lurked man-eating monsters. A few centuries of solitude wax tedious. What bringeth thee hither?"

"A difference of opinion with King Gwennon's minister, the jester-magician Corentin," said Eudoric.

"Meanst thou this King doth employ his fool as an officer of state?"

"Aye, sir; I mean just that."

"A strange conceit. What manner of man is this minister in motley?"

"From what I have seen, I hold him an able officer, if a low-minded princox and a belike a trifle mad."

"What of the King?"

"A doddering dotard, far gone in drink and gluttony and, methinks, not long for this world."

"Ha!" said the voice. "We are not surprised. Armoria hath had no monarch of truly royal quality since our own reign. Now relate the history of the nations since our demise, above four hundred years agone."

Eudoric told what he knew of the history of the Empire and its neighboring nations. Yolanda amplified his account of the Franconian past.

"So!" said the ghost. "Thou art sib to Franconia's reigning monarch, eh? How fare your royal brother and his kingdom?"

"Well enough," said Yolanda. "We have recovered from the revolt of the Jacks and have had no great wars for a generation."

"Be this Clothar a man of kinglier qualities than most of the royal ninnies whereof ye twain have told us? We wish the plain, unprettified truth, not the usual flattering panegyric wherewith kings are wont to stupefy their subjects. Speak, Madam!"

Yolanda hesitated, sighed, and then said: "I have tried to bring up my brother and to infuse him with a sense of royal responsibility, but, wellaway! to little avail. He is neither a monster of cruelty like Gundevec, nor a sot like Evatrix, nor a halfwit like Merovic the Fourth. He is amiable and not unintelligent; but he lives not up to his mind's potential. Poring over treasury statements doth bore him; so off he goes to revel in some light-minded game or sport, leaving the drudgery of's office to Minister Brulard. Hence the insolent rabble call my brother 'Clothar the Frivolous'—not, of course, to his face."

"A disease whereto monarchs oft are subject," said the voice. "Now tell me of yourselves."

"Let Eudoric speak," said Yolanda. "He has traveled the most and has had the most adventures."

Eudoric launched into the tale of his journey to Panthenia in search of two square yards of dragon hide, and of the adventures that befell him there. When the first candle burned down to a stub, Forthred lit a second.

"Four-wheeled wagons, with seats for wayfarers and canopies to keep off the rain, running hither and yon and bearing any who can pay?" said the ghost in marveling tones. "An ingenious notion; but 'twould never do in Armoria, because of the straitness of the roads. Go on, Sir Eudoric."

Eudoric suppressed a yawn. "Night has fallen, Your ghostly Majesty—"

"And ye are fatigued. Well and well, ye are welcome to pass the night in this our small domain," said the voice, "if ye do promise to tell more tales upon the morrow."

"Gladly," said Eudoric. "If you will excuse us whilst we fetch our blankets from the horses—"

"Ah, nay!" said the voice. "Thinkest thou that we

will suffer you to depart our tomb, leaving poor King Balan with no company except a brace of spiders? We do assure thee, spiders make dull company. Ye shall remain here till my craving for companionship be sated."

"How long would that be?" asked Eudoric.

"Mayhap a year or two."

"I beg to differ with Your Ghostliness," said Eudoric, rising, "but we have our own business to attend. So, thanking you for your hospitality—"

"Ha! Nay, do but essay to depart, and thou shalt see!"

Yolanda and Forthred had also risen, and now Forthred cried out in astonishment. Turning towards the entranceway, Eudoric saw that the passage had vanished. They were in a completely circular chamber without a visible exit.

" 'Tis but an illusion," said Yolanda. "Feel along the walls until you come upon the opening."

"So?" said the voice, adding a ghostly chuckle. The encircling wall, with its mortuary recesses, began to rotate. Faster and faster it went, until the recesses blurred into a pattern of black bars encircling the entire chamber between wider bars of buff-gray stone.

"Still an illusion," said Yolanda. "Go on, touch it, one of you!"

Forthred put out a cautious finger to the speeding stony surface. "*Autch!*" he cried, snatching back his hand. " 'Tis real to the touch at any rate."

Eudoric picked up a leg bone of the half-eaten fowl and tried the wall with it in several places. Each time, the bone met resistance and made a loud scraping sound.

"The entrance passage should be here," mused Eudoric. "The bone should penetrate this illusory wall with ease; but it does not."

"Well, my hero," said Yolanda nastily, "what now?

Sit here telling tales until we starve? Will our crumbling bones be found some day by another foolhardy snooper?"

"I'm thinking," said Eudoric.

"What with?" she responded.

Mustering his self-control, Eudoric ignored the gibe. "Hast no magical counterspell to neutralize our captor's?"

"Nay. My magical paraphernalia lies packed in the smaller chest, and that is still lashed to your mule."

"Have you no familiar spirit, such as the jester Corentin commands?"

"Nay. I had one, which on this plane took the form of a badger. But upon my arrest, Corentin pronounced a spell that manumitted the creature. It vanished, and I've been unable to summon it ever since."

"Master," said Forthred, "why not tell our ghost about—"

A quick glare and a shake of the head by Eudoric silenced the apprentice. After a long hiatus, Eudoric spoke: "Very well, Your Majesty, I'll tell of my adventure in Pathenia—"

"Meseems thou hast already spoke thereof," grumbled the voice.

"Oh, did I forsooth? Then of a surety I shall recall more details on the second narration. When my old teacher, the retired wizard Baldonius, needed two yards of dragon hide for his alchemcal experiments. . . ."

Eudoric awoke, stiff and sore, in total darkness. The second candle had guttered out. He felt around and located the bodies of his companions. Both moved and muttered at his touch but did not awaken. He found the pack containing their food and drink; but lighting a candle with flint, steel, and tinder in utter blackness baffled him. He raised his voice:

"Your Majesty!"

"Aye, Sir Eudoric?"

"Could you, pray, permit us a little light?"

"If thou regale us with more tales of thy life."

A faint gray glow, as of an overcast dawn, suffused the chamber, as if early morning light were filtered through an illusory wall of rock, or a pane of heavily clouded glass. Yolanda and Forthred stirred. Eudoric got the third candle going while his squire set out more food. Forthred muttered:

"Sir, I fear me this beer won't last the day. What shall we then do for drink?"

"Perhaps King Balan would suffer you to fetch water whilst holding the princess and me hostage," began Eudoric.

"Never!" boomed the ghostly voice. "An we opened the way for thy servant, ye twain might dash for freedom ere we could reëstablish the spell. Thou motest bethink thyself of something better."

"But, Your Majesty! If you keep us here, we shall die."

"Then your ghosts shall keep ours company."

"I am no theologian, and those gentry disagree amongst themselves as to what befalls our spirits after death. But I am sure we shan't be immured here like your royal self."

"Some day," said the voice, "we will tell thee of the curious curse that caused us to be clapped up here. Meanwhile, how shall we make certain that, if we permit the departure of the one, the others will not likewise show a fair pair of heels, leaving old Balan to his inarticulate spiders? Surely so clever a wight as thou art can devise a solution."

After a long silence, Eudoric said: "Your Majesty!"

"Aye?"

"How were it if one of us securely tied the wrists and ankles of the others? Then he who tied the knots could go out and return without danger of the bound ones' flight. After all, we must go forth betimes or pollute your tomb."

"We will give thy proposal a trial. What wilt thou use for cord?"

"Strips cut from the hem of my wife's gown."

"Indeed?" said Yolanda. "What makes you think, husband—"

"Enough!" roared Eudoric. "Your dress is nought but a mass of mud at best."

"Then you shall buy me another as good, once we are back in civilization."

"Eh?" said the ghost. "What is this about regaining civilization? If yon female imply that Armoria be not civilized, we will hold her imprisoned here forever and ay—"

"Please, Your Majesty!" said Eudoric hastily. "In the tongue of Franconia, 'civilized' means only one who speaks Franconian, regardless of his learning and manners. My wife meant no slight to Your Majesty's fertile realm."

Yolanda seemed about to speak again, but a murderous glare from Eudoric stopped her. The ghost said:

"Humph! That is as may be. Think not to bind one another with bastard knots, which fall apart at a tug! We know somewhat of knots, for in our youth we commanded a ship of our sire's navy. Oh, and one thing more: We heard the lady mention wizardly gear in her chest. Think not to fetch it into our demesne, to cancel our spells!"

"What would you do if we did?" flared Yolanda.

The ghost chuckled. "Thinkest thou we'll shoot off every shaft in our quiver in practice, leaving none for the battle? Do but try it, and we warrant on the word of a king that thou shalt not enjoy the results."

"What could he do?" whispered Eudoric.

Yolanda shrugged. "I know not. Wouldst take a

chance that 'tis but empty bluster? He may slay us, but I fear not death."

Eudoric shook his head. "When there's no way to reckon the odds, I hedge my wagers with caution."

"Tradesman!" sneered Yolanda under her breath.

At last the bindings were tied to the ghost's satisfaction. The wall stopped whirling, and the entrance reappeared. The three prisoners were let out in turn. Returning from one such expedition, Forthred said:

"Master, we should unload the poor beasts. Leaving them tethered and laden will afflict them with sores. But I cannot perform that task alone."

"Later," said Eudoric. "And now, Your Majesty, I shall tell of my adventures in Pathenia. . . ."

When Eudoric had plodded through the tale for the fourth time, Yolanda muttered: "How the spook feels I know not, but I am bored to the point of screaming."

Eudoric smiled and started the story over again. When he had finished, the ghost said: "We thank thee; but is there no other tale that thou canst tell? This one groweth weary with repetition."

"Alas, nay, sire," said Eudoric. "Aside from this one foray, I have led a sheltered, uneventful life." (Yolanda and Forthred hid their smiles; Eudoric was pleased to note that the ghost's abilities did not include the detection of lies.) "Have I mentioned the curious custom of the Pathenians, of making their homes in the shells of the gigantic snails that infest that land?"

"Aye, yea, forsooth and eftsoons! Thou hast told us of those snailhouses, not once but thrice! Get thee and thy companions hence, ere we die a second death from tedium!"

XIII

Heroes in Hiding

In Knokani, Eudoric addressed a shopkeeper. Not knowing the Armorian for "map," he said: "Tell me, goodman, hast a picture of the land hereabouts as it would look to a bird in flight?"

The merchant scratched his head. "Dip me in ordure if that bean't a strange thought! How could a man make such a picture, less he could fly above the land like a bird or a bodiless spirit?"

"It can be done, I do assure you. Men measure the distances along roads and fields and draw their lines accordingly. Have you no such charts to sell?"

"Nay, Master. What need have we for such, who dwell in Knokani all our lives and know the land like the palms of our hands?"

"But travelers like unto us would lack this knowledge."

The shopkeeper shrugged. "That's their plight. Belike they make such pictures in great cities like Ysness."

Eudoric sighed. "Well then, canst sell me a sheet a paper?"

"What's paper?"

"A new stuff used for writing; a kind of felt made of linen rags. If there's no paper, how about a sheet of parchment?"

"What's parchment?"

"A sheepskin treated to make a good writing surface."

"Oh, aye, sheepskins I have; albeit I know not if they'll serve your turn. The only wight hereabouts who knows reading and writing is the priest."

Eudoric left the shop with a roll of sheepskin, with the fleece still attached. "No map, Shorty?" asked Yolanda sharply in Franconian. Eudoric winced.

"They've never heard of maps. We shall have to make our own as best we can."

"That will merely tell us where we've been, not whither we must go. Meanst we shall wander about this countryside in circles until we perish of old age, or some peasant hears we're wanted by the King's men and sets them on our trail?"

"We are *not* wandering in circles," said Eudoric, stung. "I keep track of direction by sun and stars."

"But two days out of three are overcast. You should have thought sooner to fetch a map along."

Eudoric felt his temper slipping. "And when have I had time to shop for maps, what with you and the monster and the jester Corentin? Why don't you work your magic to find the right direction?"

"I could, had I the apparatus I left behind in Letitia. And methinks it bid fair to rain. Wilt make us sleep in that leaky little tent, though I awaken with Forthred's foot in my mouth and it give us rheumatics ahead of our years?"

"Sir," said Forthred in a low voice, "I beg your pardon, but people are staring at us. Were it not better to belay disputes until we be out of town? Ye ken how suspicious these villagers be of strangers."

"You're right," growled Eudoric. "Wedge this sheepskin under a pack rope and mount up."

Yolanda mounted, remarking: "Could we not for once enjoy the luxe of an inn? Foul though I know these wretched excuses for inns to be, after that tent 'twould seem a paradise."

"Nay," said Eudoric, swinging into his own saddle. "You know as well as I that, if we bed in a village inn, or even in a peasant's barn, we're like by morn to discover a squadron of King Gwennon's finest with blades to our throats."

She sighed. "Had I but known the hardships this flight entailed, I should have enjoined you to leave the Rock and suffer the monster to devour me."

"And had I known the sweet temper of my bride-to-be," snapped Eudoric, "I should have obeyed that command with a right good will."

For a while they rode in silence. Then a sound brought Eudoric round. Yolanda was weeping. Through her tears she blubbered:

"Oh, Eudoric dearest, why do I so misdemean myself? I'm sorrier than I can say. I hate myself. It's as though some demon from time to time possessed me, making me savage the kindest and most patient husband any woman could ask."

She collapsed into sobs and outcries. Eudoric petted and tried to comfort her. When she recovered, she became positively angelic, insisting on doing more than her share of the work of setting up camp. She even undertook to cook their supper, although the product of her first attempt proved so inedible that even Eudoric, inured to rough fare, could not stomach it.

Next day, another village loomed out of the drizzle. Eudoric said: "I see what looks like a tavern. Let's stop for a bit of food and rest."

Beyond the front door of the tumbledown structure, a plank floor extended out a few paces, and overhead the eaves of the building projected an equal distance. Two small tables stood on the planking, at one of which sat three old men, drinking and gossiping. When Eudoric and his party took chairs at the other table, the three oldsters fell silent and turned to stare. The one on the near side of that table even turned his chair around to get a better view of the newcomers.

"One would think they had never seen a human being eat or drink before," muttered Yolanda in Franconian.

"A traveler must needs get used to this sort of thing," replied Eudoric. He gave his order to the taverner for bread, cheese, and perry. As they waited, Yolanda said:

"Dear Eudoric, I truly grieve that I have so often yerked at you without just cause. My rank, alas, has shielded me from the need to govern my temper."

"It's never too late to learn," said Eudoric noncommittally.

While Yolanda and Forthred were occupied with their repast, Eudoric looked the nearest oldster in the eye and said in Armorian: "God den, goodman. How goes it with you?"

The man started, then pulled himself together. "Well enough, save for the rheumatics. And ye, sir?"

Eudoric had to strain his attention to follow the local dialect. "Well enough. And your companions?"

"Well enough," said one of the other old men, "save for a shortness of the breath."

"Well enough." said the remaining oldster, "but for a dimness of the eyes."

"Ah, well," said Eudoric, "when I reach your age, I shall doubtless suffer the same ills and more. Couldst tell me what lies yonder?" He pointed eastwards.

The old men exchanged glances, and he to whom Eudoric had first spoken said: "Well, now, there's one more village, clept Gaura. Beyond that, nought but forest. They do say that, an ye push on through the woods, ye'll come to the border of Franconia; but none I ken hath ever ventured thither."

"There are no roads thereabouts?"

"Nay, nary a road. None goes that way save perchance smugglers, to catch whom our King's soldiers patrol the border. An ye'd enter Franconia, ye maun turn back and travel many leagues to northward, where there's a proper road—or at least so 'tis said. I've not been thither to see. What would ye with roads to Franconia?"

"We are on a wedding journey," said Eudoric, "enjoying the countryside." He suppressed a smile as he caught a murderous glance from Yolanda.

"Oh, ah!" said the oldster. "Strength to thy yard!"

When Eudoric had paid and he and Yolanda were mounting, Forthred hastened out of the tavern to join them. As soon as they were out of hearing of the tavern, Forthred said: "Sir Eudoric!"

"Aye?"

"As I came out from the jakes, I heard those three old fellows talking. Ere they marked my presence, I heard one say: ' . . . smugglers without a doubt. If they force their way east from Gaura, they'll come upon the orthodox ogre."

"The *what?*"

"The orthodox ogre, sir! I heard them plainly."

"Art sure you mistook not the Armorian words? Neither of us is at home in that speech."

"Nay, sir; a man in the servants' quarters at the palace was a pious knave, who sought to save my soul from damnation by converting me to Bishop Grippo's Triune Creed. So I know the Armorian word for 'orthodox' when I hear it."

"What then?"

"Nought; they fell silent when they saw me, albeit laughing and chuckling as at some fine joke."

"Armorians," said Yolanda, "would deem it a rare jest for us to be eaten by this ogre."

"My dear," said Eudoric, "couldn't you conjure up a bigger demon, to overawe the ogre? Perchance one of those marids whereof you told me?"

"The spell works not, so far from the Saracenic lands. I have marid servants in my palace; but when I sought to evoke more in Armoria, none responded to my call."

"Have you any other magic against ogres?"

"One spell for routing a foe; but I've never essayed it. The result might be worse for us than for the foe."

"Well then, what is your idea?"

"We must retrace our way to the main road and enter Franconia at the regular crossing, as the old man urged."

"And be seized at the border by Gwennon's men-at-arms? Art daft, woman?"

"Nay, Shorty; you are now the besotted one. If I call out my name and rank when we reach the border port, the Franconians on the other side will rush across to rescue me."

Eudoric hated being called "Shorty," but he was sure that if he made an issue of this sobriquet, Yolanda would only use it all the more whenever she was displeased. He feared that, despite her pleas of wifely devotion, she would be angry over something most of the time. Mastering his irritation, he took refuge in logic:

"Imprimis, the Armorians might seize us ere we came within calling distance of the border post. Secundus, even if we drew nigh the post, your people might not understand that a Franconian princess was beset. Tertius, they might be under strict orders not to violate the border. Quartus, your royal family is far from popular with the lower orders, wherefore the soldiers might decide to let you stew in your own juice. Quintus, if they were partisans of the Duke of Dorelia—"

"Oh, you vile tradesman, calculating odds instead of rushing in to succor the right! Where is your knightly courage?"

Eudoric gave a mirthless smile. "My mammet, if you know your own history, 'twas but a decade ago that your gallant Franconian knights, serving in the Carinthian army, lost the day for their side and their lives as well, at Polovotsograd. They made one of those gallant, headlong charges, against orders, into the midst of the Pantorozians."

"At least they died with their honor bright! As for you, you're not even the other kind of swordsman. You've pranged me but twice since we left Ysness. My third husband, with his nose forever in ancient books, was no Huano of Tarraconia; but he could still futter thrice to your once!"

"Your third—" Eudoric stopped with his mouth agape.

"Aye, my third husband, the scholar Sugerius. What about him?"

Eudoric took time before answering, being somewhat shaken by this revelation. "I realized on our wedding night that the Armorians had stretched the truth in calling you a 'maiden'; but I knew not what a monstrous taradiddle it was."

"Well? And what of that? 'Twas all perfectly legal. 'Tis not my fault that I am thrice widowed."

"You told me you were single," said Eudoric, "when I asked you as we sat awaiting the monster."

"So I was then. I said not that I had always been so."

Eudoric rode for a time in silence, then asked: "Tell me of my predecessors. What befell them? Didst turn them into frogs?"

"Nay. Art sure you wish to hear this painful history? I would not wound your feelings beyond necessity, for despite all you are dear to me."

"I'm sure, Yolanda," he said. "I believe in scouting territory ere I invade it."

"Well, my first mate was chosen for me, as is usual with the children of royalty. He was Gontran of Tolosa, a duke's son and a famous warrior. But he proved a stupid, drunken brute, who laid vile hands upon me in anger."

"What happened to him?"

Yolanda shrugged. "He disappeared one day. 'Twas thought that, like many another dissatisfied husband, he'd run off, changed his name, and taken up a new life elsewhere."

"But then, how could you—"

"Oh, I see what meanst. As I once told you, there's no divorce in Franconia; only annulment, to be had by lavishly bribing the priests of the Triunitarian hierarchy. But if a spouse vanish and nought is heard of him, or her, for a year, he may be declared legally dead. This has the same effect as an annulment; and thus it was with Gontran."

"What if he reappear?"

"Legally, that has no effect. But I dread the thought; for Gontran was a rancorous, vengeful man, who never forgave what he deemed a slight or let bygones be bygones. Hatreds and grudges so filled his mind as to render him impervious to reason. I hope you'd be prepared to confront him, should he—ah—manifest himself in the flesh."

Eudoric sighed. "I can only do my best. How about Husband Number Two?"

"He was a poet from your Empire, Landwin of Kromnitch."

"Forsooth? Methinks I knew that fantastioo a few years agone. A tall, thin, fair-haired wight?"

"Aye. He had some vague claim to noble descent, which I credited not; but he sang such sweet songs and made such tender love that, being young and foolish, I overlooked the vileness of's blood, I persuaded Clothar to knight him for his verses. Still and all, to marry off a royal to such an one did bend the framework of our social order until it creaked."

"How fared the pair of you in wedlock?" Eudoric asked. He was a little surprised to find that his emotion on learning of Yolanda's much-married past was less jealousy than a consuming curiosity.

"I could not complain of his lectual performance," said Yolanda. "For all his meager frame, he had lust enough for three. The trouble was, he wouldn't confine his interest to his wedded wife, but must need futter the scullery maids behind the door to the buttery. So we quarreled, and he disappeared as did the other."

"And Number Three?"

"That was Sugerius, Count of Perigez. An imperceiverant bookworm, who cared nought for the usual amusements of the nobility: hunting, drinking, gambling, fighting, and fornication. He neglected me for his musty tomes and moldy manuscripts until he drove me to seek consolation in other beds. When Sugerius found out, he had the insolence to strike me—me, a royal princess!"

"And then he disappeared," said Eudoric, suppressing the skepticism from his voice. This tale of the three absconding husbands had to Eudoric an odor of fish. He wondered what had truly befallen them. Had they been dropped through a trapdoor into a cellar or a well containing something man-eating? Had they been bricked up alive in the walls of her palace? He asked: "Were there others betwixt Sugerius and me?"

"Nay; you're Number Four, and I hope you will outlast your predecessors. It were worth your while to try, since you will have my royal brother as your patron.

"I am sorry to have betimes been bad-tempered; but I have suffered great vicissitudes of late. Nor are you an ever-present ray of sunshine. Still, you are a man of many virtues, whom I am sure I shall truly love."

"Thankee," said Eudoric dryly. He wondered whether even the enormous advantages of being a client of the King were worth the risk of being dropped into a monster-haunted pit. "Let me tell you a little secret. A man's ability as a swordsman of the other kind, to borrow your words, hinges much upon his health of body and peace of mind. If you'd fain cause his—ah—resolution to droop, you have but oft to berate him in harsh and wounding terms. If you're fain to have him serve you with vigor, flatter and praise him; make him think himself worthier than in his heart he knows himself to be.

"Meanwhile, we shall go on to Gaura and thence through the forest to the border."

"What of this orthodox ogre?" asked Yolanda.

Eudoric shrugged. "If it exist, we shall cope with it as best we can. From what I know of peasant legends, it's but a tissue of dreams and moonshine. Trot!"

XIV

The Orthodox Ogre

"Forthred!" called Eudoric. "Mark!"

For half a day they had plodded through the forest east of Gaura. Since it was an ancient forest, where no timber had been felled for many decades, there was little underbrush. The only obstacles were an occasional stream, or a ledge, or a giant tree trunk athwart their path. The leaves had just begun to turn to yellow and bronze. From time to time they fell, rocking and spinning earthward in the cool, calm, autumnal air.

At Eudoric's command, Forthred, far in the lead, thrust a yard-long stake or wand into the ground. Yolanda, leading her horse, followed at a distance. Behind her came Eudoric, leading the remaining animals with one hand and grasping a bundle of wands in the other. When he reached the aftermost stake, he halted and, squatting, sighted over this stake and the next one. "A little to my right!" he called, waving. "Yolanda, step aside that I may see."

When Forthred had moved his stake to right and

left until all three stakes were in a straight line, Eudoric called: "Good!" and pulled up the stake before him. Forthred inserted his stake upright in the soft soil and called:

"That's my last marker, sir!"

"Yolanda!" said Eudoric. "Hold the animals, pray."

Hastening forward, he thrust the reins into her hands and continued on to where Forthred stood. He handed the apprentice the bundle of wands he bore and went back to where Yolanda waited. By this simple form of surveying he hoped to keep the party traveling in a fairly straight line. Otherwise under the canopy of leaves, especially on overcast days, they could easily lose track of direction and wander in circles until they dropped.

They resumed their deliberate march, halting at intervals to plant and pull up stakes. Presently Forthred cried out shrilly: "Master! Sir Eudoric! Come speedily!"

Eudoric again handed the reins to Yolanda and ran forward. He found his squire staring fearfully at a singular being. This was a man-shaped creature half again as tall as a man, with a thick, warty hide. Webbed fingers and toes ended in claws. A pair of horns surmounted pointed ears. From beneath its blob of a nose, like a grotesque mustache, sprang a pair of yard-long, tapering, serpentine tendrils, which twitched and writhed. Smaller tendrils depended from its chin and rose from its scalp. The club it carried was nearly a fathom long—as long as Eudoric was tall.

"God den," said Eudoric. "Are you the orthodox ogre whereof we have heard peculiar tales?"

"We do not call ourselves 'ogres,'" rumbled the giant in a guttural accent. "It is a name ye little folk have given us, meant in no flattering spirit. As for my orthodoxy, we shall soon see about that, when it is decided whether ye three shall be eaten or not.

Think not to flee, for I can outdistance you as a hare outruns a tortoise."

Eudoric made sure his sword was loose in its scabbard, although he did not highly rate his chances in combat with the ogre. The creature's pachydermous hide furnished armor of a sort, and its size and reach would enable it to squash Eudoric like a bug before he could get close enough to inflict a mortal thrust.

"Really?" said Eudoric, assuming a composure that he did not feel. "Then how would you prefer to be addressed, sir?"

"Our name for our own kind," said the ogre, "is *Ghkhlmpf*." At least, it sounded like that to Eudoric.

"I fear I could never master the ogerish tongue," said Eudoric. "But what's this about your orthodoxy?"

"Know, little stranger, that until a few years ago, in my ignorance I devoured all who came my way, regardless of sect. But now that Bishop Grippo hath converted me to the Triune Faith, I give those whom I stop a chance to earn their lives by questioning them about the tenets of the True Faith. An they give truthful answers, they are suffered to proceed. My first question—"

"Your pardon, Sir Ogre," said Eudoric, "but I must have a word with my servant." In Locanian he said to Forthred: "Go back—walk, do not run—to see what Yolanda is doing. If the ogre attack me, I'll try to hold it in play long enough for you two to mount and gallop away." He turned back to the ogre. "And now, sir, what are these questions?"

"First," said the ogre, "ye shall recite the sixteen essential points of the Triune doctrine, as formulated by the Supreme Archimandrite, Alexanax the Third."

Eudoric tightened his grip on his sword. With a forced smile, he said: "I fear you have the advantage of me. Though not a religious man, I was reared in the Empire, where the official creed is that of the Divine pair—"

"Ho!" roared the ogre. "Bishop Grippo especially impressed upon me the need for utterly extirpating that vile heresy!" He hefted his club and took a step forward, each mustache-tendril writhing like an angleworm on the hook.

"On the other hand," continued Eudoric as if unperturbed, "my recent bride, the Princess Yolanda of Franconia, could probably answer your questions better—"

"I care nought for your bride!" growled the ogre. "When I have finished with you, she shall have her chance to escape mine inquisition. Die, pygmy!"

With a frightful roar, the ogre bounded forward and swung his club. Eudoric's head would have been smashed like an egg had he not leaped backwards as the wind of the blow fanned his face. The ogre moved with agility remarkable in one of its bulk. As Eudoric noted that the toe claws, digging into the humus, gave the ogre the needed purchase, he knew that he could never outrun those colossal legs.

He thrust at the ogre's arm as the monster recovered from its swing; but the distance was too great for the weapon to be effective. His point merely scratched the hide of the forearm. With his left hand, Eudoric fumbled for his dagger. Perhaps, he thought, his best chance would be to leap in close, inside those rugose, ape-long arms and try to stab the ogre in one of its thinner-skinned parts.

"A lively minikin!" grumbled the ogre. "But it will not save you!"

The ogre brought its club in a shooshing arc straight down. Eudoric sprang aside, but the club grazed his left arm and thumped against the humus with the sound of a muffled drum. The glancing blow made Eudoric stagger, and his dagger went spinning away.

"We will soon end your dance!" roared the ogre, aiming a wide, sweeping sidewise blow at Eudoric's ankles. Eudoric had just time and strength to leap into the air as the club passed beneath him.

"Last blow!" howled the ogre, heaving up its club and crouching to spring. Eudoric tensed himself to bound forward into the ogre's embrace. He could not recover his dagger in time, but a shortened sword might serve the task. If it did not, this would be his last adventure.

Then came an interruption. With half an ear, Eudoric heard Yolanda cry out a phrase in an unknown tongue. A heartbeat later, amid a rising hum, the air about the battling pair was filled with flashing, swirling, black-and-yellow objects. A howl from the ogre told Eudoric that a swarm of huge hornets had streamed past him and attacked his foe. They thrust their stings into the ogre's leathery hide and especially clustered on its face, neck, and other thin-skinned parts.

Roaring, the ogre danced about, its footfalls shaking the forest floor. It swung a futile club until it dropped the weapon to swat its tormentors with its web-fingered hands. At last it conceded the contest and fled, careening and crashing through low-hanging branches in its flight.

Wincing at the pain in his battered arm, Eudoric picked up his dagger and returned to the glade where Yolanda and Forthred crouched beside a brazen tripod. A slender column of turquoise smoke ascended from the dish of brass suspended beneath the tripod's apex. Beside the tripod stood the viridine vase that Eudoric had urged Yolanda to leave behind in Ysness. The horses and the mule were tethered to nearby trees.

"What on earth—" began Eudoric, but Yolanda laid a finger on her lips. So Eudoric watched in silence. Then Yolanda rose; she made a trumpet of her hands and called: *"Rudi sasa upesi! Rudi sasa upesi!"*

For a while the glade was silent, save for the stirring of the animals. Then Eudoric heard the hum of the hornets. Strung out in a long column, the swarm wound through the air among the tree trunks as they flew towards the travelers. Eudoric prepared to fight them off, but the hornets streamed directly for the green ceramic and plunged into it. By the time the last of the hornets had vanished into its depths, Eudoric felt sure that the total volume of the insects was several times that of the vase; but, as he told himself, such paradoxes were common in magic. Yolanda clapped the lid back on the vase and smiled triumphantly up at him.

"Well!" said Eudoric, helping her up. "Princess, your magic assuredly saved our gore that time. My profoundest thanks!"

She shrugged. "That was the spell whereof I was not sure. By good hap, it worked just right. Aren't you glad you failed to persuade me to leave my jar behind? Pray help me to pack up again."

Eudoric said: "Lend a hand, Forthred. You must excuse me, my dear, for my left arm was somewhat banged by the ogre's club."

"You are hurt? Oh, darling, let me see. . . . What a ghastly bruise! I have an ointment. Hold still. . . ."

Eudoric relaxed as she got out a small jar and rubbed a pungent salve on the bruise. "Thank you, Yolanda. I'm glad the bone be not broken."

"I'm sure 'twill be well by the time we reach Dorelia."

The rest of the journey through the forested borderland was uneventful, save that for one day the fugitives were shadowed by a pack of wolves. The wolves never came close enough to alarm; but the sight and smell of them, slipping around the black tree trunks in the middle distance, drove the beasts of burden frantic and so delayed their progress while

Eudoric and Forthred strove to bring their animals under control.

The travelers never knew when they crossed the border into the duchy of Dorelia and hence, in theory, into the kingdom of Franconia. When they were sure, Yolanda said: "At last I can show my true colors and get the respect that be my due, instead of slinking along pretending to be some lowly tradesman's lass!"

"Oh, no, you shan't!" said Eudoric. "This is the demesne of Sigibert of Dorelia. If the Duke should learn we are within his grasp, he might arrest us to use as bargaining counters with your royal brother."

"Then how," Yolanda asked, "shall we find our way across the duchy without trouble from the Duke?"

"The same way that Forthred and I came hither: by moving softly and swiftly, showing no token of rank or pretension. How didst manage the transit to Armoria?"

"Oh, that was last year, when Clothar and Sigibert were in one of their spasms of undying friendship. Moreover, Sigibert's son, young Lord Theodad, was then at the court of Letitia and thus in Clothar's power. And further, my witchly repute perchance made the Duke more cautious than he might otherwise have been."

"So," said Eudoric, "we shall still be humble travelers, atoms in the sea of the faceless multitude."

She gave an exaggerated sigh. "Life with you, Shorty, is but one long train of escapes and disguises. Where's the pleasure in't?"

"I'm sorry, Your Royal Highness," said Eudoric in his most sarcastic tone. "At the next recess, I'll see that the servitors have a grand banquet laid, to be followed by a ball with ten thousand candles, a hundred musicians, and a company of comedians. We shall dance the galliopter and the minurka, and bid

Berthar of Sogambrium to sing *The Lay of Erpo Giantkiller*. We'll invite the King of Carinthia, the Emperor, and the Grand Cham of the Pantorozians. The dinner shall include roast breast of peasant—"

"Shut thy gob!" screamed Yolanda. Then she burst into tears. "Oh, Eudoric! Why dost goad me into making these disgraceful scenes? All I wish is to be the true and loving wife of a virtuous man—a man of suitable rank, of course. With Forthred you are kind and patient; why can't you be the same with me?"

"Because, my dear, you and Forthred differ to no small extent, do you not?"

"Certes; he's a mere hilding of low degree. Whereas I—well, you ought to make allowances for my rank and position and use me gently."

"So who was gentle when the Heavenly Pair created the first man and woman?"

"My brother has hanged men for remarks less subversive than that! You sound like one of the villainous Jacks, who revolted when I was a child and went through the country burning and slaying. They'd have taken your head in a trice, for carrying pen and ink. They wished to extirpate the art of letters, holding it a means whereby the nobles oppressed them; for they sought a fantastical commonwealth of equals, where none could command another."

"We heard of that in Arduen," said Eudoric. "How the highways of Franconia bore thousands of bodies of Jacks, hanging from the roadside trees."

"They did but get their just deserts, for rising against their natural lords. I confess that one tenet of their prophet Gundolf did appeal to me: namely, that women should have rights like those of men, instead of being treated as mere chattels."

Eudoric smiled grimly. "You, Yolanda, would never let any man enslave you. If aught, you'd insist that the usual spousely rôles be reversed."

"Fair enough, were't not?"

"Certes, if you could find a suitable man: some human rabbit who'd jump at your bidding."

"I could never be happy with such a witling."

"Then belike you'll never be happy, short of mating with some hero of legend like Sigvard Dragonslayer; and Sigvards are in short supply. Philosophically, as my old tutor Baldonius says, you may have right on your side; but as a practical means of achieving your wishes—"

"Practical! There speaks the tradesman! No man of truly azure blood would trouble his head with thoughts of practicality!"

Eudoric shrugged. "Suit yourself, Your Royal Highness. I do but try to see beyond the end of my nose—as your sire did not. He hanged so many rebellious peasants that the next year famine swept Franconia, for want of hands to till the soil."

"I tire of this dispute," she said.

"So, my dear, do I." They rode in silence.

XV

Stultified Seduction

Where the road from Turonax to Carnutis crosses the river Ust by a rickety bridge, Yolanda said: "Eudoric, we haven't bathed since we left Ysness. Clothar has tried to persuade his courtiers to bathe at least once a fortnight, but so far with little success."

"A worthy idea!" said Eudoric. "If we lead the animals round yon river bend, we can unfoul ourselves out of sight of the bridge."

A quarter-hour later, they found a spot with space ashore to set down their apparel and a clean, sandy river bottom before them. As Eudoric and Forthred began to shed their jackets, Yolanda said:

"Ho there! I cannot expose myself before a person of Forthred's low degree!"

"Mean you that, were he a count or baron, 'twere all right? Where draw you the line? Would a mere knight—"

"Oh, cease your quibbling, Shorty! Forthred, lead the animals back around the bend and tether them

199

out of sight of your master and me. If you are fain to wash whilst we do, that's your affair."

Eudoric resented Yolanda's issuing orders to Forthred, as if he were her servant; but, not wishing to provoke another tirade, he said nothing. He liked clean-cut lines of authority.

Another quarter-hour, and he and Yolanda were standing waist-deep in the water, scrubbing themselves with handfuls of sand. Yolanda said: "You should have thought to get soap in Ysness."

"Aye, so I should. Failing that, I should have spent hours hunting for soapwort by the roadside. And I ought to be King of Locania, which indeed I might have been had the parents of a forebear of mine been legally wed."

"I'm sorry; I mean not to chide you."

Encouraged by her occasional efforts to be companionable, Eudoric remarked: "You're a fine figure of a woman, Yolanda."

"It rejoices me that you think so. When we reach lands where—"

"Ahoy there!" shouted a rough voice. Standing on the shore where they had left their clothes stood eight men-at-arms, five of them aiming cocked crossbows. The speaker, a burly, red-bearded fellow, shouted: "Come ashore instanter, ye twain!"

"What shall we do?" whispered Yolanda. "From their badges, those are Dorelia's men!"

"I fear we must obey," muttered Eudoric. "We're at their mercy. The range is too short to miss. If we run, we get bolts in the back, and the river's too shallow to escape by swimming under water."

"Well?" roared Redbeard. "Art coming? Or would ye fain be the butts at target practice?"

"Coming," said Eudoric. He and Yolanda dawdled towards the shore while one of the men consulted a piece of parchment, saying:

"Aye, these are the genuine twain whereof Bishop

Grippo hath written our master: a vagabond from the Empire, hight Eudoric, and the King's sister, the witch Yolanda. These match the description, and those tethered beasts we passed must bear their baggage."

"Hold your aim steady!" said one of the crossbowmen. "Shoot if the witch begin to utter a spell, lest we be turned to swine."

"That were small change," said Yolanda.

Redbeard laughed. "Fear nought; she cannot work magic, standing naked in running water without her potions and devices."

"Sirrah!" As she reached the shore, Yolanda addressed the redbeard. "It is not proper for persons of your rank to see a royal princess unclad. Pray turn your backs whilst I do clothe myself!"

Redbeard guffawed. "Since we've already seen all there is to see, what were the point? Methinks ye could give a lusty man a lively canter."

"You dare, you scum!" cried Yolanda, bringing her palm against Redbeard's cheek with force enough to stagger him.

"So!" he shouted, and slapped her back.

For a heartbeat, Yolanda's expression was of pure amazement; as if she had never before been struck in her life. Then she brought up a fist in a whistling arc against the soldier's jaw. Redbeard went sprawling.

"Seize her!" he shouted, scrambling up. "Hugo! Dagobert! Yare! For that, my lady fair, we'll have a tryout in the saddle. Toss the wench on her back and hold her down! Back off there, Master what's-your-name, or you'll get a bolt in the guts!"

Throwing Yolanda supine proved easier said than done. She gave Dagobert a punch in the solar plexus that sent him staggering off doubled over, and Hugo got a fist on the nose that started a runnel of blood.

But two of the arbalesters laid down their weapons and joined Hugo in seizing the woman.

As Yolanda struggled in the hands of the soldiers, and Redbeard fumbled with the fastenings of his breeks, Eudoric's mind raced. If he sprang upon Redbeard, his match in height and weight, could he swing the fellow around as a shield? Or could he dive for his scabbarded sword before the crossbows shot him?

A call in a foreign language wafted around the river bend. A swarm of formidable black-and-yellow hornets filled the air with their buzz and fell indiscriminately upon the eight soldiers and the two bathers. As the pair holding Yolanda released her to bat at the insects, Eudoric seized her wrist and dragged her back into the Ust.

"Take a deep breath and hold it!" he shouted, and threw himself backwards. As he submerged, the hornets that had alighted upon him flew away. When he brought his face out long enough for a quick breath, he saw that Yolanda had likewise gone under.

A glance to shoreward showed the eight soldiers, staggering back upstream towards the bridge, still slapping and yelling. As Eudoric watched, one of them fell, crawled a few paces, and then lay, rolling and thrashing. Presently his movements ceased.

Eudoric nudged Yolanda. When she raised her head, he whispered: "Methinks they're gone."

Again they waded ashore. Yolanda was hardly recognizable, with a face so red and swollen that her eyes were nearly shut, and her body marked with angry scarlet swellings. The knuckles of her right hand bled from the blow she had landed on Dagobert's metal-studded leather coat. Eudoric supposed that he looked much the same.

The fallen soldier lay still with eyes staring blankly, as Forthred approached from around the bend, saying:

"Are ye all right, Sir Eudoric and my lady? Oh, pox! They stung you also!"

Through swollen lips, Yolanda mumbled: "Forthred, didst unpack my magical gear and work the spell with the green vase?"

"Aye, Your Highness. I was out in the river, washing, when the soldiers came by. They'd seen our beasts; they tied their own near the end of the bridge and, leaving one man to watch the horses, came down the river path afoot. I crouched low in the water, so they saw me not. I'd watched Your Highness work your spell aforetime, with the ogre; so I got out the gear and did as nearly as I could remember."

"You did not remember quite all the spell," said Yolanda, "or you would have commanded the hornets to assail the troopers only. Still, my lad, you did surprising well."

Eudoric thought of pointing out that, had not Yolanda insisted the beasts be taken upstream and tied up in sight of the bridge, they might have avoided discovery by the soldiers in the first place. But he thought it better not to bring up the matter. Instead, he said:

"Baldonius warned me against my squire's attempts to play the wizard; but this time it was lucky that he did. Forthred, help us on with our garments. We are too sore from our stings to dress unaided."

This time, Yolanda said nothing about exposing herself to a baseborn churl, but gratefully accepted Forthred's help. Eudoric said: "We must find some safe place where we can lie up to recover. Can either of you propose such a refuge?"

Yolanda said: "I have a minor spell, to detect the presence of magic. Could I locate some country wisewoman, she were more like to give shelter to a fellow practitioner than would the local folk."

"Good!" said Eudoric. "Have at it!"

Half an hour later, Yolanda had set up her tripod, whence rose a plume of smoke. Then, kneeling, she held a crystal ball in cupped hands and stared into its depths. Slowly she turned to face all the compass points. At last she straightened up and pointed northwest.

"The vibrations come strongest thence," she said. "Belike our goal lies beyond those low hills."

It took the rest of the day, with three more halts to work Yolanda's directional spell, before they located a cottage in the woods near the village of Carnutis. The house looked like any other modest Franconian country dwelling, the sort a farmer, neither rich nor poor, might keep; but it lacked such a freeholder's barns, byres, and other outbuildings. Yolanda said:

"If I mistake not, that is whence come the vibrations."

Leaving Forthred to hold the animals, Eudoric and Yolanda approached the door. Eudoric knocked, then stood aside to let Yolanda talk.

A woman opened the door, saying: "Good-afternoon. What would ye?"

Eudoric had the impression that all female magicians were either young and beautiful like Yolanda, or withered and old like Svanhalla of Hasselbourne. This one was neither. She was a robust rustic goodwife in well-preserved middle age, plump and rosy-cheeked, with blond hair lightly streaked with gray. She must, Eudoric thought, have been a pretty girl, and she was still attractive.

The woman and Yolanda exchanged a long series of greetings and responses in an unfamiliar language. At last Yolanda said:

"Eudoric, this is Riguntha of Carnutis, the local healer and seeress. Mistress Riguntha, I present my husband Sir Eudoric of Arduen and his squire Forthred. I have explained our plight."

"Come in," said Riguntha cheerfully. "I have a few

simples for your stings and can harbor you for a few days. I can also feed you, provided your man go to the village to buy extra provender. Come in!"

An hour later, Eudoric and Yolanda were seated on a settle in the witch's parlor, while Riguntha dabbed ointment on their stings, talking the while: ". . . and when ye opened the door, methought ye were the fabled giants made of bladders, so swollen were ye. I'll be bound if your swellings have not already begun to shrink: but I misdoubt ye'll be in fettle to travel again on the morrow. Now then, I'll help you dress.

"I see, Princess, that ye wear those newfangled linen undergarments. When they're worn out, ye can sell them to the makers of that new parchmentlike stuff called paper. As for you, Sir Eudoric, how is't that ye do not the same? All Franconians of gentle birth use linen nowadays, whilst ye go about with rough wool nigh unto your skin."

"I fear," said Eudoric, "that in this matter the Franconians be ahead of us of the Empire. I must try out this novelty in Letitia."

"Aye, aye. 'Tis the same with us countryfolk, being too poor to afford this practice. It reminds me of the time when my husband lived, he went out one day to catch a fish for our supper. . . ."

Eudoric listened politely, although he found the story of little interest, and he had to pay close attention to follow Riguntha's country dialect. When the anecdote had run its course, he said:

"Tell me, Madam Riguntha! As a child I heard that, for the practice of magical arts, one should forswear the pleasures and pains of intimate commerce with the other sex. Back home, I know an eminent adept: Svanhalla of Hasselbourne. I understand that she has lived celibate all her life, the evidence being her assistance to me in capturing a unicorn. But 'tis plain that this stricture has not applied to you ladies. Explain, pray."

Riguntha giggled nervously. "A shrewd springald! Know, O Eudoric, that 'tis a matter of degree. An ye'd ascend to the very pinnacle of our profession, such as were needed for feats like flying on broomstick, or inflicting mortal ills upon a foe, or living over a hundred years, such self-denial indeed is requisite.

"But I lack such lofty ambitions. Happy am I to attain some modest success in predicting storms, and alleviating diseases of man and beast, and warning the folk against bands of brigands or Duke Sigibert's tax collectors. Not that there's a muchel of difference betwixt the two! If the Triunitarian bishops persuade the Duke to outlaw all magic within the dukedom, save that which they themselves command, the poor folk of Carnutis will lose even the slight succor I can afford 'em. Have some more beer!"

She smiled charmingly at Eudoric. "And now, good my sir, tell me somewhat of the Empire and thy adventures therein." (Eudoric noted the change to the familiar form of address.) "For mine arts do inform me that thou have undergone enough of such for a man of thrice thine age. Here in Carnutis, we get but little news of the world without, aside from what I can glean by mine arts. Therefore I shall hang upon thine every word!"

Flattered, for the next hour Eudoric told of his journey to Pathenia, of his hunt for the spider Fraka, and of his capture of the unicorn.

When Riguntha carried the plates to the sink, Eudoric cocked an eye at Forthred, murmuring: "Water!"

The apprentice hurried out, hoisted the pail out of the well by the windlass, and brought in a bucketful. Eudoric took a towel to dry dishes. Yolanda sat looking uncomfortable. At last she said:

"Riguntha, can—may I help?"

" 'Tis good of you to ask, Princess. But tell me: How oft in your life hast washed and dried dishes hitherto?"

"N-never; I was never taught such tasks. But if Eudoric, a dubbèd knight, can do such menial work. . . ."

"Then I fear that your aid, however well-meant, would cause more grief than would its absence. These are my only set of crockery; if they be broken, my next guest must dine on wooden platters. But fear not; I shall have other household tasks for you, if ye can gird up your spirit to tackle 'em."

Eudoric suppressed a smile. He was pleased to hear his arrogant, class-conscious princess offering to turn a hand at commoners' tasks. Perhaps, he thought, there was hope for her after all.

The couple's bed was an oversized pallet spread on the floor of the main room. Riguntha had the only bedroom; Forthred took a smaller pallet to the pantry. Before Riguntha closed her door, she said:

"Pleasant dreams, ye twain. An ye want aught, hesitate not to call on me."

She threw Eudoric a dazzling smile, as she and her candle disappeared. Yolanda murmured:

"I am loath to complain, but meseems, were I in her shoes, I should have given my visitors the bedroom."

"Have you seen her bed?" Eudoric held up his hands two feet apart. "We could never have slept therein unless intertwined like serpents. Of course, if she gave *you* the bedroom, she and I could make do here—"

"Eudoric! That is no proper jest!"

Eudoric laughed. "Then be glad for what we have. Good-night, my dear."

An hour later, the hearth fire had died to a clutch of coals. Eudoric found himself sleepless, although the pain and swellings of stings had much abated. His mind kept coming back willy-nilly to Riguntha of Carnutis and her pregnant smile. He sternly told himself that a midnight assignation would be utter madness; the risk appalled his prudent soul. Perhaps Riguntha would gasp and moan so loudly as to awaken the princess. Perhaps Yolanda would awaken anyway and come prowling. . . .

Eudoric's arguments were conclusive, yet something seemed to have taken possession of his wits. While his conscious mind was determined not to yield to this strange urge, his conscious mind was helpless in the grip of this mysterious compulsion. Even as he mentally shouted Stop! Stop! Go back to bed! Be not a bigger fool than you can help! he slid quietly off the pallet, picked up his cloak from a chair, and softly tried the door to Riguntha's bedchamber.

It gave at once, the hinge not even squeaking. Eudoric wondered if it had been recently oiled.

"Thou art expected," whispered Riguntha, sitting on the edge of her bed in the light of a candle. "Come in quietly, and slam not the door."

With a smile, she laid herself back. Eudoric closed the door softly, shed his cloak, and sat down on the narrow space between Riguntha's hip and the edge of the bed.

"Now," she whispered, "show me how the gentlemen of the Empire pleasure their ladies!"

Some time later, she said: "I am ready long since. Why dost delay?"

Eudoric slumped. "I'm sorry, Madame Riguntha. I'm fordone. I seem unable to rise to the occasion."

"Forsooth?" She raised herself. "I see what thou meanst. How doth the princess suffer an impotent man?"

"I am not wontedly thus. This has never befallen me before."

"Well, we must essay some more, to raise thy spirit."

Later he said: "Alas, 'tis of no avail. Something has stolen my manhood."

"That lioness whom thou hast wedded, belike. Well, go thy way. I thought to enjoy a gentleman for once; but I see I must make do with unwashed yokels."

Eudoric stole back to his pallet. As he started to straighten out beside Yolanda, he became aware, by the faint light from the hearth, that her eyes were open.

"Well?" she said. "How went it with my Huano of Tarraconia?"

"Let me explain," he said. "I had to ask her—"

"Forget the tale of cock and bull. I know what befell."

"You do? Then in the name of the Divine Pair, explain it!"

"I blame you not, Eudoric." Yolanda smiled. "I saw her slip a potion into your beer and guessed what portended. So I cast a little spell of mine own, lest you consummate the lust she'd imposed upon you."

"I hope your spell be not permanent!"

"Nay, 'twill wear off in a day or two. For a woman in my position at court, it is a handy device for nobbling lubricious noblemen. Now go to sleep; this time you'll have no difficulty."

XVI

The Gilded Guardhouse

"How far," asked Eudoric, "is Letitia now?"

Yolanda replied: "Less than a league. If we turn right at the next crossroad, my palace lies but a bowshot thence. We shall tarry there long enough to make ourselves clean and presentable ere going to the court."

"Oh, no, we shan't!" said Eudoric. "I'll fetch you before the King and his minister, render this Armorian treaty, and secure my franchise ere some unforeseen mishap prevent."

"Eudoric! Be not like a country boor! You must come before my brother as a proper gentleman, not an enseamed, mud-spattered ragamuffin! To appear as you now are might aggravate the anger he may feel upon discovering that he have an unheralded brother-in-law."

"I'm sorry, my dear, but my mind is made up. Business before pleasure! I'll warrant your royal brother have seen many a mud-spattered knight. . . ."

They began another dispute. Since Eudoric would

not be moved, Yolanda finally subsided into sulky silence. She spurred on ahead, and Forthred moved up beside Eudoric, saying in Locanian:

"Master! Sir Eudoric!"

"Aye?"

"Once ye be settled in the lady's palace, I'll ask release from my service."

"By the God and Goddess, why? Haven't I paid you well and treated you kindly?"

" 'Tis not that, sir." Forthred fumbled for words. "But I'm fain to return to mine own home, where my betrothed awaits me."

"Oh? Then you seek not the highest ranks of the magical fellowship, by remaining celibate?"

"Nay, sir. A few good spells are fine, but I'd liefer lead a normal life than spend a century learning how to raise a tempest. Besides, Doctor Baldonius' scholarship doth intrigue me more than his sorceries. And that's not all."

"What else?" asked Eudoric.

"I fear me that, an I see much more of you and your lady, I shall lose all wish to wed, albeit I've plighted my troth. The sight of you twain, one instant civil and gracious and the next bawling like Tyrrhenian fishwives, would strike the stoutest lover with terror. I should find such wedlock too vexatious to bear."

Eudoric sighed. "I understand. But, I promise, I'll not pass my days here as the royal sister's plaything. I have mine own affairs to tend. And remember that my princess have never learned to bridle the whims and endure the vexations of the moment, as all we lesser mortals must. Were she a child, one would term her spoiled rotten.

"So pray remain with me for the nonce; at least until we know what's toward."

Minister Brulard received Eudoric and Yolanda in his cabinet and dispatched a guard to the tennis court to inform the King. While waiting, Yolanda told the minister of her detention by the Armorians and of their impending human sacrifice. She had just reached the point where Eudoric appeared on the rock above her, when King Clothar strode in trailing a scuttle of flunkeys. Eudoric genuflected. When he saw his sister hale, albeit travel-soiled, the King clapped Eudoric on the back.

"Well done, Sir What's-your-name!" he bellowed. "Meseems we've promised you something for fetching home our willful sister. What was't?"

"A franchise, Your Majesty," said Eudoric promptly, "giving me and me alone the right to run a stage-coach line across Franconia."

"Ah, yea. Brulard, have the authorization drawn up forthwith."

"I have anticipated Your Majesty's wish," said the minister, pulling a large sheet of parchment out of his desk drawer. "Here you are, Sir Eudoric."

"I thank you," said Eudoric. He cleared his throat. "There's another matter, which I was compelled to undertake unauthorized, to allay the Armorians' suspicions."

"What is that?" asked Brulard.

"To avoid incarceration like His Majesty's sister's, I pretended to have been sent to contract an agreement betwixt the two kings concerning imports of wine and perry. Here is the draft, in duplicate, both copies signed by King Gwennon's minister Corentin and bearing Gwennon's seal. I trust that, since this treaty was the original purpose of the princess's journey, I did no wrong in pursuing the project. If Your Majesty and Master Brulard approve it, you can execute it and return a copy to Ysness."

King and minister glanced over the sheets. The King, toying with the waxed point of his reddish-blond goatee, said: "It appears in good order, though we shall have to study it. Ha, Sir Dorian, we see that you be a useful wight to have about a court. Would that you were amongst our kinsmen. We must needs find posts for them all, notwithstanding that some be unequal to the tasks—"

"He *is* your kin, forsooth," interrupted Yolanda.

The King frowned. "How mean you, sister?"

"He is your brother now."

"But we have no br—*What?*" roared the King. "Meanst that you and this fellow. . . ."

"Certes, I mean it," said Yolanda. "We were wed both by the True Church and by the heathen rites of Armoria."

"But—but members of our family may not marry without our express permission!"

Eudoric cleared his throat again. "Your Majesty's pardon, but we had no choice in the matter. The Armorians threatened to hold us in a dungeon all our lives unless we agreed to this union."

"And wherefore should they do such a moonstricken thing?"

Eudoric shrugged. "I thought it a silly idea myself; that jester-minister is to my mind more than a trifle mad. But they seemed to think that your sister were less of a formidable foe had she a husband to keep her witcheries in check."

"Hm, hm," mumbled the King. "If you do keep her in check, you will be the only wight on earth who can. Brulard and I must discuss this matter. You have our leave, Sir Eudox."

Eudoric bowed himself out, saying to Yolanda: "Now, my dear, I shall be happy to enjoy the luxe of your abode—and a change of clothes."

Yolanda's palace was a spacious two-story mansion in ornate Franconian style. A porte-cochère extended from the front door across the driveway.

"We stop here, Eudoric," Yolanda said, and whistled sharply.

Two shadowy, gargoylish figures, beside the front door, came to life and approached. Eudoric realized that they were not human at all. They were man-sized and more or less man-shaped, but they wore no clothes. Their heads had bestial muzzles and a pair of short horns. Their three-fingered hands grasped spears, which they leaned against the door frame before coming forward on feet that ended in three huge toes, capped by nails that were almost hooves. Each being had a ratlike tail, which waved behind its knees.

The horses snorted and rolled their eyes at the unaccustomed sight and smell. Eudoric and Yolanda managed to control their mounts; but Forthred, leading the spare animals, was less successful. His horse reared and threw him. Before the beast could bolt, one of the nonhuman doormen darted forward and seized the bridles. The other took the reins of Eudoric's and Yolanda's horses. Yolanda dismounted, saying:

"*Hutt humma lil-bayt al-khayl; khud ish-shunatna juwwa!*" She turned to Eudoric as the doormen led off the animals. "Ask me not to give lessons in Saracenic; mine own is barbarous. But it suffices to command the marids."

"So that's what these creatures are! Have you no human servants?"

"Aye; grooms, cooks, and maids. For heavy work—gardening, furniture moving, and such—I find the marids superior. They are stronger than men and, when constrained by the proper spell, docile and obedient. Best of all, so long as I feed them, I need not pay them wages."

"Does your spell compel then to swink forever?"

"Nay; the magic weakens after a few years. Then they'll vanish back to their own plane, and I shall have to recruit another crew. Let us go in. First I must show you the house, for I know that you pant to see it."

Eudoric was not at all eager to be shown the house. His main desires were for a hot bath, a strong drink, a good meal, and a long sleep. But Yolanda had her own ideas.

"And this," she said, "is the library. Most of the volumes are mine own acquisition; neither my sire nor his sire were much for reading. Feasting, jousting, and venery—in both senses of the term—were more to their taste. My royal brother, I fear, takes after them. Some of the books were brought hither by my scholarly husband, Count Sugerius.

"That suit of armor yonder was worn by my great-uncle, the Duke of Albi, at the battle of Novambio. You can see the dents. And those swords on yonder wall have belonged to generations of martial forebears; for ensample, that two-handed monster with the prongs. . . .

" . . . and this is the dining room. The table once belonged to King Merovic the First, my great-great—anyway, I forget how many 'greats'—grandfather. And those candlesticks were taken as booty in the Third Carinthian War—"

"Your pardon, Yolanda," said Eudoric, "but when do we break our fast?"

"Oh, belike two hours hence. The kitchen staff knew not that we were coming and so had let the fires go out. If you had taken my advice to stop here ere going on to the court. . . . Now the portrait on yonder wall is that of Lord Clodomir, an illegitimate son of King Merovic. A mighty warrior; there were those who said he'd have made a better king than the legitimate scion. . . .

" . . . and here is the master bedroom. The mirror over the dressing table is Saracenic; one of my great-uncles brought it back from a pilgrimage to Philistia—"

Eudoric blinked and shook his head to fight off

sleep. "This will be my first night in a decent bed since leaving Ysness. For a copper sesterce I'd pull off my boots and fall asleep with my clothes on."

"We cannot so do now," said Yolanda implacably. "Notice the bedspread, made by a peasant family in Drufort. Because their ancestress succored King Charivald when he was wounded in the battle of Segni, he conferred on her and her descendants in the female line the sole right forever to make spreads for the royal family. And now we must tour the kitchens and laundry."

She led him forth. On the way down the hall, Eudoric paused at a door, whose wooden surface was blank except for a knob. "What's in there?" he asked.

"That, my dear husband, is where I keep my magical paraphernalia."

Eudoric gave the knob a pull, but the door remained immovable. "Locked, eh? I can see why you might; but this door has no keyhole."

"Think you I'd entrust my direst secrets to an ordinary lock and key, which any burglar could pick in three ticks of the clock? Nay; that door has a magical lock, which only I can open. Come along, dear; I have not shown you the half. . . ."

"Tarry a while, Yolanda! I am fain to see this room of wizardly apparatus. Work your little spell and show me in."

"Nay; I let none, not even the marids, enter here."

"But after all, I am your husband—"

"Harken, Shorty! When I, Princess Yolanda, say that none shall go thither, I mean none! Now come along and blow no further bluster."

Eudoric's lips tightened. He was about to make an angry retort when she continued: "Nay, dear one, take no offense. 'Tis for your own safety. Some presences in there might harm you ere I could bring them under governance."

Eudoric's anger subsided, but he shot a skeptical

glance at the door. Then, with a small sigh, he followed her, wondering from what sorcerous source she obtained her boundless energy.

Yawning, Eudoric came awake after nine hours of his heaviest sleep in years. As he turned over, he realized that Yolanda was no longer beside him. He raised his head, to see her seated at the dresser in her nightrobe and doing things to her long, caledonian-brown hair.

"Dearest!" he called. "Come back to bed!"

She turned with a frown. "Whatever for?"

"You shall soon see!"

"Oh. You mean that you lust."

"Aye. Last night I was too wayworn; but today—"

"There's no time for that now, " she said shortly.

"No time? Why? What's toward?"

"As soon as I've broken fast, I must to town."

"Why?" said Eudoric. "I should think you'd rejoice in a day's idleness."

"You understand not. A message has reached me, revealing that Clothar and Brulard are furious at our marriage. They planned to wed me to a half-witted son of the King of Carinthia. So I go to forestall any dire plans they might hatch anent you. I would not lose my fourth husband ere I'd had time to break him in!"

"Oh? Well then, I'll go with you to confront them. I'll explain—"

"Be not a noodlepate, Eudoric! In three breaths you'd be hauled off to Riculf's Tower, whilst the headsman gat orders to sharpen his ax. Nay, stay you quietly here. I can handle those good-for-naughts."

"Humph," grunted Eudoric. "Then I'll ask one of your stablemen to saddle up some likely nag and explore your estate, with a groom to guide me."

"Nay; you must stay within doors, lest you fall into ambush."

Eudoric's irritation burst out: "Curse it, woman, it's time we sorted out our duties to each other! If you'll not come hither when I ask, I'll—"

"Attempt force? You'd not only find me your match, but also in three heartbeats you would be borne off by a dozen marids to my personal dungeon, there to languish whilst I concocted a spell to clip your claws. Let us have no more of this nonsense! In this place, my word is law, and think not but that I can enforce it!"

Yolanda rang a little bell on her dresser. Her tiring woman came in and helped her to dress. While Eudoric, seething and still in bed, gloomily contemplated the day ahead, she said to her servant:

"Eufronia, tell Leo to have the carriage ready within the hour." To Eudoric she said: "Remain abed or break fast, as you list. You must needs move sprackly, if you'd join me at table." She swept out.

When Eudoric, newly shaven and freshly clothed, arrived at the breakfast table, Yolanda had departed. He ate in solitary silence. He would have liked to question the marid servants, but he knew no Saracenic and they, apparently, spoke none of his several languages.

Afterwards he wandered restlessly about the palace. As he passed the door of the magic room, he cast a sharp eye upon it. Seeing that no servants, human or otherwise, were about, he grasped the knob and gave a mighty pull, without result.

He drifted into the library, where he spent an hour reading a history of Franconia. Then he asked that Forthred be sent for.

"Are you comfortable?" he asked his squire.

"Oh, aye, sir, if ye don't mind these horned, inhuman creatures peering at you. What's to be our fate?"

"I know not," growled Eudoric. "The princess thinks

I'm in danger if I step outside the palace. How about a game of draughts?"

Yolanda returned in the early afternoon, bringing her dressmaker, with whom she spent the next few hours closeted. When she emerged, she found Eudoric engrossed in his twelfth game with Forthred.

"Eudoric!" she said sharply.

"Aye?"

"This morn you expressed—ah—certain wishes, which I lacked time to gratify. We have an hour ere dinner. If you're still fain, I can give you the time for it now. Horses must be fed and watered, and husbands must be—"

"Madam!" said Eudoric, taken aback. "In the first place, it's not proper to put it so roynishly before others; in the second, were not this eve—"

"This evening my head bailiff reports to me on the gains and losses of my estates; 'twill keep me occupied until the small hours. So it is now or never! Or, at least until the morrow."

Eudoric glanced at Forthred who, coloring, stared at the floor. "Forthred, set the game board where none shall disturb it; we'll finish the play anon." Following Yolanda towards the bedchamber, he continued: "But tell me, how went your visit to the King and his minister. Where stand I?"

"Still ambiguous," she threw back. "I gat no promises from that precious pair, save that they commit no bale without further consultation. Forsooth, I know better than to trust the promises of kings, even mine own brother."

Eudoric wondered whether, in this hectic atmosphere, he would fare any better than he had with Riguntha.

The next day, Yolanda again departed early for Letitia. Increasingly dissatisfied, Eudoric determined to have a look around the estate. But when he opened the huge front door, two marids barred the way.

"*La'! La'!*" they said, holding arms out. "*Mush rûh!*"

"Out of my way!" shouted Eudoric, putting a hand on each bare leathery chest and shoving.

Instead of his pushing them aside, they seized his arms, hoisted him into the air, carried him back across the threshold, and tossed him in a heap. These beings, he realized, were so much stronger than any mortal man that wrestling with them would be as futile as with the orthodox ogre. By the time he had scrambled to his feet, the door had closed behind the demons.

Boiling with rage, Eudoric prowled the palace. There were three other ground-floor entrances, all guarded by marids. He went up the marble stair and investigated the second-story rooms. Wherever he looked out a window, two or three marids were patrolling beneath, now and then glancing up.

Eudoric summoned Forthred again, saying: "It transpires that I am clapped up here at Her Highness's pleasure."

" 'Tis and easy form of jailery, sir, if ye'll excuse my so saying."

"True; nobody's beating me, and the fare will make me swell like a bullfrog if I limit not my aliment. But I will be no noble lady's lapdog. Have the marids hindered your movements?"

"Nay, sir. I went to the stables early this morn, to make sure that our beasts were properly cared for, and none gainsaid me."

"Whence I infer that their orders include not you. Go to the stables, take one of our horses, and tell the grooms the nag needs exercise. Then ride in to Letitia and find the old Serican magician Tsudai." Eudoric gave directions for finding the palace and, in case Tsudai should be at home, his dwelling. "Ask him to come out here to see me. He owed me for saving him from assault."

"Hath he a beast of burden or a carriage?"

"I know not. Belike he could fly hither if he wished. Lead the mule, saddled, and give him his choice of mounts. He looks aged and frail; but having seen him hold off a band of bravos single-handed, I suspect his appearance to be deceptive."

From a window in the princess's bedroom, Eudoric watched his helper ride off leading the mule. The autumnal wind blew a shower slantwise, bringing with it an armada of leaves transformed to bronze or gold.

Back in the library, Eudoric tried to read the history of Franconia but found it hard to concentrate. Further examining the shelves, he came upon a group of books on love, marriage, and the female temperament. These seemed so out of keeping with the rest of the library, whose content was heavily historical and political, that Eudoric suspected the works had once belonged to husband number three, Count Sugerius. He pulled out a fat volume and settled himself to read.

Two hours later, Forthred returned with Tsudai astride the mule, and the marids made no attempt to stop the two from entering the palace. After greetings, Eudoric said:

"Learned Doctor, know you aught of the King's intentions towards me? The princess keeps me locked up here, like a felon, on the pretext that otherwise, Clothar and Brulard would have me shortened by a head."

Shedding the voluminous black cloak that he wore over a robe of purple silk, the Serican gave a squeaky little laugh. "This person doth assure your noble self that there be naught to the tale. After the King and minister had thought on the matter, they decided they were just as pleased. They would that ye tame this fair if formidable lady. They admit that the task doth call for a hero of legend; but lacking genuine giantkiller, they hope ye will qualify."

"Easier to tame a bull olifant in rut," grumbled Eudoric. "My one burning wish is to burst from this gilded guardhouse and return to my homeland. Any remaining scruples have been laid to rest by the knowledge that my bride has sought to deceive me."

"Leaving loving bride behind?" asked Tsudai. "That seems to this superficial person a departure from usual course of love amongst round-eyed Westerners."

" 'Twas a marriage of inconvenience," said Eudoric. "If she's fain to follow me to Arduen, we shall see how it fares with us; if not, be hers the choice. There will be no broken hearts in any case."

"Will indissolubility of Franconian marriages cause your noble self perplexities?"

"I think not; the Empire allows divorce. Next: Canst get me out of here?"

"Aye; this inferior one can put marids to rout. When wouldst depart?"

"As soon as Forthred can pack our gear. Whilst he is so occupied, let me show you the door to her magic room. She refused me admittance; so, naturally, I am curious as to what's within."

Tsudai said: "Sir Eudoric, your humble servant is eager to please your noble self. But if ye remember the fairytales, curiosity oft leads the curious one to do things that he later regret. Are ye sure ye wish me to open this portal?"

"I'm certain, Doctor; be the responsibility mine. Go ahead, if you can."

XVII

A Surplus of Spouses

Tsudai whipped a wand out of a sleeve of his robe and pointed it at the door. He moved the wand in patterns, muttering.

A marid bustled up, crying: *"La'! La'!"*

Tsudai turned on the demon, pointed the wand, and said: *"Rûh! 'Imshi!"*

"Ya shayy!" roared the marid, lunging towards Tsudai with three-fingered talons outspread. As if came within reach, the Serican rapped one of the reaching arms with his wand. There was a crack, a flash, and a smell of something scorched. The marid recoiled. With a cry of *"Istannani!"* it whirled and fled back down the corridor.

"It hath gone for reinforcements," said Tsudai. "This feeble person cannot hold them all off with little stick. Must summon aid from superadjacent world." He threw back his head and cried in a high voice: *"Lung jin! Lung jin zher!"*

A crowd of marids appeared in the corridor, running towards Eudoric and the magician. Their hooflike toes clop-clopped upon the marble. Amid the clatter, Tsudai cried out again. The foremost marids halted their charge and flinched back, although the pressure of those behind shoved them forward.

Aware that the marids were staring goggle-eyed at something beside him, Eudoric looked around and also flinched. Next to him, almost touching his shoulder, had appeared the head of a reptilian monster somewhat like Druzhok but smaller, with scales of a vivid vermillion, tendrils sprouting from the sides of its muzzle, and a pair of stubby antlers above its eyes.

As Eudoric watched, the head advanced, followed by a scaly neck, then one five-clawed forefoot, then another. The creature seemed to be crawling through a hole in an invisible barrier between its world and Eudoric's.

As more and more dragon came into view, its scales made an unpleasant scraping sound against the edges of the hole. A pair of hindlegs pushed their way into visibility, and a crested tail scraped after. The new arrival bulked huge in the hallway.

The marids at the forefront shouted and struggled to melt back into the pushing throng, but the pressure of the crowd still drove them onward. The scaly, horned head shot out, and the fanged jaws clamped shut on the foremost marid, which shrieked as it was hoisted high above the floor. There was a horrid sound of crunching bones.

The marids in the rear, at last realizing their danger, ceased to press forward. In a flash, they turned as one and fled down the hall, around a corner, and out of sight.

The dragon tossed the mangled body of the still-struggling demon into the air and caught it as it descended head-first, like a cormorant eating a fish. The reptile jerked its head in a series of colossal gulps; with each gulp, more and more of the marid disappeared until only its hoof-toed feet protruded from the slavering jaws. With a final jerk, these, too, vanished. A bulky bulge traveled slowly down the dragon's throat, merged with the creature's trunk, and disappeared.

Eudoric, a little shaken, asked: "Is that the demon you would have evoked when you were attacked in Letitia, save that you had promised it a holiday?"

"Nay. This person doth not oft evoke the *lung*, for on this plane I must find aliment wherewith to feed it, lest I risk becoming such myself. That were no small task; but with a whole marid within its belly, my bodyguard should not hunger again for several days." Tsudai addressed the dragon: "*Ni zhu zher!*" He explained: "It will secure us against further interference."

The Serican resumed his work on the lockless door. The second try followed its course without interruption; the wand flashed blue and the door swung open.

"Forthred!" said Eudoric. "Fetch a couple of candles."

When the apprentice returned with two candlesticks, the three went into the cryptic chamber. The light of the candles shimmered on the iron and brass and silver and gold of pieces of magical equipment stored here and there on dusty tables and shelves. But Eudoric's attention was riveted on three life-sized human figures standing stiffly in the center of the room.

When Eudoric moved his candle closer, he saw that one of the trio was the figure of a massive man, stocky of build like Eudoric but larger in every direction. He wore a coat of chain mail and had a huge two-handed sword slung across his back.

The second statue was that of an older man, lean and stooped, whose wispy gray hair and beard framed wrinkled, aquiline features. Were he alive, Eudoric guessed, the man would be in his fifties.

The third, the youngest-looking mannequin, was a tall, slender, blond man garbed in doublet and hose of a gaudy green-and-purple pattern. With surprise in his voice, Eudoric said:

"I know this one: a poet and troubadour, hight Landwin of Kromnitch. He guested at our castle at Arduen a few years past. I thought him a bit of an ass, but I'll warrant he deserved not being turned to a statue. These three must be Yolanda's prior husbands. She told me their names, but I forget."

"The warrior hight Gontran of Tolosa," said the Serican. "The graybeard is Count Sugerius. This person never met either of them but hath heard much about them all. Then your noble self knows of your predecessors? I forebore to speak of them, lest I stir up a whirlwind of strife."

"Are these my lady's three authentic husbands, or simulacra of wax or plaster?"

"The veridical spouses, held fast by a spell of stasis."

"Can they be returned to life?" asked Eudoric.

"Yea, that they can. Wouldst do so?"

"Let me consider."

"If they regain consciousness, there might arise discord as to who shall have rights to the lady."

"Hmm," said Eudoric. "Landwin may be a bit of a fool, but he's an amusing fellow who means no harm. Whilst I'm not famous for softness of heart, 'twere cruel to leave these poor abjects hanging betwixt life and death. Restore them, if you'll be so kind."

"Art certain? The responsibility is yours."

"Aye, I'm sure. Proceed, I pray."

Tsudai scratched his straggly gray goatee. "How long have we ere Her Highness return?"

"Perhaps two hours. She said she'd not be back till dinner time."

"Very well, this unworthy one will do his best."
Tsudai prowled the room, looking over the magical
gear. "Ah, it doth appear that this be what we need.
Help this inferior person to move the object."

The object was a kind of multiple brazier, with
seven little brass dishes hung by chains from a framework of slender rods of a similar alloy. Tsudai shuf-
fled and puttered and mixed his powders. At last he
lit a small fire in the base of the apparatus. As
varicolored smoke ascended from the dishes, he mumbled and chanted. Whisking a fan from his purple
sleeve, the Serican fanned smoke towards the three
ensorcelled husbands.

" 'Tis done," he said at last. "Abide a moment;
they will not leap to full vitality at once."

As Eudoric watched, the chain-mailed warrior
blinked his eyes and began to stir, at first moving
slowly as if his joints had rusted. Then the scholar
likewise stirred, and finally the troubadour. Voices
came slowly and creakingly from parched throats,
the first words pitched so low that they were almost
inaudible. At length, slowly, their speech waxed
intelligible.

"Where—am—I?" creaked Landwin of Kromnitch.

"What—hath—befallen?" grated Count Sugerius.
"Water!"

"Fetch them water, Forthred," said Eudoric.

"Who—are—ye—scrowles?" groaned Gontran of
Tolosa.

"You have been released from an enchantment,"
said Eudoric, "which my—which your wife, the Princess Yolanda, cast upon you."

"And who are ye?" said Gontran, glowering.

"Sir Eudoric Dambertson of Arduen. This is the
room in Yolanda's palace where she keeps her magical equipment."

"And what do ye here?" persisted Sir Gontran.

"I've brought Yolanda back from captivity in Armoria."

"Where's the hussy now?"

"She's in Letitia but is expected home for dinner."

Gontran's forehead wrinkled in thought. "Count Sugerius! Methinks I know you from aforetime. What do ye here?"

"The same as ye, Sir Gontran. I was her third husband; and when she tired of me, she cast a spell of immobility upon me and set me up here with you and Master Landwin, the sweet singer ye see beside me."

"*Sir* Landwin, if you do not mind," said the troubadour.

"By the toenails of the Holy Trinity!" roared Gontran. "Meanst that ye twain enjoyed her after my ensorcellment?"

"If 'enjoy' be the word precise," said Landwin. "I know not the full tale of your several tenures as Yolanda's husbands, but from mine own experience I'll warrant it was no bed of rose petals. You are Eudoric Dambertson, are you not?"

"Aye. Sir Eudoric, now."

" 'Tis an unanticipated pleasure to meet you again, if under such strange circumstances. How fare your family?"

"Alive and reasonably well," said Eudoric, "albeit my sire has given up the hunt."

The troubadour turned to the scholar. "Count Sugerius! Your servant, sir. What befell you in wedlock with Yolanda?"

Sugerius replied: "She found the rôle of a scholar's wife prolixious and took a lover. When I learned of this, in a rage I slapped her. 'Twas as ill-chosen an act as punching the nose of a tigress; she beat me to a jelly ere casting a spell upon me. How was't with you?"

"Much the same," said Landwin, "but I never

struck her. She caught me futtering a chambermaid and threw me out the window; she hath the thews of a blacksmith. I essayed to flee the grounds, but she sent marids after me. Being swifter than greyhounds afoot, they caught me and dragged me back. She threatened to cast upon me a spell of impotence. When I essayed a second time to flee, she did unto me the same as to you."

"I had strife with her, too," said Gontran. "She sought to confine me to this palace, save when we rode abroad together. When I defied her, she bloodied my nose with her fist; wherefore, being a hardened warrior, I knocked her down. Howsomever—Sir Eudoric, what do ye here, in Yolanda's absence? Are ye her hireling?"

"Nay," said Eudoric. "I should have departed for my home in Locania, but that she keeps me mewed up here, guarded by her demon servants."

"And why should she do that?" asked Sugerius. "Are ye her lover?"

"Nay, her current husband. Methinks that—"

"By the gods of the Saracens!" cried Landwin. "Four husbands! Here's an intrinse knot to unravel! The Franconian laws permit but one spouse at a time, to my mind a foolish, archaic prejudice. The Saracens are wiser. Sir Eudoric, has it ever come to fisticuffs betwixt you twain?"

Eudoric shook his head. "I was brought up never to strike a woman, albeit at times with Yolanda the temptation has been strong. I daresay I could hold my own in a box match with her, for all that she has the advantage of height and reach. I've seen her knock down a man of my size."

Landwin leered. "Tell me, co-husbands, how found you Yolanda as a bedmate? Come, there's no need for reticence amongst us in the matter."

"I found it interesting," said Sugerius judiciously, "that a woman of so voluptuous a form should seem to have so little interest in the carnal act. She submitted with good grace, but methinks she gat no joy therefrom. I am writing a book on amorous passion in women. How with you, Sir Landwin?"

"I, too, found her cold," said the poet. If you'll pardon my boast, I count myself proficient beyond the moiety in the art of bringing a woman to the vertex of passion; but with Yolanda, I might as well have plied my skills on one of the statues in her gardens. Meseemed her thought was: Hurry up and get it over with, thou apish buffoon! Therefore I sought others who might, I hoped, display more ardor. I had minded less, save that she sought to mew me up here as she did Lord Gontran. Sir Gontran?"

"I pay no heed to such matters," grunted Gontran. "A warrior true hath no time for fancy courtship ere sheathing his blade. I leave such japes to counterfeit knights, who claim the dignity of 'sir' without a single manslaying to their credit."

Landwin's lips compressed and his nostrils quivered at the insult, but he turned to Eudoric. "And you, Sir Eudoric? How fares it with you?"

"It is my opinion," said Eudoric carefully, "that Yolanda's passion be not for the rites of love but for the aggrandizement of power. She submits to her husbands' desire, neither for love nor for lust, but to keep them where she can rule them best. She approved a proposal of the leader of the Jacks, to give equal rights to women."

Gontran snorted. "How utterly ridiculous!"

" 'Tis not at all ridiculous," said Sugerius. "I have deeply studied the female mind. Somewhat to my surprise, I found it, not the same as the male, but on balance quite as able."

With a disdainful sniff, Gontran turned to Eudoric. "Do ye adhere to such nonsense?"

Eudoric smiled. "In foreign lands, I dispute not

matters of religion or politics. I fear, howsomever, that Yolanda gives the doctrine of women's equality a bad name."

"Exactly!" said Landwin. "She were never satisfied with mere equality; she'd reduce any man in her grip to total subservience." The poet paused, beating time with a finger, then burst into verse:

"Oh, ask not a warrior princess so bold
Who's born to lead men of a militant host
To cook and to sew and to sweep out your hold;
She'll mangle your shirts and she'll blacken your toast!

"What perplexes me," he continued, "is why, if she care so little for amorous congress, she's so furiously jealous if her man cast a friendly eye upon another. Hath she, think you, a passion to conceive?"

"I think not," said Sugerius. "If none of us four hath impregnated her despite our valiant efforts, either she's naturally barren or employs a spell against conception."

Eudoric: "Meseems 'tis but another aspect of Yolanda's drive for power. If her man fail to tup her often, or *a fortiori* if his roving eye alight on a rival, he is slipping out of her grasp. That she cannot endure."

"Howsomever," said Landwin, "entrancing though this discussion be, we must needs agree upon which of us shall be husband-in-fact, and that ere her return."

"We could play cards—you have playing cards, have you not?—or throw dice," said Eudoric. "But should the winner be high man or low?"

Sugerius fumbled in his robe and put on his spectacles. Gravely he said: "Ah, Sir Eudoric, I do perceive your import. Each of us might conclude that the pains of union with Yolanda exceed the pleasures. 'Twere like a foot race, wherein the prize doth go to the last to finish. Ye'd see all the runners hopping up and down on the starting line, each waiting for the others to outdistance him."

"Well," said Landwin, "we could take turns—be husband-of-the-day in rotation, like a relay race. Since she's more than a match for any one of us, belike by confronting her in succession we could wear her down."

"Ye jackanapes!" said the count. "Ye know the court would never permit such doings."

Gontran growled: "A manlier way were to fight it out. We'll choose two pairs by lot, who'll fight to the death. The two survivors shall then meet—"

"Ho!" said Landwin. "That were unfair! The count is well on in years, and I'm a poet, not a bully-rook. You'd cleave me in twain with that monstrous thing you bear!"

"Coward!" sneered Gontran. "Count, ye are the most learned amongst us. Who is Yolanda's legal husband?"

"Certes, ye are! Since your marriage came first and was terminated neither by annulment nor by death, it still abides. The rest of us are but unwitting adulterers, who thought we were wedding a virtuous widow—"

Eudoric interrupted: "But Gontran has been declared legally dead, in consequence of his 'disappearance.' So for that matter have the other twain of you. Were your marriages not ended by this procedure?"

"Under some circumstances, yea," said the count. "But where the spouse averring the disappearance hath actually immured the vanished one, keeping him or her incommunicado, the rule is that of the case of Chararic versus Thrasamund—"

"Adulterers!" roared Gontran, whose mind had at last caught up with the implications of the count's words. "Then ye've made a cuckold of me! By the Three True Gods, this stain upon mine honor must needs be cleansed with blood!"

"Seize him!" shouted Eudoric, hurling himself upon Gontran. He bore the warrior to the floor while Landwin, Sugerius, and Forthred grasped the Tolosan's limbs. Gontran was as strong as a bear; but the combined strength of the four proved too much for him. After he had struggled until he was red in the face, he finally subsided. Gripping Gontran's massive right arm with both of his, Eudoric looked up at Tsudai, who was busy removing magical apparatus from nearby tables to place it out of danger of breakage.

"Doctor! Canst tie him up?"

"This minor person can better that, noble sir. Tell him that, an he be not quiet, I'll put him back into stasis, as he was ere I cast off the spell."

When the thought had been repeatedly explained to Gontran, the warrior yielded. "And we'll borrow that great sword of yours," said Eudoric, pulling it out of the scabbard, "lest in a moment of passion you injure someone."

Gontran subsided, sitting hunched on the floor against a table, muttering: ". . . stain on mine honor . . . stain on mine honor. . . ."

"Now, gentlemen," continued Eudoric, "what are your plans? Mine is to flee forthwith back to Locania. We had better move yarely, for the hour of Yolanda's return comes on amain and apace. Forthred, pray pack us for departure."

"My palfrey must yet be in Yolanda's stables, unless the poor beast have died," said the count. "I'll find the horse and hie me back to my demesne of Perigez, to complete my doctoral thesis, 'The Incest Motif in Helladic Drama.' It grieves me to leave behind a parcel of my precious books, but one must weigh the alternatives."

"I'd go with you, Sir Eudoric," said Landwin, "had I a horse; since Kromnitch lies nigh to the path to Arduen."

"Good!" said Eudoric. "I have a spare horse for

you. That leaves you, Sir Gontran, master of the field, if one can call the fair Yolanda that. Alas! She's a splendid woman in her way; or would be without this passion for tyranny."

"I may depart also, when I've thought about it," rumbled Gontran.

"She would have been king instead of Clothar," said Landwin. " 'Tis pity your laws permit not reigning queens. But if the rest of us flee, Sir Eudoric, why remain you not to tame this proud beauty? Meseems you be the one best qualified for this task, and she's a worthy prize for a hero."

"Gramercy," said Eudoric, "but the liontamer's part becharms me not. It calls for a Sigvard Dragonslayer or an Erpo Giantkiller; and I do not deem myself fit for that rôle."

"But think of the perquisites! Think of having a king for patron!"

Eudoric shook his head. "For a while, during our journey, meseemed the adversities of travel would render her a more tolerable companion. But once on her own ground, she waxed as imperious as ever. I went fishing for perch and caught a whale.

"Besides, back home I know a more companionable lass, who if a trifle less beautiful is infinitely more even-tempered."

"That were easy," said Landwin, "since our wife-in-common is the least even-tempered person I've ever known." He picked his lute off a shelf. "I'm ready."

Gontran rumbled: "A word of advice! Honor forbids me to punish you libertines ere ye depart; but guard yourselves if we meet anon upon the road."

"Thankee for the warning," said Landwin, opening the door. Instantly he leaped back with a screech. "By all the fiends, what's this?"

"Doctor Tsudai's pet dragon," said Eudoric. "It will hold off the marids whilst we make our escape. Then he'll return it to its proper world. Come on, everyone!"

XVIII

Flowers in Fall

Landwin and Forthred were down at the River
Mosarn, bathing. Eudoric, who had already had his
bath, did on his forester's garb and set himself to
kindling a fire. Another day's travel would bring
them to the borders of the Empire.

The snap of a trodden twig brought Eudoric round.
At the edge of the glade, Sir Gontran of Tolosa
strode out from under the lofty, leafless trees, wearing his mailshirt and grasping his sword in both
scarred hands. When Eudoric sprang up to face him,
he said:

"Ha, my fine lecher! I warned you to guard your
vile self! Have at thee!"

As he lofted the two-handed sword, Eudoric drew
his own weapon. The thought flashed through his
mind to yell for his companions; but what could they
do, arriving unarmed and naked, and neither one a
fighter? Eudoric's armor and his crossbow, either of
which might have shifted the odds, were lashed in a
bundle on a spare horse.

237

Eudoric feared that, if he parried so as to meet the big sword squarely, his lighter blade might break. He parried the first swing slantwise, so that the two-hander skittered off.

"Be not a zany!" he shouted at Gontran. "If neither of us wants the jade, what are we fighting for?"

"Honor!" roared Gontran, making another swing. "Methinks ye Imperials know nought of honor. Well, I'll teach thee!"

Another swing, another parry. Eudoric's arm tingled with the impact.

"Honor, hell!" said Eudoric. "You wear a mailshirt; I, nought but this leathern jack."

"That's thy misfortune. I warned thee."

Another swing; Eudoric's heel caught on a root, so that he stumbled back and barely avoided another powerful slash.

"Stand and fight, dancing master!" howled Gontran.

Round and round they went, swords clanging. Eudoric began to tire; but so, he saw, did Gontran. The warrior's face was scarlet with effort and dripped with sweat, even in the cool autumnal air.

Then came the instant for which Eudoric had been waiting. Gontran paused to catch his breath, standing with feet widely braced and the long sword held before him with the blade slanting up towards Eudoric. Eudoric whipped up his own blade and captured Gontran's near the tip in a *prise*. He forced the hostile blade around in a circle, which threw it out of line. A quick advance brought Eudoric past Gontran's point and within his own sword's reach of his foe.

Eudoric lunged. Instead of aiming for Gontran's mailed chest, he drove his blade into the warrior's right thigh, protected only by woolen breeches. He felt the point bite through.

Gontran gave an animal-like howl and started to raise his sword. Eudoric skipped back out of reach as Gontran's wounded leg folded beneath him, spilling him into the leaf mold. As Gontran struggled into a half-sitting position, still gripping his sword, Eudoric aimed a mighty cut at Gontran's neck. The warrior threw up his left arm, into which the blade bit. Eudoric sent a backhanded blow towards the other side of the exposed neck; he missed and laid open Gontran's cheek.

Landwin and Forthred ran up, dripping. Landwin said: "What's—we heard the clash—"

Eudoric made a thrust at Gontran's throat. Gontran jerked aside, so that the blade pierced his shoulder muscle; the push toppled the massive man over on his back. He lay moving his heavy limbs like a wounded insect.

"Methinks he's cut up enough to be harmless," said Landwin. "The knightly codes ordain giving a fallen foe a chance to yield."

Eudoric hesitated. Then he knelt beside the fallen man and spoke: "Sir Gontran!"

"Aye?" The voice came out half strangled by blood.

"Do you yield and swear by your honor never more to molest your co-husbands?"

For a few heartbeats, Gontran was silent; then he suddenly spat blood and saliva at Eudoric. "That for thee, thou coystril!" he coughed.

Eudoric, rising, sighed. "I would not only have let him live; I'd have patched up his wounds if he'd spoken me fair. But to spare one who would spend his life looking for a chance to slay me were mere folly." He brought his blade whistling down on Gontran's throat, half severing the neck. Gontran lay staring at the sky while his blood poured out on the forest litter.

Eudoric wiped and sheathed his sword, saying: "You are my witness, Landwin. He asked for it, in case anyone seek to make an issue of this."

"We had better bury him," said Landwin, "and

swear ourselves to silence. He was somewhat of a
Franconian national hero."

"How did such an arrant blockhead achieve the
name of hero?"

" 'Twas he who led that fatal charge of the Franconian
knights at Polovotsograd, and he alone survived that
field of blood."

"How so?"

"He cut his way out of the swarming Pantorozian
hordes. He may have been a blockhead, but so mighty
were his strokes that every blow laid low an oppo-
nent. So—"

"We have no shovel," said Eudoric. "Forthred!
Don your breeks and boots and go find the simpleton's horse. Methinks he may have brought a shovel
with him, intending to bury us therewith."

Forthred departed. Landwin, his head cocked quiz-
zically, said: "You think of everything, do you not?

> "Sir Eudoric, knight,
> Puts monsters to rout;
> Prevails in a fight
> With a murderous lout.
>
> He chaffers with lords
> And roisters with churls;
> He's handy with swords
> And loved by the girls,
>
> But flees like a hare,
> Although without blame,
> The sorceress fair,
> Yolanda by name!"

Eudoric laughed heartily. "Would that I had half
the virtues you attribute to me! Especially that part
about being loved by the girls. The only girls who
seem taken with me—Yolanda aside—sell their affections for ready money. With you, I'm told, 'tis other-

wise. What have you that I lack, aside from your gift of tossing off rhymes?"

Landwin squinted knowingly. "I mean no dispraise, Eudoric; but to me you seem a bit of a cold-blooded contriver—too much so to be a very prow lover."

Eudoric shrugged. "You are right. At Saalingen University they called me 'Eudoric the Calculator,' because I excelled in reckoning. I fear my classmates did not much like me; but I went my own way regardless, as I've done ever since."

Forthred returned, leading a horse with one hand and bearing a shovel in the other. Eudoric held out three grass stems.

"Take one each, my friends," he said. "Short straw takes first turn at the shovel. Oh, murrain, 'tis mine! Give me the shovel, pray."

Doctor Baldonius called: "Come in! Come in! And leave not the door ajar; 'tis cold. . . . By the God and Goddess, if it be not Eudoric! How art? Didst have more fantastic adventures in the western kingdoms?"

"Nought much." Eudoric shrugged. "Save a few incidents like saving a maiden from a sea monster; being forced to wed her only to learn that she already had three living husbands; and being snatched from durance vile by a Serican wizard and his pet dragon. I'll tell you all about it, but meanwhile—"

"Where is Forthred?"

"Calling upon his sweetling. He'll be along shortly."

"How fared he?"

"He's a worthy lad and a dutiful squire. He once attempted a spell from the princess's armory; it went a little awry but natheless saved our skins. What's new here?"

"Knew ye that Baron Rainmar's dead?"

"Aye; my family told me when I arrived yesterday. Skewered by a shaft in the back, and no man saw the archer."

"Divine justice caught up with Rainmar at last," said Baldonius sententiously.

"Oh, yea? Rainmar murdered scores in's sanguinary life. Since no man can be slain more than once, where's the justice in balancing one death against dozens?"

Baldonius laid a finger beside his nose and winked. "I confess, that thought hath also flickered through mine aged brain. But such queries might bring one to trial for heresy, especially since King Valdhelm got religion, as they say, and decided that all Locania must do likewise. Now Rainmar's son-in-law, and a cousin, and Count Petz are locked in a legal broil over the title. Since the son-in-law hath the castle, methinks he'll prevail." Baldonius pushed his spectacles up his nose to see more clearly. "By the axis of the universe, what's that in your hands? A bunch of flowers, *now*, when we expect the first snow any day?"

"Fresh from Master Yvain's greenhouse in Zurgau. I bethought me—"

"And that other packet; what's that?"

A shy smile crossed Eudoric's sober features as he set his packages on Baldonius' reading table. "Sweetmeats from Goodwife Ingunda's shop in Kromnitch. You see, I stopped in the town to sound out Count Petz on a joint enterprise of a new kind, whereof I learned from the Serican wizard. If we can persuade the Royal Locanian Council to amend the law, and enlist the support of men of substance, we can expand our carriage business, refurbish roads and inns, and vastly better conditions of travel in the kingdom. As it may chance, we also stand to make our fortunes."

"Indeed? How is this joint enterprise conducted?"

Eudoric explained the *hong* and its body of shareholders. "Thus, under the direction of leaders chosen by the holders of shares, these shareholders act as one individual, with far more effect than if they transacted their business separately."

"As if the group were merged into a single artificial person?"

"Precisely, Doctor. What would one call such an artificial person?"

Baldonius pondered. "In Helladic, the suitable word were 'corporation.' To form such a group would, I suppose, be termed 'to incorporate.' I see possibilities in this, my dear lad. If I could prevail upon some of my colleagues, such as Svanhalla and even that faker Calporio, to join me in setting up a similar group to bring order to the practice of magic. . . ."

"I wish you all success. And now, where's Lusina?"

Baldonius picked up a book, riffled through the pages, and drew out a folded and sealed sheet of parchment. "One more matter, which meseems next in order of urgency. Yesterday a messenger came by, after a long and furious ride from Letitia, with a letter for you, bearing the seal of some high and mighty person. Here it is."

Eudoric took the folded parchment. "Grammercy. But why left he the letter here 'stead of at the castle?"

"He stopped to inquire the way, and I told him I'd deliver it to you. Methought ye'd prefer to have it out of the reach of meddlesome kin."

Eudoric laughed. "How well you know my mother! She'd have had it open in one heartbeat. I suspect who this missive's author be." He broke the seal. "It must have cost her a pretty penny." He fell silent as he scanned the letter.

"Bad news?" asked Baldonius.

Eudoric shook his head. "I'll read it aloud, since it may concern matters of moment to the twain of us." He read:

H.R.H. Yolanda of Franconia to Sir Eudoric Dambertson of Arduen.

Dearest:

When I returned from Letitia, I found all my husbands flown like caitiff knaves. Had any been within my grasp, he should have smarted for it; but what's done is done. When I had recovered from the shock, it struck me that, of all the four, I regretted the flight of only one.

I must tell you that, of the lot, you are the only one I could truly have loved, since you are neither stupid like Gontran, nor lewd like Landwin, nor yet old and reclusive like Sugerius. You are he for whom I yearn by day and by night. You are therefore commanded to return forthwith to your adoring spouse's arms.

As for the delicate legal points arising from the revival of your predecessors, transforming me from a virtuous widow to a polygamist, I have the word of the Archimandrite that there shall be no difficulties. We shall have a proper legal marriage, wherein I will endeavor to make you the happiest husband ever. I am not unaware of my faults, which I swear to overcome. Only come back! You cannot abandon me after all we have endured together. I love you!

                                                                    Yolanda

"Belike she does," said Eudoric, thoughtfully refolding the missive, "as far as she loves aught but power. But it matters not to me."

"I grasp the nib," said Baldonius, "although I burn to hear the rest of the story. Where stood ye in the file of husbands?"

"I was the fourth; or so I was told. She had stricken my predecessors with a fixative spell, which kept them statuelike in a cryptic chamber. Of her quartet of nuptials, only the first has any claim to validity. But of that, more anon. Where can I find Lusina?"

"Oho! So that's the why of those unseasonable posies! I might have guessed."

Eudoric's face showed a worried frown. "Has she another suitor?"

"Nay. A brace of local swains have asked my leave to pay her their addresses, but she denied them. She hath never forgiven herself for her folly."

Indulgently, Eudoric smiled. "Who can go through life with never an indiscretion? I have committed more than I care to think about."

"Even my prudent, calculating pupil hath gone astray?"

"Aye; but I strive never to commit the same blunder twice."

"What wilt do about that letter? I must know, if ye think of courting my chick."

"I shall ignore it. As saith Helvolius the Wise, only a fool pets a biting dog a second time. Emmerhard's lawyer, Doctor Rupman, has assured me that any spousal claims by Yolanda would have no more weight in the Empire than a puff of smoke. If my business compel me to visit Letitia again. I shall be most careful not to cross paths with this overweening witchprincess. But about Lusina—"

"She's in her room in back. Take care that she flee not at sight of you."

"However fast she run, I'll follow faster," said Eudoric as he picked up his presents and hastened down the passage.

Baldonius chuckled softly. He adjusted his spectacles and opened his great iron-bound encyclopedia to "Incorporation."

POUL ANDERSON

Poul Anderson is one of the most honored authors of our time. He has won seven Hugo Awards, three Nebula Awards, and the Gandalf Award for Achievement in Fantasy, among others. His most popular series include the Polesotechnic League/Terran Empire tales and the Time Patrol series. Here are fine books by Poul Anderson available through Baen Books:

THE GAME OF EMPIRE

A *new* novel in Anderson's Polesotechnic League/Terran Empire series! Diana Crowfeather, daughter of Dominic Flandry, proves well capable of following in his adventurous footsteps.

FIRE TIME

Once every thousand years the Deathstar orbits close enough to burn the surface of the planet Ishtar. This is known as the Fire Time, and it is then that the barbarians flee the scorched lands, bringing havoc to the civilized South.

AFTER DOOMSDAY

Earth has been destroyed, and the handful of surviving humans must discover which of three alien races is guilty before it's too late.

THE BROKEN SWORD

It is a time when Christos is new to the land, and the Elder Gods and the Elven Folk still hold sway. In 11th-century Scandinavia Christianity is beginning to replace the old religion, but the Old Gods still have power, and men are still oppressed by the folk of the Faerie. "Pure gold!"—Anthony Boucher.

THE DEVIL'S GAME

Seven people gather on a remote island, each competing for a share in a tax-free fortune. The "contest" is ostensibly sponsored by an eccentric billionaire—but the rich man is in league with an alien masquerading as a demon . . . or is it the other way around?

THE ENEMY STARS

Includes for the first time the sequel to "The Enemy Stars": "The Ways of Love." Fast-paced adventure science fiction from a master.

SEVEN CONQUESTS

Seven brilliant tales examine the many ways human beings—most dangerous and violent of all species—react under the stress of conflict and high technology.

STRANGERS FROM EARTH

Classic Anderson: A stranded alien spends his life masquerading as a human, hoping to contact his own world. He succeeds, but the result is a bigger problem than before . . . What if our reality is a fiction? Nothing more than a book written by a very powerful Author? Two philosophers stumble on the truth and try to puzzle out the Ending . . .

You can order all of Poul Anderson's books listed above with this order form. Check your choices below and send the combined cover price/s to: Baen Books, Dept. BA, 260 Fifth Avenue, New York, New York 10001.*

THE GAME OF EMPIRE • 55959-1 • 288 pp. • $3.50   _____
FIRE TIME • 55900-1 • 288 pp. • $2.95   _____
AFTER DOOMSDAY • 65591-4 • 224 pp. • $2.95   _____
THE BROKEN SWORD • 65382-2 • 256 pp. • $2.95   _____
THE DEVIL'S GAME • 55995-8 • 256 pp. • $2.95   _____
THE ENEMY STARS • 65339-3 • 224 pp. • $2.95   _____
SEVEN CONQUESTS • 55914-1 • 288 pp. • $2.95   _____
STRANGERS FROM EARTH • 65627-9 • 224 pp. • $2.95   _____